heart SICK HATE

EVA SIMMONS

Published by Eva Simmons

Editing by Kat Wyeth (Kat's Literary Services)

Proofreading by Vanessa Esquibel (Kat's Literary Services)

Cover Photography by Wander Aguiar

Cover Model: Gustavo L.

Cover Design by Eva Simmons

ISBN: 9798863324081

For anyone who has been given two choices and said:
Fuck it, I'll make a third.

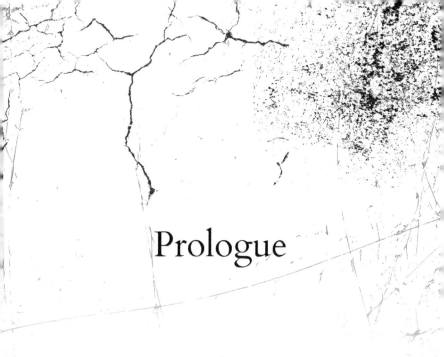

Prologue

Echo

NOTHING IN LIFE IS FREE, and I'm broke.

Never a good predicament to find yourself in.

I skim my fingers over the rich, buttery leather couch as I circle the room. Warm bulbs are hidden inside gold sconces to keep the space dim. A thick burgundy rug sits in the center. And paired with the charcoal wallpaper, darkness drinks all traces of light.

Dad's and my apartment could fit inside this single room, and the Kingsley family uses it to store their spare furniture. There is not one hint of an ass imprint on the perfect cushions.

I'm not sure why one room needs so many seats when it's clear no one spends any time in here. A layer of dust collects on the ridges of the floorboards and mantle. Above the fireplace is a collection of pictures, but they're outdated. The three boys in the photos are young, but Dad told me his friend's sons are seventeen, twenty, and twenty-seven now.

Sinking into one of the chairs, I grip the copper armrests. The white cushions are hard and unforgiving. The cool metal studs nip at my skin. Everything about it is uncomfortable. Like the energy in this room.

I stand up and make my way to another, larger recliner. Sinking into it, the soft cushions drink me. The ripe scent of old cigars and apples floods my senses. Everything from how I mold into the cushions to the stale aroma of the polyester is overwhelming.

Climbing out of the recliner, I make my way to the mantle to inspect the photos more closely. One draws my attention—a magnetic pull of steel eyes summoning me toward it.

Two cool gray orbs I can't help but focus on. So crisp and bright they're nearly translucent. But something about the distance in his gaze feels as lost as I am in this dark castle he calls a home.

We couldn't be more different, given his world is made of gold and mine is the cheap copper that paints a green ring around your finger. But in his eyes is infinite chaos.

Sick rage.

Hate in its purest form.

Beauty.

I sink into a chair facing the photo. This one is black leather, slick and cool. The arms are decorated with gold studs, curving around me in a way that feels protective.

While everything else in these walls is haunted, this chair somehow feels safe from the ghosts.

"Whatcha up to, Goldilocks?"

I jump at the sound of a voice coming from the doorway, popping out of the chair as it snaps me from my thoughts. And when I face the direction of the sound, I'm once more met with those steel-gray eyes from the photograph.

The youngest son, most likely. He looks only a year or two older than me.

Crew—I *think?*

Dad told me all their names, but as his eyes hold their focus, I can't swallow, much less think.

"So?" He smirks, leaning against the doorframe. "Whatcha doing?"

"Nothing." I roll my shoulders back.

A broken chuckle leaves his lips. "You sure?"

He lifts off the doorframe and grows a few inches.

His eyes hunt me as he circles the room and closes in, while somehow still maintaining a safe distance. Just enough to give the illusion I could escape when I have no doubt he'd find a way to stop me.

"You were awfully deep in thought to be up to nothing." He rakes his fingers through his thick brown hair, hitting me with the full force of his predatory stare. "What's on that pretty little mind of yours, Goldilocks?"

"Why do you keep calling me that?"

If he was anyone else, I'd assume it's because of my golden hair. But something about how he watches me with each step—how he seems to see everything—tells me it's not that simple.

"You were trying out the chairs, weren't you?" He smirks, his gaze darting to each one I sat in. "Too small, too overbearing, until you found the one that was just right?"

Finally, his stare lands on where my fingers clutch the black leather chair I jumped out of when he walked into the room.

Releasing it, I quickly cross my arms over my chest. "No."

At least, I don't think I was. Not intentionally.

He continues to circle until he closes in on me. Ten feet away. Five. Until he's right in front of me, drawing out the length of my neck, so I can look up at him.

Close enough to smell cedar and old oak trees. The chill of midnight in fall sends a shiver up my spine. He's cold and splintered.

"Sure you weren't." He dips his chin. "I've got two brothers. Planning on testing us out next?"

Heat floods my veins as he pulls back. His tilted smirk is a challenge as his gaze drops to my warming cheeks. And I'm sure he doesn't miss the bob in my throat as I try to swallow.

The nerve of him.

My fingers clench.

Crew is probably used to precious, sweet girls, and how it's so easy to ruffle their feathers. Ones who wear pleated skirts and walk around school with golden spoons in their mouths in a display of their parents' money. And maybe he thinks I'm one of them, with my blonde hair in a tight ponytail on top of my head, and a white dress that hits me at the knees.

But my elegance is a mask, just like the one I sense he puts on for those who underestimate him.

I'm Echo Slater.

I'm rotten.

I've already seen the worst, which means I don't get caught off guard or surprised. And I don't let boys get to me.

"Let me guess." I narrow my gaze, smoothing my fingers over the front of my dress and rolling my shoulders back. "You're the one that's *just right*?"

Amusement ghosts his cheeks. A beautiful sight if it wasn't unholy.

"No, Goldie." He shakes his head, cool eyes darkening their focus on my lips. "I already know I'm too much for you. Not that I'll turn you down if you want to see so for yourself."

"Give it up, Crew."

Another person walks into the room, and he must be the middle brother, Rhett. He's early twenties, handsome, overly confident.

Crew's jaw clenches and his back stiffens as he turns, positioning himself between us. It's a move that would feel protective if Crew didn't strike me as someone more interested in making me his captive.

Rhett smiles, softer and not as menacing as his brother. He has a golden-boy aura with his styled hair and collared polo shirt. He looks like he belongs in this mansion, unlike

Crew, wearing faded jeans and a Nightmare on Elm Street T-shirt.

And as Rhett walks toward us, brushing his sandy brown hair off his forehead, he's almost welcoming. If only I didn't find better comfort in darkness.

"You're Echo?" He stops in front of me, and I nod.

Rhett offers a warm smile, while Crew stands like a cool steel wall between us. They're opposites, while I'm a girl torn down the middle.

The girl I was born, and the girl who was saved.

My dark and light battling the same as these brothers.

Crew turns at my silence, examining me as his brother does.

Which part of me are they looking at? What I show or what I hide?

Rhett tilts his head and offers another soft smile. A gesture that would be sweet if I was capable of trust.

"Your father's looking for you," he says.

Crew chuckles and Rhett's smile falls, his attention snapping in his brother's direction.

"Knock it off."

"Or what?" Crew steps toward him—a rubber band of tension on the verge of snapping. "Maybe Goldie and I weren't done yet."

"We were." I step around them both, not sure I trust myself to keep talking to Crew given the way he stirs up my insides. "And just for the record, I'm no Goldilocks."

She had three choices. I've only got one.

"See you around." Rhett waves and I give him a nod as I dip out of the room. Purposefully avoiding Crew's eyes when I feel them on me. No good comes from looking into eyes like his.

I make my way through the maze of hallways, finding the path toward the foyer. Everything about this dark castle in the Los Angeles hills is grand and expensive. If it didn't feel like a prison it would almost be beautiful.

Turning a final corner, I find my father waiting for me. He's clutching the cross around his neck, deep in thought, like it has the power to crucify the demons we sold our souls to here.

"Ready?" he asks when I stop in front of him.

His expression is tense, and the gray patches of hair at his temples draw out his age with his frown.

"I'm ready." I thread my arm through his and find the gravity I've been searching for since we walked in.

Dad leads me out of the house, to our beater parked at the curb. He swings the door open for me and holds it while I climb inside. We're both silent until he circles around and gets in himself. The wheezing of the engine cuts through the night.

"It's done then?" I ask, clutching the hem of my dress.

Dad nods, wiping away the slight sheen of sweat from his forehead with the back of his hand. "You don't have to do this. I shouldn't have involved you in the first pl—"

"Stop." I turn in my seat to face him. "You didn't involve me. This was my decision. I know the terms."

"There are other ways."

"And you'll die searching for them." Tears sting my eyes. Needles prick my throat with every word. "You need a heart, and he can get you one. That's all that matters. It's done."

Dad swallows hard, keeping his eyes on the road. "It's done."

"Which one do I need to marry?" I turn once more and face the road, trying to slow my breath as my heartbeat throbs between my temples.

"Rhett." He lets out a heavy breath and I feel the weight of it. "Not now. We'll wait until you're older and it makes sense."

"Rhett," I repeat. "Good."

He's nice enough. Safe enough.

Just right if I had to guess.

If only I wasn't haunted by the lingering ghost of Crew's cedar scent when I close my eyes and let the road rock me to sleep.

If only the darkness in me didn't wish for a different decision.

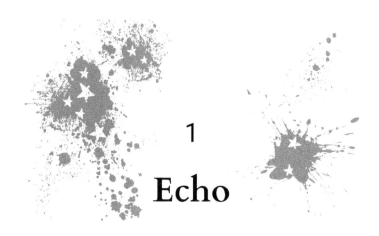

1

Echo

Eight Years Later

CREW POPS THE CAP on a bottle of vodka and pours a shot. "What the fuck is taking Jude so long?"

Sage snags the shot Crew poured for himself and slams it before Crew can stop him. "They're probably fucking."

I can't help but groan at Sage's comment. I know more than I ever wanted to about the three of them and their sexual escapades. One of the downsides to co-owning a tattoo shop with three guys.

It's disgusting.

Crew shakes his head and pours another shot. "They can fuck later—for the rest of their miserable lives, as a matter of fact. I don't get it."

I roll my eyes, leaning my elbows on the counter. "Well Crew, when a man loves a woman, sometimes he actually wants to spend more time with her than just the five minutes it takes him to fuck her. Hard concept for you to grasp, I know. But Jude loves Fel, believe it or not."

"Cute." Crew smirks, those devilish eyes focusing on me as he plants his hands on the counter and leans forward to square off with me. "Is that all my brother gives you? Five minutes? Explains why you're so fucking uptight, princess. Need someone to bend you over and give you a proper climax?"

"You offering to help her out?" Sage smacks Crew's shoulder and laughs.

It's what Sage says every time Crew makes a joke about how I'm uptight or how I need to be properly fucked.

I've learned to ignore it. He can think whatever he wants. He's only saying it to piss me off.

"He's just jealous," I say to Sage, flipping my hair off my shoulder and hopping off the stool to walk around the island. "What is it they say about always wanting what you can't have?"

It's bullshit, but when Crew pushes, I'll push back.

Every. Time.

"You wish, princess." Crew doesn't fight me when I grab the vodka bottle out of his hand and the backs of our fingers brush.

Electricity that pisses me off on contact. And I hate that he smirks when he senses it.

Because I hate Crew Kingsley. He's arrogant, rude, sadistic. And worst of all, he's my boyfriend's brother, so there's no avoiding him.

"Help, please." Maren walks into Crew's apartment frowning, her shoulders slumped back. "I locked my keys in the car when I went back to get my bridesmaid dress."

"Don't worry, I'll save you." Sage winks and Maren rolls her eyes at him.

Sage is a flirt, interested in any girl with a nice pair of legs, and Maren is smart enough to see straight through it.

Sage knocks Crew in the shoulder before scratching the stubble forming on his jaw. "Be right back. You two try not to kill each other while I'm gone."

"Easier said than done." I force a smile.

Sage follows Maren out of the apartment, and I wish my body didn't tense as the door shuts behind them.

Crew and I might see each other all the time at work or family gatherings, but I've never been to his apartment. No one has. Not until Jude bought the place across the hall for him and Fel.

I spin the top off the vodka and pour myself a drink, trying to ignore the fact that Crew is standing really close. Our arms nearly brushing as I draw the shot glass to my lips and down it.

"Drinking away your problems?" he asks as I set the glass down and start pouring another.

"You're one to talk."

He steals the shot when I'm done pouring, and I set the bottle down, turning to face him.

"Thanks." He takes the shot and grits his teeth, before setting the empty glass down.

"That wasn't for you."

"Just doing you a favor, lightweight."

I fold my arms over my chest and glare at him. "I don't need you monitoring my alcohol."

"Right." He leans in closer, hovering over me like an ominous cloud I should probably run from. "You've got my brother for that. Where is he, anyway? Wasn't he supposed to come to the wedding with you?"

"He's busy."

It's a lie. Rhett forgot. As much as he cares about me, he cares about the church more. And the moment I got the text he was dropping something off for Sunday's service, I knew he'd get distracted and wouldn't make it to Jude and Fel's wedding.

Not that it really matters. Our relationship is a show for them. A deal signed in blood. I don't owe Crew an explanation.

"Where's your date?" I toss back at him. "Couldn't find a girl with poor enough judgment on such short notice?"

He must notice my tone catch at the end because he smiles, reaching up to brush back the piece of hair hanging in my face. "Now who's jealous?"

"Not in your lifetime." I clench my teeth.

"You sure, Goldilocks?" His finger trails down my arm.

He's toying with me. Like he's so good at.

"Does it bother you, Crew?" I straighten up, tipping my chin up and facing him. "All this teasing and I can't help but think maybe you're just mad your brother got to me first."

"That's bullshit, and you know it."

"Is it?" I purse my lips. "Or is that denial I'm hearing?"

"Denial is you pretending you aren't dating my brother just to piss me off."

"Why would it?" I shrug. "Thought you didn't care."

"I don't." He smirks. "Not since you went and made yourself my brother's whore."

Rage pulses and my vision goes black.

My knuckles crack as they connect with Crew's nose, but he doesn't so much as flinch. His neck barely even moves with the hit. Besides the blood now pouring out of him, he's otherwise unaffected.

"Fuck." I grip my knuckles with my other hand and wish it was enough to make the throbbing subside.

I've been to the guys' underground fights plenty of times. It always looked like *being hit* was the painful part. But as my hand pulses and my fingers numb, I'm not sure why the guys at the shop fight people for fun because even the hitting part hurts.

Bad.

Crew smirks, grabbing a towel off the counter and holding it to his nose as blood pours down his dress shirt. He's proud of his vile comment because there's nothing Crew Kingsley loves more than getting a reaction.

This asshole brings out the worst in me.

Even now as he stands in front of me with what is likely a broken nose, he looks more amused than anything.

Figures. He's a sadistic dick who feeds on taking pain as much as he enjoys inflicting it.

"Quite the right hook you've got there, Goldie."

I hate that he calls me that—still. It's a threat as much as it's a taunt. A reminder that he knows all the little things we both bury on the outside.

"Feel better now?" He winks at me.

Actually fucking *winks* at me.

"Fuck you, Crew." I turn and walk away, blood boiling in my veins. Molten hot and coursing through me.

Sage and Maren are walking back into the apartment as I storm toward the door. Maren's eyes go wide when she spots Crew covered in blood, but Sage just starts laughing.

"What'd you do this time?" I hear Sage ask, but I don't stick around for Crew's answer.

I already know Crew won't tell him anything.

We'll continue this dance like we always do until he finally throws me off a building and puts me out of my misery.

"You okay?" Maren follows me into the hallway. "I didn't realize Sage was being literal when he said try not to kill each other."

"I'm fine." I pull out my phone. "Just need a second."

She nods, her dark curls doing a shimmy as she does. I only met her a few months ago, but she's quickly becoming one of my closest friends.

Guess that's not difficult when I don't have any.

Maren leans against the wall and pulls out her phone while she waits for me to make my call. It's one of the things I appreciate most about her. She won't ask what happened unless I offer it up.

The phone rings only once before Rhett picks up.

"I broke your brother's nose," I say before he gets a chance to even say hello.

"Crew?"

"Obviously."

Adam is too busy running the Kingsley empire and spending time with his girlfriend, Lakeyn.

There's a long pause on the other end of the line, broken with a giant laugh that finally bursts out of him. "You're serious?"

"He deserved it."

"Oh, I have no doubt about that." Rhett can barely speak through his choked laughing. "I can't wait to hear that story. But I gotta go, so catch me up later, okay?"

Of course he has to go. He always has to go. I might be his girlfriend, but it doesn't mean I rank on his scale of importance. Especially when it's all for show.

"Just thought you should know." I hang up, annoyed.

I've made my fair share of bad decisions in my life, but involving myself with the Kingsley family is the dumbest of them all. Saints and villains raised in their dark, haunted house. Minds as twisted as their morals.

If I thought I escaped the hands of the devil when Dad found me, the Kingsley family proved me wrong.

Demons never let you truly disappear from their sight.

I spin the ring that sits on my left hand around my finger, wishing it could ground me. It's all the purity I have left, and soon it won't matter. I'm not sure it even matters now that my fate is already sealed. But a girl can hope.

"Ready?" Maren stops at my side when I tuck my phone into my purse.

No.

But I roll my shoulders back and nod. Today isn't about my uncertainty, or Crew being a jerk, or the avalanche of promises caving in on themselves. It's about our friend, and that's all that matters.

Maren knocks on the door across the hall from Crew's apartment and Jude answers. He and Maren share their usual snide comments before he lets us in and disappears to go find the guys. I should probably care that it suddenly feels like time is skipping, but my hearing is fuzzy, and my mind is scrambled.

Something about what Crew said sits like lead inside me. It forces me to pay attention to things I'd rather ignore.

Choices.

I pop a piece of gum in my mouth and try to bury the thought, bouncing a step as I follow Maren into Fel's apartment. There's no going back. I may not like the path straight ahead, but I know better than to veer off course.

"You look like a fairytale princess." Maren's voice snaps me back to reality just as I almost run into her.

She's stopped in the doorway to Fel's bedroom as Fel spins around.

I swear the girl moves in slow motion sometimes.

Delicate, peaceful.

She's all the things I'm not with her long, wavy red hair that lands at the center of her back. Her white dress sparkles with the sun shining through the windows. Lace hugging her soft curves and a smile that might as well be a beacon of light in the center of the city.

She's the kind of brightness Jude needs in his life. And I'm thankful they have each other. They've been through hell together and not all people find peace at the end of what they experienced.

"Do I look okay?" Fel bites her lip nervously.

"Okay?" Maren practically snorts, walking over to her and brushing Fel's hair off her shoulders before planting her hands on them. "Girl, you look drop dead gorgeous."

"Stunning, sweetie." I pop another piece of gum into my mouth and blow a bubble to settle my nerves.

I need to smoke a joint—anything to keep me from crawling out of my skin again. The last time that happened ended in blood. As long as I'm moving, pacing, running at full speed—I don't have to think.

Fel breathes out a laugh. "I can't believe this is really happening. He wants to get married right now."

She's still in shock from Jude's impromptu wedding, but I'm not surprised. Jude is the grumpiest asshole at the shop—which is saying a lot since Crew also works there—but Fel brings out a side of Jude I've never seen.

"Of course he does. Look at you." Maren guides Fel to a chair and starts working on her makeup. "Can't blame the guy."

"I guess." Fel laughs.

Maren smiles wide, her eyes darting in my direction. "Speaking of women bringing men to their knees, you're not going to believe what Echo just did."

"He deserved it." I point out.

"You don't have to explain yourself to us." Maren shakes her head. "Crew is a total dick, so I've no doubt he did."

"What did you do?" Fel spins in her seat to face where I'm propped against the wall.

"I might have punched him in the face."

Her eyes blow wide with shock.

"She *might* have broken his nose." Maren laughs. "And by *might*, I mean girl definitely broke his nose."

It sounds worse than it is. I think?

Teasing me is Crew's favorite hobby, and even if I have thick skin, he hit a tender spot today.

So much for pretending I'm unaffected.

"What did he do?" Fel's eyebrows pinch in curiosity.

"What didn't he?" I ask in return, diverting her question.

They laugh and return to Fel's hair and makeup like it's any other day of Crew saying dumb shit at the parlor, itching to get punched in the face. They're blind to the fact that I'm glass shattering inside.

Because no one really knows me.

While Maren and Fel talk hairstyles and wedding night sex, I walk to the en suite bathroom and smooth my hair in the mirror. Half black, half bleach blonde, straight down the middle where my part is.

While most people use their appearance to project perfection, I use mine to remind myself of the only truth

I have left. Nothing is mine but my body. Nothing but the two sides waging a war inside me.

Which side will win out in the end?

My phone pings, and I look down to see Rhett's name lighting up the screen the same way it should light me up inside.

He's sweet. He cares. He's a good friend. He holds up his end of our arrangement.

Arrangement.

I should probably start thinking of it as a relationship when that's what it's supposed to be. After all, Rhett Kingsley will be my husband someday soon. A title thousands of women at the church would die for.

Preacher at Eternal Light, my father's church. Leader in the trendiest way to practice Christianity in Los Angeles. Blinding smile, golden boy presence. He's everything I'd want if I wasn't permanently broken.

I look down at my phone, buzzing once more in my hand.

Rhett: Sorry I had to rush off the phone earlier, babe. Hope your day gets better.

He probably means it, even if he's clearly forgotten where I am right now, or that he promised he'd be here with me.

Echo: All good. I know you're busy.

Guilt is pointless when it won't get us anywhere.

Rhett is sweet, honest. We know we stand in this to-gether and are both willing to make the sacrifices neces-sary.

Rhett is my future, as promised.

And it's the one promise I can't break.

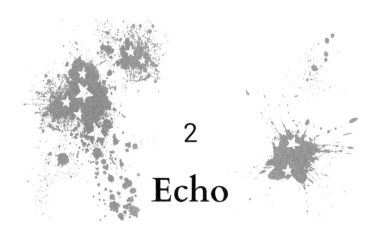

2

Echo

THE NEEDLE DRAGS ACROSS skin, and it's the only time I'm calm. Focused. At peace.

Nothing clouds my mind when I'm inking. Not my past, not my future. Not even punching Crew in the face last night.

All that matters is the burst of color painting Claudia's flesh. A wild rose blooming from the cracks in the skull. Beauty in an ugly world.

Growing up, art was the one thing that was mine. The one thing from my past life I held onto.

Pencil on paper stopped me from drawing with razor-blades on skin when all I wanted to do was crawl out of my body.

My mom was a druggie with no money, and my dad didn't know I existed. Half the time I was either alone or crashing on random people's couches. Besides my one stuffed bear with a missing eye and a hole in his leg, I didn't have many things I considered mine.

Art was it.

I could leave my mark. Create pretty things in chaos.

Something I almost lost when they locked me up. Until Dad found out he had a daughter and came for me.

Saved me—some would say.

It sounds like a second coming. Religious when I don't have much faith left. But in technical terms, it's what he did, and I'll forever be in his debt because of it.

He pulled me from that place with white walls and pills so big they hurt to swallow. He saved me from the system when mom overdosed and extinguished any hope she'd someday try to be a parent. And he gave me art again. He helped me find a purpose.

I'm not religious like him. Faith is wasted on pointless things most of the time, so I don't understand it. But I do believe him finding out I existed in that dark moment was fate.

My mom and dad met when they were young. She was in school and he was already on his path to becoming a pastor. From what dad has told me, she had dreams of being a teacher and enjoyed helping people. They got married at twenty-one and were already talking about babies. But then mom got into a car accident. And what started as a pill addiction quickly spiraled. Dad watched her slowly disintegrate, and when he tried to get her help, she disappeared.

It wasn't until she left him that she found out she was pregnant. And she was too deep in her own mess to reach back out. If she hadn't overdosed, and if I hadn't been taken away, he might have never known about me.

He wouldn't have found me.

But he did. And not only that, he accepts me for who I am, what I do, and how I act. He doesn't frown at my yin and yang hair or my choice of profession. He loves me as is.

When I got the idea from Crew to start an apprenticeship at Twisted Roses, I expected Dad to put up more of a fight. It was no secret that he wanted me to take his place in his church, or at the very least, become more involved. But that was his path, not mine.

Which is why, when I had the chance to pay him back, I did.

I always will.

No matter the price.

The needle glides across skin, and I'm at peace with my decision. I owe him.

Two knocks come at the door to my room at the shop, and I look up to see Jude standing in the doorway.

"Aren't you supposed to be on a honeymoon or some shit?"

"Something like that." Jude brushes his shaggy hair off his forehead. "But I had to get some things in order before we take off to Seattle."

I'm still not sure how Seattle is an exciting place for a honeymoon, but who am I to judge? I've never left California. Even when I started making money from my quarter ownership in the tattoo shop, every spare penny has gone to medical debt or been stashed away *just in case.*

It's easy to separate people who have come from money versus those who have always lived without.

Just in case.

A perpetual state of existence where it doesn't take more than a bad day to fuck up every plan you've made. I don't trust money any more than I trust people. Neither are promised to actually stay.

"Well get shit done then." I draw the final bubble of red to finish the rose on the half sleeve. "Then get the fuck out of here. We've got this."

Jude's always been the most responsible of the guys at the shop, even if he's just as unhinged as the rest of them. When it comes to keeping things in order around this place, he never fails. Which is why, he's standing in my doorway instead of disappearing with his new wife like he should be.

"Promise, I've got this under control."

"I know *you* do."

"Then trust me to keep Sage and Crew in line. It's a week, we'll be fine."

I set the needle down and squirt green soap on a rag before cleaning off my client's tattoo.

"Nice work." Jude admires the bright, fresh tattoo.

Every artist has their own unique style, and mine involves lots of color. Big bright pieces bursting with energy and life.

Claudia stands up and smiles as she examines her fresh tattoo in the mirror. I've been inking her for a few years now. We finished one arm about six months ago, and she's finally ready to tackle the other.

Her eyes brighten as she looks it over. "Thanks, Echo. It's perfect."

I nod, snapping off my gloves. "We'll start the forearm next time."

"Sounds good." She does a little twist of her arm, taking in every defined crack in the skull.

The shading around the eye sockets came out perfect, thanks to some advice from Sage. He might annoy me with his constant antics and how he flirts with every girl who walks in, but his talent when it comes to tattooing can't be matched.

Claudia sits back down so I can wrap her tattoo up, and she watches Jude as I do, her cheeks reddening. Too bad for her, he's only got eyes for his new bride.

"Is there something else?" I ask Jude when he hasn't moved.

"Oh, yeah." He stands up tall, snapping out of whatever thought had him pulled under. "Rhett's here."

I almost burst out laughing.

"Rhett?"

He never comes here. Rhett is too clean-cut to be caught at Twisted Roses. And even if he's outwardly supportive, he still thinks my tattooing is a hobby he'll convince me to drop once I'm a preacher's wife.

Which is why, every time he says shit like that, I get more ink.

My future might be decided, but my body is mine.

"Barely believed it myself." Jude shrugs.

The guys don't understand my relationship with Rhett, which means we need to get better at faking it. Trouble is, the longer Rhett and I do this dance, and the more real it gets, the more I'm instinctively pulling away.

Resisting.

Needing something more.

I force a smile and try to bury my hesitations.

"I'll take you up front," I tell Claudia, before turning back to Jude. "Tell Rhett I'll be there in a minute, please?"

If I had to guess, he's here for damage control after forgetting he was supposed to attend Jude and Fel's wedding with me last night. I don't actually care. But I can't say that because I'm supposed to.

After leaving Claudia with the new girl working the front counter, I make my way to the office.

The hallway closes in on all sides as I try not to suffocate with every step.

I pop a piece of gum in my mouth like it's enough to calm my nerves when I should have smoked a joint instead.

My stress has me smoking more lately. I probably should find some healthier coping mechanisms.

Sure enough, Rhett is in the office with his ass propped on the desk and arms crossed over his chest. His polo and khakis look pretentious and out of place in this part of LA. I'll be surprised if his BMW still has tires when he leaves.

Rhett smiles when he sees me, and I remind myself that at least we don't hate each other. This could be worse. We're just two people in the same fucked up predicament, doing what we have to for our families.

I stop in front of him, and his gaze runs over my exposed skin, which is a lot in my short shorts and tank top. I'm pretty sure if it were up to Rhett, I'd wear a turtleneck twenty-four-seven to cover up my sprinkling of tattoos.

A preacher's girl should be understated and appropriate. She should choose one color for her hair and not lace her skin with ink. I'm still not sure how I'm supposed to fit that mold.

"Sorry about last night," he says as I stop in front of him.

At some point, he must have realized where I was, and that he promised to go. I should be thankful it didn't completely slip his mind.

"It's fine, I know you were busy. You would have hated it anyway."

We don't share mutual friends or interests. And even if he likes me as a person, our only commonality is my father. I'm his own personal path to his holy calling.

"You're not mad?"

"Why would I be?" Rhett and I don't have the kind of relationship where I get angry or jealous.

That's me and his brother.

"We're good," I tell him, dropping my hands to my sides. "Promise."

Rhett smiles, offering a blinding grin.

He's the clean-cut Kingsley. The star child with obviously handsome features and a welcoming smile that draws people to him. Dark hair and striking blue eyes. Tall with solid muscle. Perfectly put together and every girl's dream husband.

If only my favorite flavor was vanilla.

I want all of them mixed together, a different taste every time it hits my tongue.

"Did you get everything done that you needed to?" I ask.

"And then some. We'll be streaming Sunday's service. Finally spreading the word worldwide."

Rhett lights up when he talks about the church. It's his calling, and I pretend to understand it. But Rhett's approach is different than my father's and the way he wants to grow Eternal Light to such a large scale doesn't feel genuine at times.

"Good."

Rhett reaches out and grips my elbows, pulling me to him.

It takes everything in me not to recoil at his grasp, or how his hips press against me at the closeness. Friendly or not, I don't like being touched.

"It'll get easier," Rhett says, squeezing my elbows, likely sensing my hesitation.

"I know."

"I'm serious, Echo." His smile drops and vulnerability slips out. "As long as we're in this together, we'll be okay."

I hope he's right.

"Do you ever worry we didn't give it enough time?" I ask. "Are you really ready for all this?"

We agreed when I was a teenager that we would put our plan into motion when I turned twenty-three because, at the time, it sounded like a good idea. Now, I still feel young, and I don't feel ready. But maybe that's just because it's him, and this isn't real.

Rhett works his jaw, thinking through his answer. "I don't think it's a question of if we're ready. No one's ever really ready. But it doesn't matter because the time is right. Your dad is ready to step down, and I'm ready to take his place. They love him, and with you by my side, they'll love me too. It's my calling to guide them, Echo. And this is how it has to happen."

I'm sure he thinks he's doing God's work, but I can't help but wonder why his comments sometimes make it all sound like a cult.

"We're taking it slow for now." Rhett brushes my arm with his hand, and I fight the reaction wanting to burst out. "Do what you need to do, because as your friend, I understand this is a difficult transition when it's not by choice. But we both know what's at the end of this road."

I'll be his wife.

I nod. "Are you still... you know..."

"Seeing other people?" He cocks an eyebrow.

"Yeah."

"I won't when we're married." He frowns. "But you said you didn't care while we're still figuring this out."

"I don't." It's the truth. If anything, it absolves me of all my conflicting feelings. "I was just checking."

"Good." He releases my arms and chuckles. "It's not like you're a virgin either."

"Right." Instinctively, I spin my ring around my finger.

"You'll still be my wife." He smiles. "And when we say our vows, we'll both accept our roles under the eyes of God."

Judgment might as well burn me on the spot. I'm not sure what role he thinks I'll be accepting, or if I can meet the expectations.

"So have your fun." He winks at me. "You know I am."

My stomach twists because I should be taking his direction. I shouldn't be saving myself when my future is decided for me. But that's what I've been doing.

Movement in the doorway draws my attention, and I turn in time to see Crew walking into the office with his head down as he stares at something on his phone. And when his eyes lift—those steel gray orbs meet mine, and my heart plummets straight to hell.

Or maybe it's the fire in his gaze lighting me up.

"You got him good, baby." Rhett laughs, turning me, so he can toss an arm over my shoulders, slipping into his role of pretending to be my boyfriend. "What did you do to piss off my girl?"

My girl.

Two words that slither through me, leaving a chilled path in their wake.

Crew, the master of projecting exactly what he wants you to see, doesn't so much as flinch at his brother's comment. He tucks his phone in his pocket and grabs the top of the doorframe, smirking. The movement tugs the bottom of his T-shirt up just enough that it shows off a hint of his tight, muscular stomach, and my core throbs as the muscles clench with the dark chuckle that comes out of him.

Why does my body have to betray me like that?

You hate him, remember.

"Why do you care? Worried I'm riling up *your girl*?"

Two words that don't sound any better out of Crew's mouth. If anything, it stings more.

Rhett chuckles, holding me closer to his side. He might be blind to most things, but the way Crew reacts when it comes to me isn't one of them.

"Rile away," Rhett says, squeezing my shoulder. "My girl knows I've got her."

The faintest tick of Crew's jaw makes my stomach sink. He drops his hands as Rhett pulls me along beside him, and we make our way out of the office.

"Oh, and I almost forgot, we're all expected at dinner tonight. Dad's request," Rhett yells back to Crew, not looking at him as we pass.

But I do. Because I always do, no matter how much I hate Crew's stupid, broken face.

I can't help it.

Crew watches me walk away with his brother wrapped around me, and I can't help wondering if it will always feel this way. Eternity with every step.

I'd like to believe things could have been different. But that's the kind of thinking that led Eve to take a bite out of the apple. Wishing for more.

After all, temptation is a powerful thing.

But it's not love. Love doesn't exist. At least, not for me.

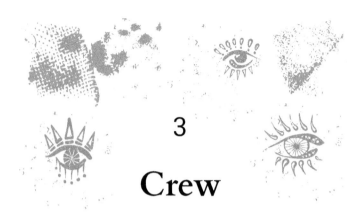

3

Crew

"In God's name. Amen."

What a fucking joke.

There's nothing less holy than sitting at this table. We're chess pieces in my father's game, and sometimes I think I'm the only one who notices.

He's at his throne at the end already cutting into his steak. His dark hair is perfectly oiled, like his personality, and he's wearing one of his most expensive suits when no one here gives a shit about his money more than him.

At the other end sits Echo's father.

The two of them couldn't be more different. While my dad is a viper, with enough money and power to make some of the worst men in the city fear him, Echo's dad is one of those true, down-to-earth, good men.

Most churches in LA feed on money and the status of the members of their flock, but Ryan Slater actually started his church with the honest intention of helping people. And even if my brother has been shifting the direction recently with viral streaming and mainstream religious hooks, Ryan still believes it's all for the good of his congregation.

I'd be impressed if I didn't feel sorry for him. People don't survive in LA on good intentions and pure hearts.

Which is why he doesn't see he's a pawn. A means to an end so my father can help my brother fulfill his need to be the center of attention. The favorite son—the good son. Why strive for money and power when you can aim for religious influence? People love Rhett. They *believe* in him.

Another reason I don't have faith. People always place it in all the wrong things.

My gaze skips from one end of the table to the other. A crevice in the middle feels like this whole scene could crack.

Ryan made a deal with the devil eight years ago to grant my father's favorite son a spot in the most influential church in town. But I still don't know what it is Ryan got out of it, besides a cookie-cutter, Jesus Ken doll for his daughter.

Echo fidgets with her fork, pushing her food around on her plate. Instead of eating, she's chewing gum and playing with the steak like it's still bleeding. She wraps one hand around the tail end of her ponytail and spins it around her finger, before settling it in front of her shoulder and covering the star tattoo that lives there.

The girl irritates the hell out of me. She's too upbeat.

And between our family ties and the fact that we both work at the same tattoo parlor, there's no avoiding her. So I do what I do best instead—pick at her and piss her off every chance I get. If I'm going to have to endure her endless energy, I might as well at least enjoy the entertainment of fighting with her.

Girl is energetic when I prefer things quiet.

Loud when I like to think.

The fucking sun when I'm used to the dark.

Why she actually started dating my brother five months ago still baffles me. I'm convinced it's only because she wants to make her father happy. She and Rhett don't have anything in common.

Either way, now that she is, there's no escaping her.

She's everywhere.

Oil spreading over the surface of the ocean, and it won't stop spilling out. Like her black hair mixing with the white blonde.

I hate the irony of her edge when she still tries to pretend she's prim and proper. I hate her outward optimism when I know her mind is much darker. I hate her energy when I'd like her to just sit still for five seconds.

I hate her.

But when Rhett wraps his arm around the back of her chair, and she ticks with an almost insignificant flinch—I decide I hate that more.

She doesn't like him, but she's dating him. Not that he sees it or cares. His eyes are set on his pathway to heaven, and with Echo at his side, the congregation loves him.

Echo's gaze drops to where I'm gripping my knife, and I realize my knuckles are white. I hate that she notices everything I don't want her to. After dinner, I'm going to head to the ring and punch someone unconscious just to wipe the judgment of her golden eyes from my brain.

"I hear Rhett gave his first sermon last Sunday." Dad points the tip of his knife at his favorite son.

"It was beautiful. He's a natural." Ryan beams because he honestly doesn't see past this bullshit. "And we'll be recording the next one. Rhett's been working out the logistics."

Dad nods, pretending to care, while Ryan drones on about the importance of spreading the word of God to the people. And even if we're all listening, I can't help but wonder how many of us at the table believe this shit.

Echo goes to church because her dad's a pastor. I avoid it entirely. And my father is only caught inside if he's needed for a business meeting.

"Rhett's a natural, right sweetie?" Ryan smiles at Echo.

She returns one so big and bright, it's out of place in this dark house my father still calls his home. The walls are nearly black with the deep charcoal wallpaper. This manor is a casket for light, while Echo sits in the center of it burning every last atom of oxygen in the room.

"It was good." She nods.

Rhett plants his palm on her shoulder and shakes it. "Just good? Come on, babe. Be supportive."

The laugh that bursts out of me is so sudden all eyes fly in my direction. But my brother is a fucking joke, and the fact that he depends on constant praise is pathetic.

Echo narrows her sparkly golden eyes at me and rolls her shoulders back. "The sermon was perfect, Rhett."

I'm not sure if anyone notices the sweet slip of venom with her statement. Beautiful anger dripping with each pause in her words.

"I loved how you tied moral dilemma to survival instincts. It was..."—she pauses, pushing her food around once more, her eyebrows knitting—"enlightening."

Interesting word choice. Or maybe it's how Echo said it.

Rhett doesn't seem to notice the sadness hinted in her comment. He's too lost in the compliment to care.

Her stare moves to her plate once more. And when he unwinds his arm from Echo's chair, her shoulders relax.

It's slight.

Insignificant.

Her gold eyes flick to mine and pause. If my father is the devil, she's Lady Justice, weighing my fate and looking straight through me.

I set my fork down and lean back, wrapping my fingers around the back of my head and avoiding Echo's eyes. As painful as these family dinners are on a regular weekend, they're worse when Ryan and Echo are here. A chess game of power and faith.

Dad and Ryan dive into some mind-numbing conversation, and I all but zone out.

Even if it's stupid to get in the ring with a broken nose, nothing is going to stop me after this dinner. I need to hit someone—anyone. I'll just make sure I don't take a punch to the face.

The last thing I need is more ammo when Dad already made plenty of comments about me showing up to dinner with two black eyes. He's always got a lot to say about how I disrespect the Kingsley name, and tonight is no different. It's laughable considering I know what he and my brother, Adam, do to build the family empire.

No matter what I do, or how sadistic people think I am, I'm no worse than them.

"A fall wedding would be best."

The word *wedding* drags me out of my head, back to whatever our fathers are talking about.

Echo's face is pale as she swallows, looking on the verge of throwing up.

"Eight months?" Her dad asks my father.

He nods. "Which means an engagement by the end of February to appear natural. Does that work for you, Rhett?"

A train of thoughts floods my brain, grinding to a halt. Smoke fills my mind as the wheels of what they're talking about rip like metal tearing.

"You're getting married?" I don't intend for the question to be to Echo, but I'm staring at her. I can't take my eyes off the darkness of her own. Or how she's popped another piece of gum in her mouth and the chewing is all I hear in this deathly silent house.

"February works." Rhett ignores my question and answers our dad instead.

But I can't break my gaze on Echo as I watch her become a shell of the girl who was the sun a few minutes ago.

"What?" she says in a whisper yell when I don't look away from her. "Yes, we're getting married. Are you just now joining the conversation?"

"You guys have barely been dating."

"Why do you even care?"

Because I know she isn't on board with any of this. Not that I can say that. I don't give people reasons to think I give a shit, and questioning her motives would just make her think I do.

My gaze drops to her finger, where she's twisting the simple white gold band she's always wearing around her finger.

"Guess you'll be upgrading."

Echo narrows her eyes, and Rhett looks at where she's spinning her ring around.

He takes her hand. "Don't worry, baby. I'll replace this piece of junk with something pretty."

Once more, she flinches.

I hate everything about her, but what I really hate is that stupid flinch. Like she's been hit, but her soul is where she feels it.

Rhett drops her hand, once more not noticing, and she grabs her ring with her other hand, twisting it around. The boring ring means something to her, I just don't know what.

My phone buzzes, and I pull it out.

"Not at the table, Crew." Dad leans back, narrowing his gaze at me.

He forgets I'm a grown man sometimes and that I show up here by choice. And every time he speaks to me like a child, I'm tempted to burn his house down so there's no obligation to come back.

"God forbid we ruin this holy dinner." I chuckle. "Have fun planning the wedding of the century. I need to take a call."

Echo frowns, and it shouldn't please me how much I annoy her. But I feed on her hate—her disapproval. And when she clenches her teeth around her gum as I smirk at her, it lights me the fuck up.

"Baby." Rhett nudges Echo's shoulder. "You haven't touched your steak."

"She doesn't eat red meat."

Fucking idiot.

I swear, I'm the only one paying attention.

Standing up, I hit answer before pushing my chair in to really piss off Dad. Giving him a final "fuck you" glance before walking into the other room.

"Yeah?" I answer.

Paul is out of breath on the other end of the line. He always sounds like he's running a marathon from the amount of stress he puts on himself.

"Axel bailed." He sounds frantic when it's nothing to worry about. "And Brea is causing shit with the girls again. Now they're asking for seven-fifty each."

"Then give them seven-fifty." I'm not sure why I have Paul running logistics for these fights when he defers to me on everything. "We make enough that it's not an issue."

The perk of running an illegal underground fight ring filled with politicians and cops is there's plenty of money no one wants to actually account for.

"If we give 'em this, they'll just want more in a few months."

I pinch the bridge of my nose and am reminded it's still throbbing from Echo's punch. Girl can throw one, and I deserved it, so I didn't bother flinching or trying to stop her.

"Then we'll give 'em more in a few months. Would you rather the girls bail?"

Paul can be such a fucking idiot. I'd fire him, but then I'd have to be the face for management, and I don't want anyone knowing who really runs these fight nights.

Jude might think he's the one who introduced me and Sage to the fighting ring, but he only found out about it because I accidentally left the website up at the shop one time, and he saw it. Now I have to be careful when they're there, pretending to be any other fighter like them. The last thing I need is for anyone to know my business. Even my friends.

"If the girls bail, the guys will be pissed," Paul says.

Now he's getting it.

I don't give a shit how much money the ring girls want when we've got more than enough to cover it. Nothing mixes with blood like sex, so if we want the guys to keep opening their wallets, we need them happy.

"And what about Axel?" Paul asks, reminding me we're short a fighter tonight.

"I'll cover it." It's as good of an excuse as any.

"Alright, boss," Paul says, shuffling papers in the background. "See you soon then."

I hang up and freeze when I realize what room I've stepped into. To most people, it would seem like any other—unused and overly decorated. The large mantle in the center of the far wall is lined with photographs that haven't changed in years.

A room my father might as well have walled off after what happened. No one comes in here.

Not since we found her.

My gaze drops to the floor, and I swear I still see the pool of blood on the wood, even if it's no longer there.

I swear I still hear her screams haunting these walls.

Haunting me.

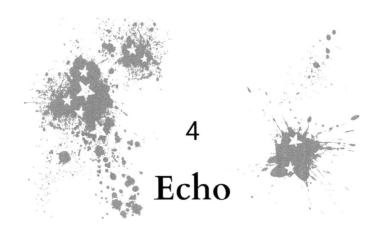

4

Echo

"She doesn't eat red *meat*."

I'm not sure what annoys me more, the fact that Rhett can't remember the simplest things about his girlfriend, or that Crew felt the need to point it out.

It's no secret Crew isn't happy I'm dating his brother. He teases me constantly, but when Rhett is around, he's meaner. There's underlying brotherly tension between the two of them I've never understood. I don't know whether it's their competitive natures or something else, but my getting in the middle didn't help the situation.

Not like I have a choice as our fathers sit planning my wedding.

"Sorry Echo, I forgot about the steak." Rhett frowns, not offering me something different to eat.

Instead, he returns to his conversation, and I'm thankful I'm not hungry anyway.

On my right, I feel my dad's eyes on me, like they've been all night. The shimmer that once resided in the blue has dulled these past few years, and his gray hair is thinning at the crown. Every year ticks a few off him and worry ages his face even more in this moment.

I force a smile and wish it was enough to convince him I'm okay with this. I need to be okay with this. Max Kingsley might be a terrible human being, but he helped save my father's life. He got him a heart and funded his treatments. We owe them for all they've done for us, and I don't back out of my obligations.

Rhett sees a future at my father's church with me at his side, and at least we're friends, so it will be tolerable. It's not like I need love anyway. That's for other people.

"I'm going to use the restroom." I push my chair out and excuse myself.

If I have to continue listening to them plan my wedding, I'm going to scream so loud the sound will embed in the walls.

But when I make it to the doorway, I almost run into Crew, who is circling back into the room, tucking his phone in his pocket. He smirks, stepping aside for me.

"I'm taking off." He waves at the room.

"Already?" Max asks.

"Shit to do."

His dad grumbles before returning to his conversation with mine, and I try to slip down the hallway before Crew can catch up, but he's too quick. The devil in orbit, always watching his prey.

"Leaving so soon." I roll my eyes as he matches my pace. "I'd say I'm disappointed, but we both know I'd be lying."

Crew chuckles, pressing close to my side in the narrow hall that leads to the main part of the house. He leans in so his breath tickles the hair on the top of my head as he flicks my ponytail with his hand.

"Try not to miss me too much." His fingers barely graze my arm and goosebumps skitter to the surface.

"I never do." If anything, with Crew gone, tonight will finally be tolerable. "Where are you running off to anyway? One of your my-dick-is-bigger-than-yours fights? Or is your nose still recovering?"

I smirk, my gaze darting up at him and his broken nose. I should feel bad, and if he wasn't Crew Kingsley, I might. But he wears it like he's proud of the fact that he let me punch him.

"I don't need to beat the shit out of someone to know I've got the bigger dick. Wanna see what you're imagining with your fingers inside you at night?"

"I can promise you I'm not."

He winks. "Sure thing, Goldie."

"You're disgusting."

"And you're a prude."

I wish it didn't sting. That it didn't bubble every insecurity to the surface.

Crew doesn't know I'm a virgin, just like Rhett doesn't. So for once, Crew's comment isn't completely malicious. But something about how the word slips out like he finds it disgusting—how me keeping my legs crossed might as well be pathetic—makes my stomach sink.

Just because I'm not working my way through every available option doesn't mean I don't have my reasons. If only today wasn't one reminder after another about how strange that is for a twenty-three-year-old girl.

Dropping my chin, for once I don't have a comeback. And I hate that Crew's capable of taking my words away from me.

"I'm stepping in for Axel." Crew changes the subject, subtly ignoring the shift in energy as we walk into the foyer. "He bailed on the fight, and someone's got to do it."

I'm not sure why he sounds like he's explaining himself to me. It's not like him.

"Have fun with that." I swallow hard, already choking on the words trying to come out.

I avoid Crew's eyes as I peel the opposite direction from him before he can read whatever is brewing inside. Between his brother assuming I'm sexually experienced when I'm not, and Crew sounding disgusted by the fact that I'm chaste, I've never been more aware of my virginity.

Tears burn behind my eyes, and I don't trust myself to face Crew as I walk away.

I hear him start to say my name in a question, but I'm already turning down the hallway to the bathroom. And it isn't until I'm locked inside that I press my back to the closed door and exhale.

Around Crew, I'm a raw nerve, and he knows exactly where to tap.

Where to prick.

What to say.

If only it felt better to relieve the tension when I punched him in the face.

Walking over to the sink, I lean forward and fill my hands with water. Splashing the coolness of it over my heated skin doesn't erase my thoughts, but at least it settles me down.

Sometimes it's wrong to do the right thing. But I'll do it anyway.

My reflection cries at me with mascara streaming down my cheeks. Wet rivers, dark like it's the middle of the night. Secrets I drown in.

With wet hands, I wipe my cheeks clean. My face. Until my skin can breathe, even if I can't.

Tonight was a bad idea, but I knew that going in. This house does nothing but bring out every insecurity I've ever had. Dark walls that refuse to let the light in. Haunted energy that whispers doubt.

The first time I was here I sold my soul, and every time I've stepped through the doors since then, I hear it somewhere in the basement, chained, and rattling around.

Dad saved me and I'm saving him now.

Penance.

Atonement.

Fate has a way of always coming full circle.

I splash my face a few more times until the mascara is washed off, before drying it. It looks like I've been crying, even if I haven't shed a tear. Doesn't matter, no one will ask me if I have.

With my hair and face presentable, I turn and open the bathroom door, only to find my father standing with his back to the wall outside it.

His gaze pinches at the sight of me. "If you're doubting—"

"I'm not." I don't even let him get his fears out.

He lifts off the wall to follow me down the hallway. No matter how tall he is, everything feels small in this manor. The ceilings tower and the decorations are gaudy and grand.

"Echo, you can be honest with me. Max would understand."

"I promise, Dad. I'm fine." I roll my shoulders back. "He got you a heart, remember? So if it helps Rhett to have me by his side, I'll do it. I'll do anything. Because they're the reason I still have you. We owe them to not back out on our promises."

"How are you two? Getting along at least?"

I shrug. "Rhett's a friend. It's not like we have to love each other to get married."

"You should."

"If this were a teenage girl's fantasy, sure. But I don't need that, Dad. I've got you still and that's all that matters."

He stops, turning to face me in the hallway.

"It's not a fantasy to want to be happy."

"I'm happy enough." It's the truth, anything is better than my childhood—than before Dad learned I existed. "And Rhett's sweet. He's a church boy, remember? He'll treat me fine. This is all for the best."

I force a smile and hope it reaches my eyes, while Dad tucks his hands in his pockets, looking uneasy.

"Promise you'll tell me if you change your mind."

"I won't."

"Promise me, Echo."

Letting out a deep breath, I tip my head back and close my eyes. "Fine. I promise."

I look back at him, knowing it's already a lie. I don't want to marry Rhett, even if it's the right thing to do after all his family has done for us. But I won't back out either.

"Thank you." Dad's gaze skims my face once more. "You feeling all right? You look a little pale."

I tuck my thumbs in my black jeans and shrug. "It's been a rough week, that's all. I just need to chill."

"Does this rough week have anything to do with Crew's face?"

"How did you...?" My eyebrows scrunch.

"Rhett."

I nod. It's not like I was hiding the fact that I punched him, but even though it felt good to work out the aggression, I can't help but feel a little guilty.

"He deserved it" is all I say as we continue down the hallway to the front of the house.

Admitting anything more gives too much away. I refuse to acknowledge that Crew has the uncanny ability to rile me up the way he does with a single comment.

"I'm sure he did." Dad pauses at the edge of the foyer. "I'm grabbing some paperwork from the car really quick. Max wants to see the blueprints for the new church."

Of course he does. Wouldn't want to take the finger off the pulse of his investment.

Dad gives me a quick pat on the shoulder before disappearing out the door. The hollow sound of it closing behind him vibrates through the dark, cold walls. It's no surprise the Kingsley brothers are twisted when they grew up in a house that feels less like a home the longer you spend in it.

Heading back down the hall to the dining room, a voice draws my attention from one of the many small sitting coves tucked off the hall.

"I'm sorry, baby, dinner's running long."

It's Rhett's voice, but it takes me a moment to put it together with the words coming out of his mouth.

Pressing against the wall, I glance around the corner, and Rhett is standing with his back to me as he runs his fingers over the old leather chair in the center. His face tips to the side just enough for me to catch the genuine smile stretching it.

"Promise I'll be there as soon as I'm finished." His voice drops an octave. "The red ones. And I want those legs spread waiting for me. I'll know if you came before I get there. Don't make me punish you."

Legs spread.

Punish you.

Rhett's been open with me about the fact that he's not a virgin, even if he lets the congregation make their own assumptions. And we both have the freedom before we're married to see other people. But knowing that and hearing it are two different things, and something foreign courses through me.

It's not jealousy, because I don't care who Rhett's seeing. It edges closer to embarrassment because I'm not doing the same.

We'll be married soon enough, and he'll have gotten all his secret desires out of his system. But I'll be settling into our cookie-cutter life still a virgin. And what does that mean?

I'll lose it to him?

My stomach turns at the thought. I can barely handle him touching me, but the idea of him doing more makes me nauseous. It's not Rhett's fault. There's only one person who doesn't incite that reaction, and I hate him—proving how fucked up I really am.

The burn in the back of my throat almost makes me vomit. The one thing I have control over in my life is my body. My promise I made to myself. And I decided that if and when I gave up my virginity, it would be to a man who deserved that piece of me.

I just never met him, and now time is running out.

I push off the wall and head back down the hall, except now I'm going in the wrong direction. The walls are closing in on me, and Crew's insult from earlier plays in a loop along with everything his brother said.

Prude.

Have your legs spread.

Just because they don't understand me doesn't mean I don't have my reasons.

Stretching my fingers out in front of me, I try to get a grip. I try to ignore the imaginary blood under my fingernails. I blink until my blurry eyes finally drip clear.

When I make it to the foyer once more, I stop at a set of stairs and drop down onto it, defeated.

I can't turn back, and I can't change fate. The countdown has begun.

Deals sealed in blood mean there's no backing out.

I'm Rhett's, and I have no choice but to play this game for them. No matter what it does to me.

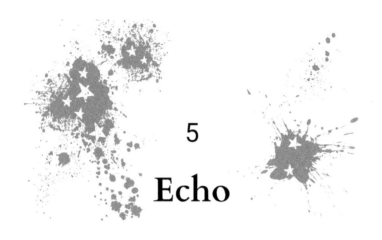

5

Echo

"Echo, you made it." Maren runs up to me, her curves on full display in her neon pink bikini.

She pulls me into a hug, before stepping back and jumping up and down in excitement. A passing fighter notices as his eyes drop straight to her bouncing chest. Something she doesn't seem to mind as she winks at him and bites her lip.

You'd never guess she spends her days working at a fancy plastic surgeon's office, and that the only reason she's here is for the thrill of watching guys beat the life out of each other. Maren fits in like everyone else.

"I think I might get his number." Maren watches the fighter's ass as he walks away.

I can't help but laugh. "These guys are not worth your time."

"To date? Of course not." She puckers her lips. "But a guy who can throw hands can toss me around the bedroom any day."

She shimmies her hips and smiles with the kind of confidence that makes me wish I was more like her. While I have no problem holding my ground in the streets of LA, or doing what needs to be done to survive, sexual confidence is something I've always been sorely lacking.

Something that never bothered me until the constant reminders have been thrown in my face today. It's why I'm here instead of in bed where I planned on going after dinner at the Kingsley manor.

Watching guys beat the shit out of each other will hopefully help me forget the clock counting down in my head.

My stomach twists, and I think I might be sick.

"You feeling all right?" Maren's eyes drop to where I'm clenching my bare stomach.

I changed before coming here, needing to get out of the long sleeves I wore to dinner. I'm more comfortable in my cropped gray top and black jeans, but Rhett would have hated the fake wolf teeth necklace and studded belt. I might not care that Rhett doesn't approve of my tattoos, but I wasn't in the mood tonight to hear his comments. Even if it didn't stop him from pointing out that I was still dressed too casually for a family gathering.

He acts like this is the nineteen fifties, and I'm some suburban housewife.

"I'm fine." I lie, forcing my best I-don't-give-a-fuck smile.

I *am* fine.

I'm Echo Slater, and I don't let men affect me. Enough wallowing over the boyfriend I don't even like. This is still my story, and I'm not done writing it.

"There she is." Maren grins, likely noticing some kind of shift at my change in mindset, as she drops her hands. "I've gotta go fix my hair, but I'll see you after the fight, yeah? I think most of the girls are getting a drink at Fusion."

She gives me a final pat on the arm as she turns and disappears, and I don't miss that the fighter she had her eyes on is lingering by the changing room waiting for her to circle back around for an excuse to talk to her. Something she doesn't seem to mind one bit as she smiles brightly at him.

I make my way through the rowdy crowd and find a seat in the second row, pulling out a joint. This isn't a crowd you have to hide openly smoking in since most people here are high or drunk. Everyone's fucked up on either booze or adrenaline.

A few guys further down in the row didn't even bother changing out of their police uniforms before showing up.

Taking a long drag, I let the weed settle my brain. Smoke filters through my thoughts and buries what I don't want to think about. In the ring at the center of the room, someone is getting their face caved in by their opponent, but I don't so much as flinch as he drops to the ground.

I've got an iron stomach for blood.

Some I've seen. Some I've spilled.

"Echo, thought that was you." A guy in the seat in front of me spins around and smiles, his gaze traveling to where my crop top shows off my stomach before trailing back up.

He's trying to act nonchalant but failing.

"Hey, Derek." I tip my chin up and take another drag of my joint.

It's strong shit. My mind grows wings, and I slowly float away.

"Haven't seen you around here in a while." Derek has fully turned sideways in his seat, holding the back of it with his arm, so he can look at me.

"Haven't been here in a while."

It's been at least six months. I used to come to these fight nights all the time because, even if I probably shouldn't enjoy watching people get hurt, I like seeing the guys fight. Every hit a reminder of how it feels to unleash what I'm not allowed to.

But then I started dating Rhett, and the strings holding my limbs began to tug. He didn't like the idea of his girl-friend being spotted at an illegal underground fighting ring. So for him, I stopped coming.

For him, I stopped doing lots of things.

I understood there is a mold my life needs to fit into if I'm going to be his wife. And for the past few months, I've accepted it, so long as he doesn't try to talk me out of working at the shop. He might not balk at my quarter ownership in Twisted Roses, but he doesn't like that I still work there. It's not appropriate enough for a preacher's girlfriend, according to him.

Like he's one to talk, pretending he's celibate for his congregation.

"I've been busy," I tell Derek, leaving the crawling itch of truth out of it because it's none of his business.

"I know how that is." He smiles. Wide eyes, big teeth. Everything about him is overwhelming. "I've been busy myself. Things have been wild at the station lately. Got promoted to sergeant."

"Congratulations." I nod my head once and take another hit.

Cops that come to these fights are usually dirty, so it's probably not a good sign he's moving up the ranks as easily as he is.

"Thanks, if you ever want to see the precinct, let me know. I'll give you the tour."

Why in the hell he thinks I'd ever care or want to baffles me. But I force an appropriate smile that's probably condescendingly sweet when paired with my pinched gaze anyway.

"Or, if you'd like to hang out after this..."

Derek reaches out and runs the back of his hand over my knee like I offered it to him. I hate that men are always touching. It doesn't matter if I've given him no reason to think I'm interested, he'll grab for it anyway.

I'm about to burn him with the end of my joint when a body passes between us and a shin kicks Derek's hand out of the way.

"Fuck off, Derek. She's taken." Crew drops into the seat beside me.

He told me he was fighting tonight, but I kind of hoped the fact that it took me so long to get here after dinner would mean his fight would already be over, and he would have left.

Derek's eyes skip to Crew, and he turns back around.

Crew is one of the few fighters who everyone is familiar with. Opponents fear him, but the crowd loves him. He's vicious—violent. And as annoying as it is that people think they need to bow down to him, in this moment I'm thankful he cut off my conversation with Derek.

Not that I'll share that with him.

"What? I'm not allowed to talk to friends?"

Crew crosses his arms over his chest, leaning closer to me, but not taking his eyes off the fight happening in the ring in front of us. "Since when are you and this douchebag friends?"

"Since I tatted his brother."

We aren't friends, but I don't need Crew thinking he's some knight in shining armor for saving me from that conversation.

"Interesting." He chuckles.

I narrow my eyes. "What?"

"Didn't know you were in the market for *friends.*" His gaze slides in my direction, and I don't like that he's insinuating Derek is something more than what he is. "My preacher boy brother not keeping you satisfied?"

If only my core didn't clench every time his steel eyes made contact with mine.

If only his vicious comment wasn't so on point.

My mouth falls open, and I almost let that slip. Almost make the biggest mistake I can by giving Crew Kingsley a peek behind the curtain. Luckily, the buzzer sounds and reminds me who I'm talking to.

"At least your brother cares about satisfying others." Not a total lie considering what I heard him tell the random woman on the phone. "I doubt *your* partners can say the same thing."

"They say lots of things." The most devilish smirk climbs his cheeks. "Yes... Please... *More*. Want to hear what I do to make them beg for me?"

Heat floods my cheeks. My skin erupts.

Crew watches my parted lips, and I feel him focusing on every quick breath. I snap my mouth shut and try to bury the volcano bubbling inside.

"No." A lie has never scalded my tongue the way that one word does. But I can't say the truth, because wanting to hear his answer is wrong on every level.

Crew shifts back, but I don't break his gaze as I hear a body fall to the mat in the ring in front of us. The buzzer sounds, and I can't help that it makes me jump. Fury boiling as Crew notices and smirks.

He doesn't say another word as he stands up and walks away, leaving the seat beside me once again empty. And I can't take my eyes off him as he makes his way up the steps to the ring, peeling his shirt off and putting his tight, tattooed chest on display.

Crew doesn't sit on the stool as he wraps tape around his hands. He's calmly swaying back and forth with whatever he's thinking while his opponent bounces in the other corner. His eye sockets are dark from where his nose is already broken, but in this light, I realize it's not as bad as I thought it was.

Or maybe it's that Crew wears bruises well. Proudly, like a badge of honor.

A girl in red star pasties circles the ring, swaying her hips with each step. Once more, the display of sexual confidence makes my stomach ache. She winks at both guys as she steps down to take her seat, but Crew doesn't acknowledge her back. He's too focused.

He's a hunter, lasered in on the kill in front of him.

He's smirking at his opponent for daring to think he might win.

He won't.

Crew doesn't lose. Even when he lets his opponent land a few good hits, it's only for his own amusement. There's no chance this guy is going to walk out of here.

The buzzer dings and they collide in the center.

Bone. Blood. Violence.

Crew smashes his knuckles against his opponent's jaw, and he smirks in pleasure as the guy stumbles.

He's enjoying this.

He wants to watch the light fade from his opponent's eyes.

He's a sick, twisted, walking disaster who destroys everything he touches simply for his own entertainment.

And as I watch him knock his opponent one final time in the side of the jaw—cracking it with such force it can be heard over the screaming crowd—I get an idea that will send me straight to hell.

It doesn't matter if I hate him. Crew enjoys making a mess, and I'm in the mood to burn everything down.

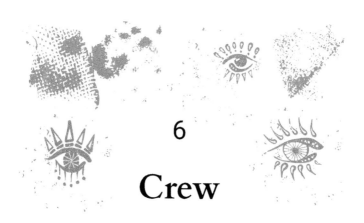

6

Crew

Rage drops like dead weight to the mat in a puddle of his own blood. Satisfaction courses through me as my fingers flex. The way my knuckles imprinted on his flesh and painted a beautiful violent picture with his face should settle me, but I'm more amped up than I was before the fight started.

My gaze moves to the empty seat Echo was sitting in earlier, and I clench my hands into fists. It's her fault for riling me up before the fight, making it impossible to enjoy it like I normally do.

Something about how Derek grazed her leg made me want to cut off his fingers and feed them to him. That and the fact that Echo offered me such a sweet inhale when I teased her about how I could make her beg for me.

The girl is dangerous. I don't like her, but she still manages to get my blood boiling.

Fuck her for messing with my head.

I left her at the house with Rhett—*her boyfriend*. She wasn't supposed to follow me here, walking around with judgment in her eyes. I can't escape the girl lately, and it's making my mind numb trying.

"Brutal." Mandi slips her hands around my arm and presses her pastie-clad tits against me.

I don't fuck ring girls anymore because I pay them, and the first couple of times I did, it got complicated. But it doesn't stop the few of them who continue to try.

Mandi bats her lashes like she thinks she has the power to break me with her silicone-infused lips. They're overinflated and unimpressive. And as much as I enjoy fucking, lately, I've had no interest.

The only thing that even comes close to releasing a little tension is hitting someone.

Jude and Sage write me off as a sadistic fucker who doesn't give a shit. Maybe that's true given the amount of enjoyment I get inflicting pain on others. What they don't understand is why I am the way I am.

Either you're the one receiving pain or inflicting it. I saw the result of one side as a child, so I made sure when I grew up to be the one who did the damage.

Shaking Mandi off my arm, I make my way out of the ring. The crowd screams for me—cheers for me. It should give me some sense of validation, but I'm not here for them. I don't need their acceptance or admiration. I did what I came to do.

If only I felt better now.

Lifting my hands, I examine my knuckles bleeding through the tape. It's another part of me ripped open, and there's nothing to be found but blood. Leaking proof that life's as breakable as anything else, no matter how well you can take or hand out a punch.

I pass the locker room and head straight to the office. Jude is on his honeymoon and Sage is busy with whatever new girl he's fucking this week, so I don't have to hide what I'm up to. Swinging the door open, I find Paul leaning back on the couch with his cock down Tiffany's throat.

"Busy?" I cross one ankle over the other and prop myself against the doorframe, not bothering to look away.

Tiffany pulls her mouth off his dick in shock and rushes to her feet, while Paul just smirks from his seat and thankfully puts his dick away. I'd like to say it's the first time I've seen it, but Paul doesn't share my feelings on not fucking the girls who work here. Which is why, as Tiffany shuffles out of the room, winking back at him, I already know this is going to be another Chelsea situation.

"You never fucking learn, man." I cross the office and sink into my seat at the desk, kicking my feet up on it.

"One blow job from Tiff, and you'd understand." Paul rakes his fingers through his curly dark hair. "Girl's a fucking hoover without a gag reflex."

"Well sorry to ruin your fun." Not really, but fucker doesn't care anyway. He'll finish what he started when I leave for the night. Either with Tiffany or someone else. "I'm guessing you told the girls about their raises. They're extra cheery today."

It's annoying. I hate happy people. Give me your pissed-off bullshit because at least it's more believable than nauseating optimism.

"Tiff was just thanking me for it."

"You're lucky I'm the one who technically pays them. Illegal fighting is one thing, but this isn't a fucking prostitution ring."

"Don't I know it." He's disappointed.

If people think I lack morals, they've never met Paul. Or maybe it's that we're on different levels.

"Seriously, boss, you need to fight less and fuck more. Makes for a happier existence." Paul stretches his arms out along the back of the couch.

"What's happiness if it isn't breaking someone's face?"

Paul shakes his head. He might run the logistics of these fights, but he's never been in the ring. He understands the back of Tiffany's throat better than he understands what it means to be a fighter.

What it means to survive walking away from the blood after you've spilled it.

I've been there, more than once in my life. Each time a victory is more important than getting lost between some ring girl's legs.

"Where are we at with the Oakland setup?" I ask, dropping my feet and getting to business.

I'd rather be at home, halfway down a bottle of whiskey, than sitting in an office that smells like Tiffany's perfume and Paul's dick.

"Almost all set. Trevor took a trip with the guys last week and nailed down a location."

"And the locals?"

"Onboard."

Los Angeles isn't the only city with dirty cops and bent politicians looking for an outlet for their aggression. And I'm happy to drain their wallets by offering up a solution.

It wasn't my plan initially to expand. These fights started five years back as a way for a small group of guys to blow off steam. One person told another, then they told another. Now we're a full-blown organization—even if technically we don't exist.

Sometimes you stumble on a need in the market before you realize it.

"Good. Let me know when the papers are ready, and I'll take a trip up there to sign off on the building."

"You got it."

I rarely leave Los Angeles anymore. As a kid, Dad forced us to tag along on all his work trips. Every month I was missing school for one of them. Not that it affected my grades when Dad donated more money than God to the school board to ensure it didn't matter whether we were there or not.

After we lost Mom, he couldn't sit still. So he drowned himself in work, forcing us to follow him while he found anything he could to replace her as a distraction.

I traveled enough in my teenage years to be tired of it. But if I'm going to expand the fights, it needs to be out of the city. Too much noise in one place will eventually draw attention.

A soft knock comes at the door before Mandi peeks her head in.

"Sorry." Her eyes dart from me to Paul. "I didn't know you were busy."

"Taking off." As much as I enjoy fighting, everything after makes my skin crawl.

"So early?"

Standing up, I circle the desk and pat Paul on the shoulder. "Yep. If you need anything I'm sure my man here would be more than happy to help you out."

Paul smirks up at me. I might not agree with his methods, but so long as he continues to get shit done, I don't give a fuck what he does.

Mandi frowns as I walk past, before stepping into the office and closing the door.

A few people try to stop me on my way out. Everyone's in the mood to drink, party, and fuck. But just like every day lately, I'm not.

Something's been off, and I don't know what the fuck it is. All I know is I'd rather focus on the throbbing of another broken bone or fracture than have to think about it.

It takes twice as long as I'd like to get back to my apartment. And when I do, I'm met with a cold, empty space.

Exactly how I like it.

I strip out of my clothes and hop in the shower to wash off what's left of the sweat and blood from my fight. Washing my face, my nose throbs a little from Echo's punch. She got me good for such a tiny thing.

Echo.

Fuck, that girl won't get out of my head or life lately.

Her judgmental golden eyes and her sweet smile try to hide the fact that she's a little devil beneath. But I see it. Sunshine bursting through the smoke covering the city. Energy radiating from every pore.

And she's marrying Rhett?

I figured our dads were forcing them to date long enough for Rhett to take his place in Ryan's church as the holy son. Then they'd quietly part ways and Rhett would find some submissive preacher-wife-type to have boring sex with on Fridays.

But he's going full steam with Echo? It doesn't make sense.

As if it isn't bad enough for Dad and Rhett to drag her into the peripheral of our family, they're turning her into a Kingsley for real. That only ends one way—and as much as I hate her most days, I don't wish my mother's fate on anyone.

Turning off the shower, I barely have time to slip into sweatpants before I'm heading to the liquor cabinet. Anything to get my mind off what my family is going to do to Echo.

My father used to tell me drowning problems in booze is for the weak. But he's one to talk. It's better than his outlets.

Downing a shot of my strongest whiskey, I start to pour another when my phone pings with an alert that someone's at my door.

No one shows up at my place this late. No one shows up here at all.

People know better when I go through a lot of trouble to make it seem like this place doesn't even exist. Most of my friends assume I live near the shop since I crash on the couch in the office so often. If Jude hadn't moved in across the hall, he and Sage wouldn't even know about it.

My apartment is the one place I can disappear. Which is why I don't even bring the girls I fuck back here. These walls are for me alone.

Pulling up the live feed, I'm not sure what I expect, but it's not Echo standing at my doorstep.

She's still wearing the same black jeans and gray crop top from the fight earlier, but she's ditched her jewelry, and her hair is down. Like she got halfway to bed and made a different decision.

The one and only time Echo has been to my apartment ended with me getting my nose broken, so I'm not sure why she's digging her thumbs in her pockets and standing at my door looking like she's the one who should be nervous.

Or better yet—why she's here at all.

If it were anyone else, I'd probably ignore it and finish my drink before going to bed. But I'm too damn curious to not walk to the door and find out what she wants. And I'm too damn tempted to make her regret showing up in the first place.

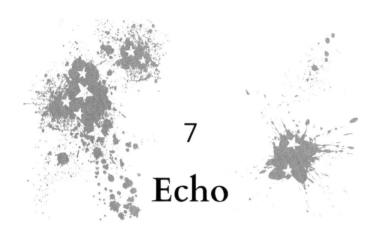

7

Echo

THIS MIGHT BE THE worst idea I've ever had.

Crew probably didn't even hear me knock. It's been two minutes, and I'm still standing in front of his door like an idiot, while there's not so much as a sound coming from the other side. I could still walk away, and no one would have to know I was ever here.

I take a step back, and like a predator sensing my retreat, Crew swings open the door.

Fuck him.

Of course he's in nothing more than a pair of gray sweatpants that hang so low on his waist his muscles draw a line straight to places I should not be thinking about. His tattooed chest is on full display, every ripple of his arms flexing as he grabs the sides of the doorframe and smirks at me.

Devilish confidence I'd like to smack off his face.

"Crew." I grit my teeth.

His lips tilt in a devious smile. "Already with the at-titude? You're the one standing at my doorstep in the middle of the night."

He's right. I am. Doesn't make me hate him any less.

"Can I come in?"

I think he'll shut the door in my face just for the fun of it. He's unpredictable, and you can never guess how he'll react or what he'll do. But instead of locking me out, he takes a step back, letting me in.

This is a terrible idea.

Why I'm walking past him instead of running doesn't make any sense. But the gravity of this place, of my deci-sion, *of him* pulls me inside. And when he closes the door behind me, air holds in my lungs.

"Drink?" he asks, brushing past me and walking into the kitchen.

A large granite island separates the kitchen from the rest of the apartment, and it feels bigger than it did the last time I was here. Or maybe I feel smaller.

The dark gray walls expand with every breath. Black and gray furniture; sleek lines that draw out the wideness of this space.

Working at the shop with Crew, in a not-so-great part of LA, it's easy to forget he comes from money. It's only when I see him here or at his father's house that I'm reminded just how far apart our worlds are.

He tips the whiskey bottle at me, and I shake my head.

The booze might give me more confidence, but I don't need anything else clouding my judgment right now. That's already twisted enough.

Crew shrugs, pouring a shot and downing it before setting the bottle aside.

He's been drinking more lately. Partying more lately.

Not that I can judge when I've been getting high more lately. *Lately*—somehow everything is escalating. I'm not sure what his reasons are, but I know mine.

"Did you come here just to stare at me?" Crew's voice snaps me out of my thoughts. Out of those gray eyes of his that root me in place.

I shake my head. "No."

This all played out better in my imagination, where I was more confident. While right now I'm standing on shaky ground as I try to pull myself together.

"Then why—"

"I want you to take my virginity," I cut him off, and I'm not sure a sentence has ever felt more vulnerable.

His eyes pinch as he works over what I said. Processing for a moment as the words float in the space between us. Only then does he react.

Barely. The smallest tick of a smirk.

"Funny." Crew shakes his head, pushing off the counter and walking across the room to sink into a big leather chair. "You almost got me with that one. Why are you actually here, Echo?"

I swallow the frustration bubbling to the surface, clenching my hands at my sides. "That *is* why I'm here."

"You're not a virgin." His eyebrow ticks as his gaze drops down my body and back up again, pausing when his stare lands on my left hand, to the solid white gold purity ring that sits there. "You're not."

I'm not sure if he's repeating it to convince me or himself, but his Adam's apple bobs with a thick swallow.

"I'm not here to explain myself to you. You can believe me or not, it doesn't really matter." I take a step into the living room, my feet itching to run but moving in his direction anyway. "I just need to know if you'll do it."

"Did my brother turn you down or something?" He looks almost angry at his question.

I shake my head. "Didn't ask him."

"So instead of the obvious option—*asking your dick-of-a-boyfriend*—you show up at his brother's apartment?"

Crew almost sounds genuinely curious.

I nod in answer. "Yes."

"But you hate me."

"Exactly. We hate each other." At least if he's moved away from the *she's a virgin* line of questioning, he might actually be considering it. "And because of that, there's no risk either of us will get attached. Besides, you have no morals, and I swear you hate your brother half the time. There are plenty of reasons for you to do this. Take your pick."

The bastard smirks and his energy closes in on me without him so much as having to take a step. Instead, he takes up all the space in this room with one look.

"That still doesn't explain you showing up on my doorstep asking me to take your virginity, Echo."

Crew usually avoids calling me by my name, which is how I know he's being serious.

"Why do you care?" I try to brush off his question. "It's just my virginity."

"That *is* why. It's your *virginity*." The word comes out through gritted teeth, and I don't know who he's mad at—me for offering it up or him for considering it.

"Is it supposed to matter?" I challenge. "Is that what you're worried about? Trust me, I'm not holding onto it for the reasons you probably think I am."

"Then shouldn't you be giving it to my brother?" He spits the words like the thought of them makes him sick.

"Probably," I agree. "But if he's going to have his fun before we get married, then shouldn't I be allowed to have mine? He's not walking into this a virgin you know. He's off screwing someone right now."

Storm clouds brew in Crew's eyes, and I realize Rhett and I might have been faking our relationship better than I thought because he looks genuinely shocked by my comment.

"It's fine. We have... an understanding."

My reassurance does nothing to relax Crew's shoulders, so I dig deeper.

"You don't know the arrangement between me and Rhett, so I get it sounds like I'm being irrational." I roll my shoulders back. "We made a promise, and we're going to keep it regardless. But he isn't my husband yet, and I'm not his wife. I know how you feel about me, Crew, you hate me, and I annoy you. And I don't particularly like you either. But I trust you with this. I know you well enough to know you'll keep it between us."

He doesn't so much as flinch.

"Besides…" My cheeks heat as I remember what he said at the fight tonight. "You've got the experience, so I know you'll make it worth it."

I swallow hard. The idea of Crew touching me sets my skin on fire—makes my throat sandpaper. While the thought of anyone else makes me cringe.

"I know I don't have experience myself, but sex is sex, right?" I shake my head, and something about that sentence makes his entire demeanor tense. "I'm asking as a friend—or enemy—or whatever we are. I don't want to get married a virgin. So are you really going to suddenly grow morals or are you going to help me out and ruin the last bit of good I've got left?"

My rant should be enough to send any sane person running. But this is Crew Kingsley, and he's far from sane. If anything, his gray eyes heat with the inferno building inside him. Amusement lights his smirk up in the most devious way.

There's a reason I came to Crew with this—apart from my body's annoying reaction to his. I hate him enough that I won't grow feelings, and he's hopefully twisted enough to take me up on this offer.

Finally, Crew stands, walking across the room. Stopping close enough that his campfire scent heats me to the core.

He brushes my hair behind my ear, ever so slowly trailing his finger along the side of my throat. With anyone else it would be sweet, but with him, it's almost a threat.

"I'm only going to say this once, Echo." He pauses his fingers on my pulse, before dropping his hand. "You should give your virginity to someone who cares about you. Because as annoying as you are, you deserve it. And I won't be sweet like your preacher boy."

"He's not sweet."

Just boring. Vanilla. Plain.

Crew tilts his head. "He's not me."

"Maybe," I agree. There's no arguing with the fact that no one is as uncaring and brutal as Crew Kingsley. "But nothing is on my terms anymore. Nothing but this."

I dare to step toward him. A flicker of interest in his eyes as I get closer to him than I've ever been before. Tipping my chin up, I'm met with those silvery-gray eyes that rattle me around.

I don't want sweet. I don't want gentle.

Which is why I react to him against my better judgment.

I want a reminder of how good I feel when I unleash my dark side.

"It's one time," I say, nearly a whisper. "Don't worry, I won't want to do it again."

"You think that now." He lifts his hand once more and fingertips brush lightly along my jaw.

"I know it." Wanting him sexually and emotionally are two different things. "Please, Crew."

The darkest smile crosses his face at my words, and he takes a step back. He turns and walks across the room, dropping into his leather chair once more and looking me over.

"Begging is a good start." Crew plants his tattooed hands on the arms of the chair and grips it tightly. "But it's better done on your knees."

My eyes narrow, fighting every instinct inside that urges me to flip him off for talking to me like that.

But I asked for this.

I want this.

It's why I showed up here instead of anywhere else.

"What do you want me to do? Pray to you, *my lord*?" Sarcasm drips from my tone, while the words make me shiver at the thought.

Crew's sick smile hitches. "I don't want your prayers, Echo. I'm no faux saint like my brother. I want your sins. I want to watch you burn for me. You want this? Then get on your knees, princess, and crawl."

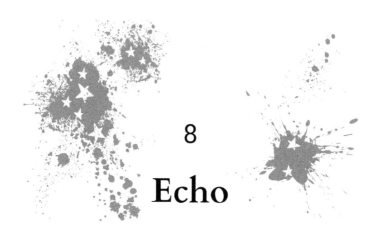

8

Echo

CRAWL.

One word that goes against all my instincts.

It's degrading. Disgusting. But worse, it sends a hot rush through me. My cheeks heat and I feel the blush crawling up my chest—my neck. In embarrassment or anticipation. I've never wanted to make a fool of myself more than with one word.

Crew watches me, not offering a flinch of an expression. He issued the challenge, and he's waiting to see if I'll accept it.

I shouldn't.

This is probably a test because he doesn't think I'm serious. He assumes if he pushes me to my limits I'll turn and walk away. I'll realize this was a bad idea and rescind my offer.

Trouble is, I can hate him all I want, but my body still responds to him in ways it doesn't for anyone else, not even in my imagination.

I want this. I want *him*. And I'm prepared to prove he can't scare me.

His sculpted chest is on display in the dark apartment. The curtains are drawn, and the city is lit beneath us. Darkness casts shadows on his features, sculpting a vicious, tattooed god my body wants to bow down to.

So I do.

I drop to my knees to prove to him I'm here for a reason.

His gaze falls, watching me, following every movement. His fingers grip his leather chair as I plant mine on the cool wood floor beneath me.

It should be degrading. But as I start to crawl, his steel eyes darken. And as his jaw tenses, I've never felt more in control.

Never felt more wanted.

I haven't held onto my virginity because it's an important keepsake. I've kept it because it's mine, and someone tried to take it years ago like it wasn't. I promised I'd do this on my terms, and that's what's going to happen.

My last piece of innocence, and I just offered it to a devil.

Crew is calm as he waits for me to stop between his spread legs. His chest rises and falls with every breath, and his nostrils flare as I sit back on my knees before him. An offering, and for some reason, I'm at peace.

I'm still.

I'm silent, lost in his every exhale.

He leans forward, planting his elbows on his knees, so he's close enough for me to feel his body heat. To smell the soap from his shower and the spice from his still-wet hair.

"You don't have to do this," he says.

Crew's never thoughtful. Always impulsive, but tonight, every comment flips between crude and caring. A tug of war I can't wrap my head around.

"I want to." It's a choked whisper and too honest.

"Do you even know what you're asking for?" His eyes narrow in a challenge, his fingers finding my jaw and running along it. His thumb rubs roughly over my lips. "Have you ever sucked a cock, Goldie? Has a man ever stretched these pretty lips to their limits? Made your jaw ache and your eyes water from fucking it hard and rough. Have you ever had a man beg for your mouth—for you to swallow his cum like it's the best thing you've tasted?"

I shake my head.

I've never wanted that. Never felt the urge—or any urge for that matter. But as Crew's thumb toys with the line of my lip, brushing against my teeth with my exhale, my core clenches and my insides flutter.

He leans in closer, so we're nearly nose to nose.

"I get why you came to me and not to Rhett, whether you hate me or not."

"I *do* hate you."

"Okay." He chuckles like he doesn't believe it. "But, Goldie, you still have no idea what you're getting into. And as much as I'd love to sink into you right now and taste that pretty little hate fire of yours, I'm not going to be a weapon for you to later use against my brother. I'm not going to be your excuse when you're too scared to make your own life choices. If you want me to fuck you—to take your purity—I'll only do it if you tell me the real reason. You're asking me because *you want me to*."

He leans back in his chair, arms stretched at his sides. Shoulders relaxed, but the darkest steel-gray eyes as he watches me sitting in front of him.

"I can't." Not because I don't want it, but because I can't open myself up to what might come from that admission.

Crew understands why I'm here, but he's trying to flip this around for his own validation. He wants me to admit I want him more than his brother—either because he's competitive or because I'm vulnerable. It doesn't matter. It's already too much that I've told him I want him to fuck me. I can't let him think any more of it.

"Fine, I won't fuck you then." He tips his chin up. His squared features catch the shadows in this dark room. "Come here."

My instincts tell me to run, but I stand instead, accepting his open palm as he pulls me onto his lap so I'm straddling him.

"What are you doing?" I grab his shoulders, hating how the skin-on-skin contact makes my insides flutter. "You just said you won't fuck me."

"Correct. Not until you're ready to admit why you really came to me with this." He rakes his teeth over his bottom lip and grabs my hips.

In one sweep, he stands up and flips us until I'm sitting in the leather chair, and he's kneeling on the floor in front of it.

"What are you doing?" My nails dig into his shoulders.

"You're lying to me, Echo." He runs his hands up my thighs, slowly inching his way inward the higher he gets. "So I'm going to have to find more creative ways to get your confession out of you. And trust me, I will."

I shake my head. "You can't."

"Hmm." He slows as his hands drag upward, pausing when they're just shy of grazing where I need the pressure. "You sure about that?"

"No." I tip my head back and close my eyes because he knows he's breaking me, and I can't stop him.

Why I'm here doesn't matter. I need to feel him.

"Didn't think so." Crew's fingers crawl upward, and he pops the button on my jeans. "Lift."

My focus snaps back to him as his fingers curl into the top of my pants. And I lift my hips so he can drag them down, sitting once more, so he can peel them from my legs. There's nothing more than the thin fabric of my underwear between us, and as his gaze moves to the spot between my legs, I'm sure he's seeing how wet I am at the thought of what he'll do.

"You drive me fucking crazy." His fingers trace over the rose tattoos on my upper thighs before his hands move inward, and he spreads my legs for him. "You piss me off in the worst ways, and then show up in the middle of the night looking like pure fucking sin, offering your virginity to me."

His fingers graze so close to my pussy that I almost come apart from him brushing against the soft skin of my inner thigh.

"Sin dressed up in innocence. Begging me to take your purity." This time when his hands drift up to my hips, his thumbs drag over my underwear, and my clit throbs at the contact.

Crew slides his fingers down and peels my underwear to the side, his jaw clenching at the sight of me spread in front of him.

"Beg me to fuck you, and maybe I'll consider it."

Before I can tell him to fuck off, he dives between my legs. His tongue drags my pussy, and I lose all rational thought. He rolls it over my clit, and I swear it vibrates. My bones shake, and my vision blurs.

Gripping his dark hair in both my hands, I'm holding on and letting go as he fucks me with his tongue. Pressure edges me to the brim of losing my mind as he holds my hips tight to his face. And when I start to clench my thighs around his head, he presses my thighs farther apart.

I'm at his mercy, and he's feasting like he's starving for every bit I'll give him.

My nails rake against his scalp as he once more moves his focus to my clit. Back and forth. In circles. Painting pictures that swirl around us as my body starts to float.

I've never done anything with a man—and certainly nothing like this.

Something that makes my legs boneless as he turns my body to liquid.

Lashes fluttering, I feel myself losing my grip on this plane of existence, just as Crew stops all movement and pulls back.

"Crew." It's a half plea, half moan.

I'm pathetic and desperate and I need him to keep going. My legs are shaking from the sudden loss of friction.

Crew sits back on his heels, continuing to press his palms to the inside of my legs to hold them open. A devious smirk on his face.

"There's only one thing you can say to me for me to let you come, Echo. You know what it is."

My jaw clenches, teeth gritted, but I can't get it out. As good as he feels, I refuse to admit how much I want him. This is a means to an end, nothing more.

"Have it your way." But instead of pulling back, he's on my clit again.

His lips kiss my pussy like I'm the best thing he's ever tasted. His tongue dances in figure eights, and my vision darkens.

I'm no longer holding his hair, I'm clawing his hands, my legs, the chair. I'm scratching to hold on while he drives me to the edge. Air beneath my feet and wind in my hair as I start to plummet.

And just as I'm about to reach it—to taste the sweet relief—he pulls back again.

"Fuck you." I try to kick at him as he sits back on his heels again, but his hold on my legs stops me. So I jab my heels at his sides, even if all it makes him do is laugh.

"I already told you what you need to say if you want me to fuck you."

"I—"

He must sense my attitude on the tip of my tongue because he pulls my words from my mouth by diving between my legs before I can finish my sentence. This time he's not slow and sweet. He's brutal, the stubble of his chin rubbing roughly against me as his tongue fucks me, and he moans as my pussy squeezes him. The invasion is almost too much. But every time I'm close, he pulls back.

Burying my face in my hands, I groan at the loss of him once more. White noise clouds my hearing, and I'm seeing stars with each blink. I'm so close and so far from pleasure, one graze of his hands on my skin might send me over the edge. But he holds me still, refusing me the relief.

He's a magician or a God or the devil.

Hanging me over the pit of hell and refusing me what I need.

"Please, Crew." I drop my hands and grab onto where his hands hold me open.

"Please what?" He's no longer smirking. A serious edge as his steel-gray eyes take in my exasperation.

"Please let me come."

I'm not sure I've ever been more desperate for anything.

"Why?" He grips my legs tighter.

"Because I need you to." I drag my fingers over his, through his. I hold him, and I'm not sure a person has ever felt as comforting as he does as his hands lace in mine and tether me to this moment. "I want you to."

Crew pulls my hand up and kisses the back of it. "Who does your body need, Echo?"

"You." I don't so much as hesitate. It's the truth, whether I like it or not.

Fire lights the darkness in his eyes, warming me to my core.

"Good girl."

This time, when he kisses my pussy, there's an intensity that wasn't there before. He keeps his fingers laced through mine and holds me through each roll of his tongue. Holds me in place through the vibrations of his hums. His lips kiss my clit, and then he's rolling back and forth over it. My hips rocking with every wave.

Darkness tunnels my vision as I watch him between my legs, and then there's nothing but Crew and his silver eyes, watching every exhale leave my lips. His hands on mine, and his tongue rocking me through it. My entire body shakes, but he doesn't pull back this time.

I can't help the scream that releases as my entire body might as well split open. I burst. I shake around him.

My nails dig into the back of his hands as he slips his tongue inside me like he wants to feel every squeeze of my climax. It isn't until I stop shivering, and my vision clears that he pulls back.

I release his hands and drag mine through my hair, pulling it off my shoulders while I try to catch my breath.

"You're welcome." He grins.

I kick him with my heels. "Asshole. That was borderline torture."

"What ends well..."

Crew bites his lower lip, tilting his head and smiling darkly, his gaze dropping to my hand.

He picks it up and draws my ring finger into his mouth, circling his tongue around it. The warm wet, massage makes my stomach tighten. My legs are practically shaking at the sensation.

This night is so far past boundaries we shouldn't be crossing, but I can't pull my hand away.

With a final suck, he drags his teeth over my finger as he draws it from his mouth, and that's when I realize my purity band is no longer on my finger. He reaches up and pulls it from his mouth, holding it between us.

"I'm keeping this." He pushes my ring into his pocket. "Until you're ready to give me the real thing."

"Jerk." I roll my eyes, but when I start to sit up, he stops me with a hand planted in the center of my chest.

"One," he says, pressing my back once more to the leather.

"One what?"

"That was one." His fingers graze my clit, and I'm so sensitive my body jumps. But his hold on my chest keeps me in place. "Now give me another."

Before I can ask what he's referring to, he's back between my legs and darkness overwhelms my vision.

Space. A universe where I'm floating. A star closing in.

9

Crew

VIRTUE IS MEANINGLESS. I don't care about doing good or being holy. Turning down Echo's offer had nothing to do with a sweep of righteousness flooding me.

I'm selfish.

And the moment I realized Echo is a virgin, my protective animal instincts kicked in.

If she thinks she can use me against my brother just because he's enjoying himself until they get married, I'll prove her wrong. I'll make her desperate until she begs for me.

Only me.

She can hate me all she wants. I don't particularly care for her either. But messy, needy—anxious for my tongue in her tight pussy—I'm tempted to fuck her until she forgets why she should have never offered herself up to me in the first place.

Problem is, if I'm going to have her, it'll be on my terms, and I can't figure out what those are anymore.

I suspected Rhett was cheating on her, but I didn't expect her to be aware of it. Him being a holy church boy, and her being mostly a good girl, I wouldn't have guessed their arrangement. But it makes sense. If neither of them is particularly interested in their inevitable marriage, and there are no vows yet to hold them back, why not?

And while Echo could have gone to anyone to play out whatever little revenge fantasy she sees fit for her situation, she came to me. Someone she hates—or at the least, someone she dislikes.

Offered herself up like a perfect virginal prize.

One taste and this girl has me feeling unhinged. A girl I've spent years butting heads with. She had to go and lace her fingers through mine as she came on my tongue, and I had the sick thought that I was the first person to do that to her.

The *only* person to do that to her.

Her mouth can deny it all she wants, but her body reacts. Her eyes watch. Her skin shudders. She gives herself away with every exhale.

She's offering one time, but I'm going to call her bluff because now I'm addicted.

Echo might think she knows all there is to know about me, but she's about to learn I'm a twisted, sick fuck who doesn't share his possessions, so she shouldn't have made herself one of them.

Walking into the shop, I'm thirty minutes late for my appointment, and I'd pretend to give a shit if I cared.

I don't.

Waking up was hard enough when I barely slept.

All because of Echo.

Her name should have been my first warning because that's what she does. Echoes inside me. Haunts me to my fucking bones.

The girl was like art while she came for me over and over again. I've never enjoyed someone's pleasure more than watching it wash through her. She shook, clawed, and grabbed until she almost blacked out from orgasms.

The purest beauty.

I carried her to my bed when she started to shiver, and she was asleep the moment her head hit the pillow. Then I lay there, staring at her, not able to sleep. Wondering why her in my sheets made my chest tight.

Women aren't allowed in my apartment, and Echo shouldn't be allowed in my life. But both rules broke with one sentence.

"I *want you to take my virginity.*"

She had the nerve to stand there like it didn't mean anything. She's lying, she just doesn't want me to know why.

Doesn't matter, she'll tell me. One way or another I'll get it out of her. Because I need to know what's held her back all these years.

She smokes and drinks. She parties, and she's hinted before that she has a dark past. But in all that time, she's somehow stayed a virgin. It doesn't make sense.

Which led to another night of restless sleep, watching her too peaceful in my bed. My dick too hard to jack off because it would just piss me off more. And when I finally did close my eyes and drift to sleep, she disappeared.

Another morning alone, but for the first time, I didn't welcome it.

I walk into the office and drop down onto the couch, covering my eyes. The moment I walked into the shop, I already knew Echo was here. She's overwhelming my senses.

All the bleach in the world couldn't disguise her lavender scent. It hangs in the air, haunts the walls. I swear it bleeds from her bones because her shampoo is some kind of berry, her lotion is cocoa butter, and her pussy is paradise. But all I smell is lavender.

Fucking Echo.

"What's got you pissed off this early?" Sage walks into the office and drops into the chair at the desk, kicking his feet up.

"Nothing." I sit up, flinging my legs over the side of the couch, trying to distract myself from my thoughts. "But I could really go for caving someone's face in. You fighting tonight?"

"Dude." Sage tips his chin at me. "You've still got a broken nose."

"So I won't get hit in the face then." I shrug. "Wasn't a problem last night."

Sage shakes his head, doubting me. But if there's one thing I do—and do well—it's fight. Not even the biggest, most fucked up guy gets to me if I don't want him to.

Perks of no moral code and a high pain tolerance.

Easy to set the rules when there are none.

"Can't. I'm meeting up with Kane tonight," Sage says, dropping his feet, his expression falling the slightest.

He probably thinks I don't notice because it's rare we talk about anything deep. Partying, tattooing, chilling, and drinking are the extent of our bonding most days. We might work together, but it's rare we let each other into the real shit going on in our lives.

But I don't miss that Sage's usually cocky grin drops at the mention of Kane. Or the dark haze that clouds his eyes.

"When'd you start doing shit with Kane again?"

It's no secret Sage still has ties to the Twisted Kings motorcycle club since his dad was Kane's Vice President before he died. But he's careful how he affiliates with them now, never actually patching in after whatever happened to his father. The fact that he's meeting with their president means more than he's letting on.

"I'm not." Sage stands up. "We just need to talk about some old shit. Nothing to worry about."

It's suspicious as fuck. No one at the shop knows anything about Sage's past, except that it must be dark because bringing it up takes him to a bad place. I'm not sure what he and Kane need to discuss, but it's not a good sign, even if he tries to play it off.

"Sage I—" Echo pauses in the doorway when she spots me sitting on the couch.

Lavender.

A cloud wafts from her and melts my resistance.

Her eyes widen and color drains from her porcelain cheeks. Fire wells up inside knowing exactly what she's thinking—feeling—picturing. I'm tempted to spread her out on this couch and do it all over again.

Sage's eyes dart from her to me because she's standing there staring, but I stand up before he can read too much into it. Tempted or not, no one needs to know what happened last night between Echo and me.

I don't do complicated.

Except, that's what this became the moment I tasted her. A sick desire for more. And more. And more.

But she's promised to my brother.

My fingers clench.

Rhett and Echo have nothing in common. She's too good for that pretentious asshole. And the fact that she doesn't seem willing to protect herself from the inevitable danger of being with him, makes me that much more inclined to do it for her.

I should have made my move eight years ago when I caught the little Goldilocks putting her paws all over our living room. I hesitated. I watched. I waited. Wondered what our dads' plans were for her and my brother.

Now I know.

I lick my lips and watch her eyes follow the movement, wondering if she knows I'm still tasting her on my tongue. Feeling her between my lips like she belongs there.

Maybe she's right, and I'm only doing this because I'm competitive and she's his. But it sure as fuck doesn't feel like it.

"You need something?" Sage asks when Echo continues to stare at me dumbfounded.

"Uh, yes." She breaks her gaze, popping a bubble with her gum and rolling her shoulders back.

One of these days I'm going to give that anxious mouth of hers something better to do.

She steps past me, into the room, and drops a piece of paper onto the desk, tracing over the design with her finger and asking Sage how he'd incorporate a dagger into the flowers. It's a pretty, colorful drawing. Like her. She tattoos with the same energy she radiates.

Leaning forward more, her short shorts ride up to just below her ass, putting those bows on the back of her thighs on full display. I want to sink my teeth into her flesh and mark her like those bows do. Bend her over and imprint myself on her skin.

She's not fully tatted by any means, but every one is pretty. Flowers, bows, stars. A kaleidoscope of the universe that doesn't make any sense, while somehow fitting together perfectly. Her skin holds dreams while my ink is demons, serpents, and shit that keeps you up at night.

"Perfect." Echo pops to standing, a wide smile brightening her cheeks with whatever Sage helped her with.

Not sure why she needs it. Girl's already massively talented.

Brushing past me, I'm sure she doesn't miss me checking out her ass in her shorts. But I don't avert my eyes, and I swear she swings them with a magnetic force that pulls me from the office down the hall to follow her.

"Don't you have a client?" Echo frowns but doesn't look at me as I follow her into her room. It's the brightest one in the shop. Every wall a pop of color.

She stops in front of the purple one and finally looks at me when I don't answer.

Lavender.

"They'll wait," I finally say, scratching the scruff on my jaw.

And they will. People pay ridiculous amounts of money to get tattooed and pierced at Twisted Roses. We might look like a bunch of loser punks, but we know what we're doing. Drawing is one of the only things I'm good at.

That and giving people concussions.

"About last night—"

"Don't." I cut her off.

She frowns. "Don't what."

"Don't start feeling guilty about it."

Echo twists her toes against the floor as she crosses her arms over her chest. "It was wrong."

"Is that how it felt?" I challenge her.

She doesn't answer me. At least, not in words. Her golden eyes avoid me, and she follows the lines on the wood floors instead.

When her gaze dares to lift again, her eyes go wide when she realizes what I'm wearing around my neck. Golden orbs as bright as the California sun in the middle of summer. Warming me up and melting my soul all at once.

"Why are you wearing that?" Her voice squeaks at the end.

It's cute.

I don't like cute things.

But I like how it sounds coming from her.

I shrug. "Not sure what you're talking about."

She storms over to me, right in my space. I'd like to chain her to me just to keep her this close at all times.

Her small fingers grab the chain around my neck—more specifically, what's dangling from it.

"This."

She holds her purity ring up between us.

I can't help but smirk. "It's your promise to me, princess. I'm just keeping it safe to ensure you intend to keep it."

"I didn't make you any promises." She drops the necklace and crosses her arms over her chest. Her shoulders roll back, showing off the stars she has tattooed on them.

"Maybe not in as many words." I grin.

"It was an offer, and you turned it down."

"Did you think I'd fuck you right there?" I take a step toward her, and she backs up, her legs hitting the chair in the center of her station. "Did you think your virgin pussy would be able to handle the things I have planned for it? What I did last night was a favor. Next time you show up at my door, be prepared to find out what happens when you offer your purity to a man like me."

"There won't be a next time." Her voice cracks with her words. "I'm still dating your brother, remember?"

"He's fucking his receptionist..." After her confession last night, I looked into it, confirming what she said. "Among others."

"It doesn't change anything."

She doesn't believe her own lies. I'm not sure who she's even lying to, me or herself. Her voice catches in her throat and she takes a step back. But I don't let her go.

I can't.

Not now that she's dragged me into her orbit. One taste of her part of the universe and I'm ready to float into her oblivion. She's the moon, and I'm the ocean reaching, even if it's subtle and she doesn't see me.

"You're still going to stand here and pretend your showing up last night was just a means to an end?" I step toward her, and she takes another step back.

Always just out of reach.

The darkest, most heartbreaking laugh crawls from her lips as tears spring to her pretty golden eyes. "You don't get it. It's not that simple."

"It never is."

"You don't under—" She cuts herself off, raking her fingers through her blonde and black hair. "This isn't a game, Crew. Even if you think it is. Showing up last night didn't mean I was going to end it with him. We're still going to get married at the end of this."

My heart stops. My fingers itch for my brother's blood. I've never felt possession over a woman, but the fact that she had the nerve to let me make her come and then shut me down the next day has my blood boiling. The fact that I'm the only one seeming the least bit torn up about the shredder she's putting us through has me unhinged.

The walls crack.

Or is that my brain?

"After last night, you're actually still planning to marry him?" My gaze moves to her bare finger as she fidgets with it. The only ring that's lived in that spot is around my neck, burning a hole in my chest.

"You don't need to understand our relationship." She pauses her twitching fingers at her sides, and even if it's impossible for her to sit still, in this moment, she manages it. "But Rhett is my future. I'm marrying him, and there's nothing either of us can do about it."

She turns to walk away, breaking gazes before the first tear manages to break from her lashes and swim over her now rosy cheek.

"You don't even like him." I point out, rage boiling inside me.

She shakes her head but doesn't face me. "I don't like you either. And look how that's going."

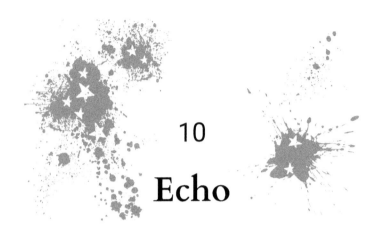

10

Echo

"This isn't what I had in mind when you said we were having a girls' day." Maren frowns, skimming the crowd of buttoned-up Christians.

"Sorry." I hand her a box of clothes, and she takes it. "Promise we aren't staying, but I had to drop off a few things to my dad."

Maren hip-checks me. "Or you're just looking for an excuse to see that hot boy-toy of yours."

Her eyes flick up to where Rhett is standing near the front of the church with the most blinding smile. Pure, holy light shining.

"Wait, what was that?" Maren crosses her arms over her chest, and I realize my hands are clenched at my sides and my jaw is tense.

"Nothing," I lie, even if it's no one's fault but mine all my emotions are welling to the surface today.

But as I watch Rhett talking to one of the members of his congregation, holding her perfectly manicured hand and smiling, I'm jealous at how good he is at hiding it, while I'm failing miserably.

Is it really that simple for him to bury any guilt, or does he not have any? Because we aren't actually in love. And for the first time since I made this arrangement that fact bothers me.

All because of his sick, sadistic, orgasm-inducing brother.

I'm going to scream, and in this room, it'll echo all the way up to the heavens.

I spin around before that happens and grab another box, trying to ignore the fire welling up inside me.

"I get the impression I shouldn't ask..." Maren starts. "But you look like you're five seconds away from blowing a gasket. What gives?"

"Rhett's fucking his receptionist." It spills out when it shouldn't. "Maybe others too. I don't really know."

It's not like Maren will judge. And if I don't talk to someone I'm going to explode. She's a better option than Crew. At least with her, I'll vent with my words. If I'm alone with Crew again I'm afraid he'll put me into submission with his tongue.

My cheeks heat at the memory of last night.

If I thought I'd experienced an orgasm before, I was wrong. My hand is nothing compared to whatever Crew did to me. It was an out-of-body experience. A baptism.

I walked through his doors one person and walked out another.

But what's worse is that it was supposed to be just sex. I hate Crew enough that there was no risk I'd fall for him. Good old revenge and a hate fuck.

Why did he have to go turning it all on its head?

First, he refused to fuck me, which is exactly when I should have left. Then he used his tongue to drive my sanity off a cliff. But worst of all, it was the look in his eyes when I was almost blacked out. It was his fingers grazing the back of mine. It was how he kissed me between the legs like he cared more about how I felt in that moment than anything else. And it was how he tucked me in his sheets after when he should have been an asshole and kicked me out.

But then he has the nerve to wear my purity ring around his neck like he's taunting me with the fact that I begged him to take my virginity. I might have offered last night, but I can't act on it now. It's already too convoluted.

I need to hate him. End of story.

"Rewind." Maren tugs my arm until I'm facing her. "Rhett's fucking other women."

I nod, my face pinching because there's only so much I should probably explain. "It's a long story."

"Because you don't actually like him?" Maren's eyes narrow as they focus on me. "Come on girl, I'm not blind. I've been egging you on for the last ten minutes trying to get you to say something nice about your boyfriend, and you haven't even batted an eyelash. It doesn't take a rocket scientist to figure out you're not feeling him. So why don't you end it?"

For more reasons than I can say out loud.

"We have an arrangement," is all I can offer.

Maren taps her fingernails on the box in her hand and quirks an eyebrow. "Whatever works."

I fold another shirt. "That's it?"

Maren shrugs. "I'm not one to judge. You do you, girl. As long as you're happy."

Our eyes lock, and I'm pretty sure my answer gives everything away, but I force a smile, trying to bury the truth likely painted on my face.

"Besides..." Maren leans against the table. "Someone's clearly keeping you happy."

I freeze. "What's that supposed to mean?"

"Come on girl." She nudges my arm. "You're the most relaxed I've ever seen you this morning—apart from when I bring up your dingbat, holy boyfriend. Someone fucked the nerves out of you last night. I just don't know who."

My jaw goes a little slack. I'm not used to having girl-friends, and Maren constantly surprises me by always seeing through everything. Things I don't even notice myself. Because she's right. I haven't chewed a piece of gum or smoked a joint in hours. I can't remember the last time I was this calm. And even if I hate him, there's only one person to thank for it.

"I didn't have sex last night." I turn my face so she can't catch the blush running my cheeks.

Maren scans me anyway, down and up. A lie detector in action. "Fine. But you did something."

Smirking, she bites her lip and continues watching me. We both know she's right. I did more than something. I didn't know a person could come that many times in a row and survive it.

"Mm-hmm," is all she hums as she walks away in her five-inch heels with a stack of folded clothes.

"Hey, babe." Hands find my shoulders and squeeze.

I spin around to find Rhett standing behind me, wearing the mask he's perfected so well. Preacher boy. Golden boy.

My friend, I remind myself.

It's not his fault I'm letting his brother get to me. Crew only wants what he can't have. He's impulsive and territorial. While Rhett is safe—expected. He's security, and that's something I can't help but need.

Rhett plants a chaste kiss on the side of my temple—the extent of our sexual relationship. It's never bothered me. If anything, the fact that he's never pushed for more is one of the reasons I'm as comfortable around him as I am. But after last night, hearing his conversation with the girl on his phone, I see it from his side for the first time. I'm a chore.

Even if he wants the benefits of us, that's the extent of it.

"What are you up to today?" He tips his chin up at the boxes behind me. "Didn't expect to see you here."

We don't really communicate outside of staged gatherings. And we don't update each other on things happening in our lives, but maybe we should. Having the title of boyfriend or girlfriend is one thing, but if people are going to believe it, he shouldn't have to ask me questions like this one.

Glancing around the room, I wonder if they see through the roles we're playing as I paint a fake smile on my face. I wonder how many of the women here are dating my boyfriend and know the truth. I wonder if it makes me inhuman that I don't care.

I should burn up on this holy ground.

Instead, I roll my shoulders back and draw on the cool confidence Rhett radiates. Like the earth isn't shaking beneath our feet. Like all of this doesn't feel one wrong move away from breaking.

"Maren and I are going to get our nails done, and then we're heading to Fusion for a few drinks."

He nods, but the slightest downturn of the corner of his lips indicates his disappointment. His eyes skim me over and land on every visible tattoo like they're burning my flesh.

"Want to join us?" I almost choke on the offer, painting the best forced smile on my face.

Rhett shakes his head, thankfully. His hair so polished and gelled it doesn't so much as shuffle with the movement. "No, I'll let you ladies have your girl time."

Sometimes I wonder if anyone else sees past the veil of our excuses for our lack of spending time as a couple. Sometimes I wonder if I should care.

"What's with all the chaos today?" I ask, changing the subject before Rhett decides it's a good idea to join Maren and me at the bar. My eyes move around him to men carrying oversized boxes through the back of the church.

He looks over his shoulder and waves one of them to the right when they start in the wrong direction. "Getting ready for the move."

"I thought the new church wouldn't be built for another six months."

"Dad's working that out with the contractor. We're aiming for two."

Rhett dips his thumbs in his pockets, not saying *Dad's throwing more money at this charade*, but we both know that's what it is. Rhett's impatient and has been putting pressure on everyone around him. He says it's for the good of the church and the people who come here, but looking around, I'm not sure they care.

"Where's your ring?" Rhett's eyes drop to my bare ring finger, and I realize I'm absentmindedly rubbing the skin there.

"Home." I clasp my hands behind my back, hoping he didn't hear my voice shoot up an octave. "I forgot it today."

"You never forget it."

Now, of all times, Rhett, the worst boyfriend in the world, decides to be observant.

"Why does it matter? Aren't you supposed to be replacing it anyway?" I divert the conversation.

His eyebrows shoot upward, and his eyes find mine. Realization and a hint of something else fills his gaze—fear? It's not something I've ever seen on him.

"Right." He swallows hard, his eyes trailing over my shoulder.

But when I turn to see what's drawing his attention, I'm met with the view of a crowd of people filtering through the doors.

"I should get back to work." He steps toward me and plants another staged kiss on the side of my temple. Only this time, it doesn't make my skin itch because there's hesitation coming from him. "Thanks for coming by and have fun with your friend."

My smile is as gritted as his.

Pausing, we stand watching each other. His hand on my shoulder and his fingers squeezing it. A silent conversation I can't read, but the crack in the earth between us has split open. And while, to anyone else, we're standing here, we're actually falling.

Guilt.

Regret.

With another gentle squeeze, Rhett walks away. He slips into the role of the man he's spent the last eight years training to be. A man fitting to take my father's place when he steps down. A man who will guide a congregation.

But as his eyes dart back at me, I see the cracks. Of what we are or what we're becoming. This place might be holy, but we're devils hiding in plain sight.

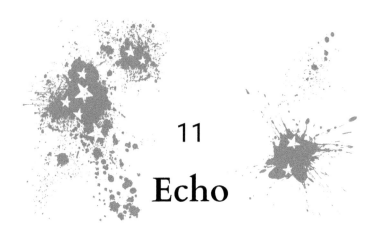

11

Echo

MAREN SLAPS HER HAND on the bar top and smiles so wide the bartender's eyes almost pop out of his head at the sight of her bright energy. "More shots."

She's a magnet for attention, and right now, she has half the men at the bar watching as she tips forward and offers the guy behind the bar her sweet smile, paired with a devious wink.

Her hair is down, curls brushing her shoulders. And her dark skin is glowing from the gold shimmer she's lightly dusted on the apples of her cheeks and collarbones. Her white strapless top hugs her chest and her high-waisted jeans show off all her curves.

Maren is the embodiment of all things sexy and beautiful. While I sit here in an oversized Black Keys T-shirt, faded jean shorts, and combat boots.

It's not that I don't know how to dress to impress or get attention—like when I made the mistake of wearing a leather skintight bodysuit to my birthday party—but we're at a bar at three in the afternoon on a Saturday, so I'd rather be comfortable.

My afternoon appointment had to reschedule, and Maren doesn't work weekends, so here I am. Day drinking and forgetting Crew Kingsley and his brother aren't waging an all-out war inside my head.

"Drink this." Maren slides a shot in front of me and narrows her eyes. "We're drinking until you no longer look like that."

"Like what?"

Lifting her glass, she holds it up between us and waves her finger in my face. "Like some sad puppy without a home. It's not becoming, and it's not you, girl. You're Echo fucking Slater. Badass tattoo artist who doesn't take shit from anyone. Especially stupid ass boyfriends. So start drinking and stop thinking."

The devious smirk that climbs her cheeks draws one on my own. Her vision of me is contagious when I could use a little confidence.

"Fine." I lift the shot glass. "To badass bitches."

"Cheers." Maren taps her glass with mine, and we both down our shots.

It's something sweet with an edge that goes straight to my head.

Setting the glass on the bar top, I let myself soak in everything Maren said. She's right. I've been letting the Kingsley brothers get in my head, and they aren't worth the time or trouble.

Rhett's doing what he wants, so I'm allowed to do the same. He encouraged it even. Guilt is for people doing something wrong, but I'm not sure that's even possible in our arrangement. And Crew might be trying to tease me with the fact that I came to him, but he's right. I did. And he can suffer knowing I'm not going to go there again.

The bartender slides us two more shots, and I down the next one. Smooth as water as my tongue is already soaking in vodka from the first one.

"There she is." Maren smiles as she pushes all the empty glasses in the bartender's direction.

"I'm done wallowing." I nod sharply. "Let's fucking dance."

"Finally." She hops off her barstool and tugs me to the dance floor.

By my fifth drink, I'm no longer thinking about anything. The shop, my commitments, my relationship. Nothing matters except how my body floats with the beat of the music. The hum of the bass vibrating inside me.

It's still early in the day, so the dance floor is nearly empty except for me and Maren, but I don't mind it. I don't mind anything as I get lost in the strobing lights flashing.

"What's that buzzing?" Maren sways to the music.

Like watercolor paint spilling across canvas as her body swishes and puddles with my vision.

"Buzzing?"

Everything is buzzing. Or shaking. Or humming. The room curls around me like a warm blanket as the alcohol takes hold.

Or maybe it's the weed I smoked in the bathroom a half hour ago. Doesn't matter. Nothing does anymore.

"Yeah, buzzing." Maren's eyes skim my body. "Is it your phone?"

The vibrations in my back pocket intensify with her question, and I realize it is my phone. Pulling it out, I roll my eyes at the name on the screen.

I can count on one hand the number of times Crew Kingsley has called me in the eight years I've known him, and it's only ever been when Rhett can't get a hold of me.

"What?" I have to yell because the music is too loud, and I can barely hear myself think.

"Where are you?"

At least, I'm pretty sure that's what he asks.

"Fusion." I laugh, not sure why he's asking when Rhett knows where I am.

The music kicks up with a change in the song, and his response is drowned out.

"What?"

I look down at my phone and see he ended the call.

Asshole.

But just before I tuck my phone back in my pocket, his name flashes on the screen with a text message.

Crew: Where are you?
Echo: Fusion... already told you.
Crew: It's four. Don't you have an appointment?

Echo: Cancelled

Crew: Are you drunk?

Echo: Maybe...

Crew: Echo

Echo: Crew

Crew: We both know you can't handle your booze, why the fuck are you drinking alone in the afternoon?

Echo: I'm not

Echo: I'm with Maren

Echo: And there's plenty of people here, maybe even one who won't turn me down when I offer myself to them

I'm trying to piss him off. Dumb enough to think I'll be able to when I know Crew Kingsley only cares about himself. But I can't help it. He turned me down last night, and I want him to suffer for it.

Crew: You better not let anyone touch you.

Echo: Why? You had your chance. Don't go getting jealous now.

Crew: I swear to fucking God, Echo.

Echo: Since when did you get so religious?

Crew: Ten minutes.

Echo: Until what?

But he doesn't respond. Not so much as the three bubbles popping up and disappearing. So I shove my phone in my pocket, annoyed Crew thinks he can tell me what to do when he wouldn't help me with a simple favor last night.

Screw him and his brother.

"Who was that?" Maren wraps her arms over my shoulders and her eyebrows pinch.

"The devil."

Maren's eyebrows knit as she scans my face, but I just roll my eyes. I'm failing to hide whatever irritation Crew's drawing out of me, but I'm not getting into it here and killing my buzz.

"You girls ready for another round?" Some guy stops beside us.

He's wearing a muscle tank with his thick arms on display. Every inch of him is covered in tattoos, but whoever did them wasn't very good. The blending is shit and the line work is sloppy.

The downfall of working in the tattoo business is that a hot guy with bad tattoos is one of my biggest turnoffs. Not that Maren seems to notice or mind because she's focused on his cool blue eyes and strong jawline.

"We are." She smiles, untwisting herself from me and grabbing my hand to lead us back to the bar.

She slides onto the stool next to Muscle-Man, also known as Brian, while I'm stuck sitting next to his friend, Wyatt, pretending I like motorcycles. I really couldn't care less about anything with an engine. Wasting tens of thousands of dollars on something to get you from point A to B seems pointless when there are cheaper options.

"That was my first Harley," Wyatt says, beaming.

"Wyatt." Brian reaches across the bar and slaps his hand down. "Shut up. She doesn't give a fuck."

At least someone notices. But Wyatt shakes his head and rolls his eyes, looking at me like his friend's suggestion is ridiculous.

"What about you, what are you into?" Wyatt lays an arm across the back of my chair, caging me in. And I can't help but squirm.

There are very few people I trust, and I don't like being cornered, even if he probably thinks nothing of it.

"You like ink?" He traces his free hand over the star peeking out of the wide neck of my T-shirt.

I shake him off and force a smile. "I'm a tattoo artist."

"Badass." Wyatt smiles. "I've got this piece I've been thinking about."

Finally, something I don't mind discussing.

"It's a lion, with a half-demon face." He holds his hand over his shoulder where I'm guessing he wants it. "I'd like it black and gray with some splashes of blood."

"I could recommend someone for you."

It sounds right up Crew's alley.

"Or you could do it?"

"I tend to tat a bit more colorful."

"Cool." Wyatt leans in, brushing my hair off my shoulder and making my skin prickle as he sets me more on edge when he grazes the star tattooed there again. "I like this one. You got any others you'd be willing to show me?"

"Good question." Crew's voice coming up from behind me hits my nerves at the same time as the scent of his woodsy cologne strikes my nose.

He's so close I feel the vibration of his tone.

My back stiffens, and Maren's eyes widen at the sight of him.

"Can I help you?" Wyatt asks Crew, looking annoyed.

"Yeah, actually." Crew leans in and brushes my hair back, revealing my neck as he presses in close. "You can take your fucking arm off her chair."

Wyatt makes no move to back up, even if it puts the three of us really close, with me in the middle and the tension palpable.

"Who the fuck are you?" Wyatt asks.

I don't have to look at Crew to feel him smirking. His energy can be felt in every pore. It's seeping through my bones, and I'm soaking in his amusement.

"I'm the guy who is going to cave your fucking face in if you don't do what I said."

I'm not sure where this possessiveness is coming from, but it bleeds out into the room.

He's seen guys hit on me before and hasn't said anything. But right now, I believe his threat. If Wyatt doesn't back up, Crew's going to let loose his unhinged side, even if I don't understand it.

"Crew, a moment?" I slide off my stool and glare at him before he gets into a fight for no reason. I turn to Maren as I step past. "I'll be right back, you good?"

"Are you?" She's holding in a laugh, and I have no doubt she's seeing through this entire thing. But there's nothing I can do about it.

"Perfect." It comes out gritted as I brush past Crew.

He's on my heels, but I don't stop, leading us across the nearly empty dance floor and down the hall that leads to the bathroom. Pushing into the women's restroom, I know he'll follow me, but I don't care. That's the point.

I'm not sure why he's here or what he wants, but I'm going to find out.

The bathroom's small and dimly lit. And when I step inside, there's no stall, just a single toilet and a sink. Spinning around, Crew pushes the door closed behind him and locks it.

"Why are you here?" I ask him, unable to bury my frustration.

"You're drunk."

"It's a bar." I wave my arms out. "In case you hadn't noticed."

He takes a step closer, and I try to back up, but there's nowhere to go when I press against the wall.

"Those guys are up to no good."

"Maybe I'm not either," I taunt him.

"You think it's that easy?" His eyes narrow, and he gets so close I'm craning my neck to look up at him. "You think you can date my brother, offer me your virginity, and then parade yourself around in front of other men? Is that what you want to do, Goldie—wreak havoc? Because I'll slice his fingers off for touching you if a reaction is what you're after."

"I don't need your reactions."

"Don't you?" He ticks his head to the side, and I'm no longer sure. "Last night you were begging me to fuck you. You sure you're not just trying to piss me off right now?"

I hate how he sees through my emotions. How he's right.

I poked the bear in my texts for a reason. I didn't like that Crew turned me down, and now I'm pushing him because I can't get him out of my head.

"You had your chance." I tip my chin up. "Now I'm moving on to other options."

I try to step around him, but he closes in on me. His fingers wrap my throat, and he pins me to the wall, holding me in place. Dipping his face to mine, we're so close our noses brush.

"No, princess." He leans closer, and he might as well be breathing me in. "You're not."

"Says who?"

He chuckles darkly. "Me."

With one hand pinning me to the wall by my throat, he runs the other over my hip, slowly moving in until he's at the button on my shorts. He pops it and drags the zipper down in one smooth movement. But instead of pulling them off, he slips his hand inside and cups my pussy over my underwear.

"Fuck." I can't help but moan as he applies pressure.

His fingers drag back and forth and the heel of his hand digs into my clit. I drive my hips forward to try and ride the waves already starting to hit. In one night, he learned everything he needs to know about my body, and right now he's using what he knows feels good against me.

"You're going to be a good girl and listen to what I tell you to do, Echo." His lips brush my ear as he pushes my panties to the side, and he slips a finger through my wetness, putting pressure on me, but refusing me what I want.

"Why would I do that?"

He rocks his hand back and forth, and my eyes close as I fight to even my breath. We both know he's in control whether I like it or not.

"Because good girls get what they want." He applies more pressure, and I feel myself starting to build.

I'm teetering on the edge, and as if he senses it, he pulls his hand away and leaves me aching. My eyes fly open, but I can't move as he refuses to release my neck. Drawing his hand up between us, he drags his wet fingers over my lips, painting them and forcing me to taste myself.

"Bad girls don't get to come." He leans in and licks my mouth.

It's almost too much. The heat of his tongue, the taste of us both together.

He steps back and releases me, which is when I realize I'm trying to hold onto the wall as my knees shudder.

"Drink some water. Sober up." He takes another step back but doesn't break our staring contest.

"I'm not yours to command."

I'm not sure I believe it, but I feel the need to say it anyway.

"Right, you're my brother's girl." His jaw clenches. "I'm going to enjoy watching you try to remember that while you're coming on my cock."

At that, he leaves the bathroom, and it takes everything in me not to collapse to the floor with my lies.

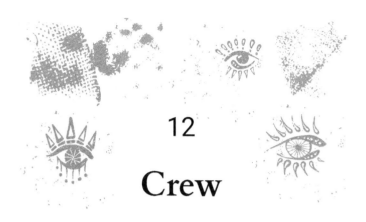

12

Crew

"WHERE'S WYATT?" ECHO SLOWS her pace, her eyes darting from her empty stool to me, before sliding into the stool he was occupying a few minutes ago.

"He went home."

She looks to Maren, who just shakes her head. "Don't ask me. Wyatt said he had something to take care of."

He did after I not-so-subtly threatened his nuts if he didn't walk away before Echo got out of the bathroom. He only spent a moment challenging me, puffing up like he was going to do something about it. And I kind of hoped he'd give me the excuse, which he must have seen in my eyes because then he backed down real quick.

Leaving Echo to me, just like I want her.

This girl's got me out of my fucking mind right now. As I drove over here, I told myself it's because I just need to hate fuck her out of my system. Convinced myself that once I finish what we started last night, it will clear my head.

Problem is, the moment I saw her with some guy's arm around the back of her chair, something darker took shape. Possession. Ownership. All the shit I told myself I'd never feel about a girl. And all she wants to do is use me as some pawn in her sexual awakening.

I'm going to make her regret ever considering it.

My little Goldilocks thinks she can walk in unannounced and mess my brain up. I'll do that and more to her.

She's mine now, whether she realizes it or not. And she's going to pay every time she tries to challenge that fact.

"You're a sick fuck," Echo says, sliding onto the stool and glaring at me.

She leans toward Maren to whisper something, and Maren doesn't take her brown eyes off me. But unlike Echo, who might as well be trying to sear me with holy fire with her gaze, Maren's expression is mildly amused, with a devious smirk ticking up at whatever Echo tells her.

Maren nods when they finally break apart, turning back to her boy-toy-of-the-day, while Echo leans back in her own bar stool and grinds her teeth as she watches me.

I slide the water I ordered her in her direction, and she's smart enough to take a sip without arguing. She might hate me, but she needs it. And I know it because I know her.

Too fucking well.

Echo can't handle her booze, and her pupils are blown wide, which means she's probably high on top of being drunk. She's lucky I showed up before that douche she was talking to tried to take advantage. If he had, I'm not sure what sick things I might have done.

My fingers clench around my beer at the thought, and I take a long drink.

It was so much easier when my contact with Echo revolved around me trying to irritate the hell out of her. When I used her bubble-gum personality as a reason for convincing myself she was nothing more than some chick who was on a mission to piss me off with her presence. It was simpler when I was under the illusion that she was just like any other person to me.

Now she's in my vision like I've got blinders on, and she's my sole focus. Every twitch, laugh, breath, movement. I can't help but see it all—want it all.

My Goldie.

I've always had a narrow focus, even as a kid. When something gets in my sights, I have to have it. Use it until the shine wears off. But whatever interest is growing with Echo didn't start last night, even if at first, I thought it did. Weeds grew years earlier. Rooting back to the first moment I looked into her sparkly, golden eyes. Sweetness covering up the darkness she's so intent to hide.

I want to see it.

Her light and shadows.

Her truth.

Then maybe I'll understand what's feeding this sick obsession spreading through me.

Echo's gaze flits in my direction for a fraction of a second, and the apples of her cheeks are rosy. She's flushed from what I did to her in the bathroom, and I fucking love it.

"You look a little tense." I lean in, and even if she avoids my gaze, she draws her bottom lip between her teeth at my closeness. "Anything I can do to help you relieve a little tension?"

Golden eyes land on me. Hate that turns my insides liquid. I'd like to bathe in her fury and watch her disappointment when it doesn't destroy me.

"I don't need anything from you, Crew."

"Still pretending." I smirk, waving a hand up at the bartender. "Whiskey sour."

He nods, passing a glance at Echo before walking away to make my drink. I'm tempted to use the spoon sitting behind the bar to carve his eyes out for looking at her. Possessive isn't something I'm used to feeling over a girl, but this one, who doesn't even belong to me, draws out every bit of my need to have her all to myself.

Especially now that I know my brother's never touched her—no one has.

Even if I assumed they weren't intimate by the way she flinched every time Rhett wrapped his arm around her, the confirmation makes me want to claim her like he never has. She'll feel me in the deepest pits of her soul. I'll carve my name inside her until there's no denying who she belongs to.

The bartender slides my drink across the bar, and I release the purity ring I'm clenching in my fist, draining half of it in one swallow. It burns my throat as Echo's eyes sear me.

Maren disappears to the dance floor with her boy toy, but Echo doesn't follow her.

Magnetism.

She can lie to herself all she wants, she's in my orbit now that I'm here.

"Speaking of tense." Echo narrows her gaze. "What's your deal?"

"My deal?"

"Do you plan on toying with me for your amusement forever? Or are you going to move on to your next victim soon?"

I smirk, finishing my drink before the truth comes out, and she tries to see through it. Setting my glass down on the bar, I spin around the splash that's left.

"Is that how you see yourself, Echo? Are you the victim in this story?" I push my glass aside and turn my body to fully face her, widening my knees so I can grab the front of her stool and pull her between my legs.

No flinch, no disgust. If anything, her lips part with a hint of excitement her glare can't bury as I force her closer.

"I'm not the victim."

"Are you sure about that?" I probably shouldn't like pushing her like I do, but it's basically foreplay at this point, and I love when she gets all fired up. "After all, you're still playing their game. Dating the holy son and pretending you want all that shit, when we both know you don't."

"You don't know what I want."

I lean back in my chair and look her over. "I know you still want me to fuck you, even if I turned you down last night."

Her glare sears me as her golden eyes narrow. "I'm not dwelling on it. If anything, you gave me a gift. It was a mistake going there."

"Was it?"

She wants to believe she was running on adrenaline and poor judgment. We both know it's a lie.

"Tell me the truth, Echo." I lean in. "Why are you still a virgin?"

"Why does it matter?"

"Because it doesn't make sense."

She pulls her blonde and black hair into a loose bun on the top of her head and secures it with one of the hair ties she has around her wrist. "I'm not the only virgin in the world, Crew. What's so confusing about it?"

"You're fucking hot."

She quirks an eyebrow. "Says the guy who hates me."

Hates her. Wants her. Needs her.

I'm going to fucking drown in her.

"Doesn't mean I'm blind. A man would have to be dead to not be attracted to you. And even then..."

"Gross."

I shrug. "Just saying. You're twenty-three, hot, badass. I doubt you haven't had any offers."

"I have." She reaches for her water and takes a hesitant sip.

Even if I'm the one who made the comment, something about her confirmation makes me pause. I'm not sure why I even care. It's not like she let anyone touch her before I did.

And I shouldn't touch her either.

I don't fuck virgins. I know better.

I should walk away and let someone else take it before this goes sideways. If ring girls who work for me are a bad idea, taking Echo's virginity is a hundred times worse. But ever since finding out she's only ever been mine, it's all I can focus on.

And not just because I could be the first man to mark her. But because I can't help thinking her purity is the key to uncovering all the dark secrets of Echo Slater.

She doesn't make sense. Her half-light, half-dark personality. Her edge and her softness. She doesn't talk about her past before Ryan found her, but I know she's been through some shit. And I have no doubt it ties to the reason she's never let a man touch her.

"You can tell me." I lower my voice.

She's chewing the inside of her cheek, and I don't know why it's unsettling that she's anxious right now when she always is. Something about this moment is different.

"You just want to know why so you can use it against me."

"You're the one who came to me, remember?" I lean in a little closer and get a hit of her lavender scent. "You didn't have to tell me you were a virgin. You could have just asked me to fuck you. But you didn't. You told me the truth because you wanted me to know it."

I can't help but brush her bare thigh with the back of my hand before backing up and crossing my arms over my chest.

"I need to know why you haven't let anyone touch you."

Desperately. Because the more I push and the more she shuts down, I need to know what makes those walls fly up around her.

"Maybe I'm saving myself."

"If that were the case, you'd be having this conversation on your wedding day with your husband, not right now with his brother."

"Maybe I'd rather do it with someone of *my* choosing."

Why does that make my stomach twist? My temples throb? Her comment means she chose me, for some godforsaken reason.

"Stop avoiding the question."

"You want to know why I'm a virgin, Crew?" She leans in, a little angry, and a tad magnetic because her irritation is what draws her to me, even if I'm sure she wishes it would push me away.

"Yes."

"Because when I was twelve my mother tried to trade my virginity for drugs." Her voice cracks, and the hard shell she's perfected falters. Whatever I thought she'd say isn't that, and my fingers clench at the single sentence. "Only, I realized what was happening and stabbed him in the nuts before he got a chance. And do you know what they did? They locked me up for it. Because it doesn't matter what a man does, I'm the one who was crazy. They committed me—at twelve—for trying to protect myself. And my mom did nothing to stop it."

Gripping the chair behind her, my sight darkens. We're in a tunnel and the white blonde in her hair is all I see. Those golden eyes breaking as she fights back the sheen starting to build. My fingers itch for the blood of the man who did this to her, and if I thought I was protective before, there's no comparison as I watch her blink back tears now.

"That's when my father found me. *Saved* me, if you want to call it that. Doesn't really matter. My mom OD'd and when the state looked for my next of kin, he learned I existed. And he took me far away from there—from everything. I'll always owe him for that."

She shakes her head and rolls her shoulders back, swallowing down the choked breaths coming out.

"Echo—"

"I'm fine." But she doesn't sound it. "You wanted to know. Well, there you have it. The reason I'm a virgin is because it's my choice when and how I give that up. Not my mother's. Not some random boyfriend's. And not Rhett's. I'll lose it how I want to, to the person I want to. And I didn't expect it to take twenty-three years, but shit happens. It wasn't like I was holding onto it on purpose."

"But now you're on a timeline." It hits me like cement drying in my stomach.

She came to me now because the wheels are in motion. Whatever deal was made eight years ago has started to take form. She's marrying my brother, and if she doesn't lose her virginity now, on her own terms, she's worried she'll never get the chance.

Whatever twisted obsession I have with this girl is one-sided.

Like always, she's Goldilocks, walking in and making a giant fucking mess, just so she can walk out unscathed.

And it pisses me off.

That some man broke her. That her mother was a piece of shit. That everything before now turned her into a girl who feels the need to even do this.

But even more, it pisses me off that she's using me, and it means absolutely nothing to her when I can't get her out of my head.

Once more, I'm the brother good enough to do the dirty tasks, brushed aside once my use is diminished.

"Come on." I stand up, sliding off my stool and putting as much distance between us as I can. "I'll take you home. You need to sober up."

Her eyebrows pinch. Anger, hurt, a collage of emotions bleeding together. Every feeling painting her face as I shut down and try to put a cap on whatever is fizzing and trying to get out.

I should be comforting. She just opened herself up to me and spilled her darkest secrets. But I'm stuck between the knot in my throat and the rage bubbling in my chest. I need to get her out of here.

Get her away from me.

Before I break her even more than she already is.

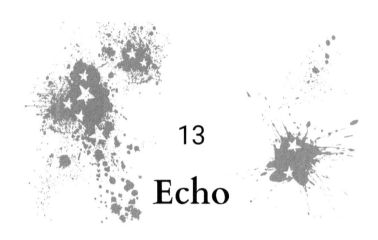

13

Echo

I'M SWIMMING.

Deep.

My fingers can't find the surface.

Pressure builds in my ears and my heart makes thunder in the silence of the ocean.

Floating, I almost reach it... hope.

But right as I do, hands wrap my wrists and drag me under.

My eyes fly open, and I shoot upright. Blinking, I grasp at my sheets and take in my room. The sun filters through a slit in the curtains, and I inhale a desperate breath.

I'm here.

I'm safe.

Dropping my head back to my pillow, I blink up at the ceiling and try to ignore that the four walls of my room are closing in.

I reach for my phone and check the time, seeing it's three minutes until my alarm goes off, and I feel like I've barely slept. At least I only have one appointment today. Then I can return to the shell I've spent the past week hiding in.

Ever since I went out to the bar with Maren last weekend, time is painfully slow.

Every day, I walk into the shop and expect Crew to say something about our conversation at the bar. For him to make me regret drunkenly opening up to him and telling him all my secrets. Every day, I'm anxious.

And every day, he doesn't.

He's been keeping his distance, and I'm not sure what's worse. The fact that I opened up or the fact that it scared him off.

I shouldn't care. If anything, it's for the best things go back to how they were before he started claiming rights to my virginity. So why does it hurt?

Rhett and I aren't even engaged, and I'm already feeling the pressure. A fork in the road, and I know what path I'm meant to go down. Another one far more tempting.

Taking in a deep breath, I gather myself. Grip my composure and drag myself from the bed. It doesn't matter how hard each day is, I have to face it.

By the time I get ready and head to the shop, I'm running late.

"Hey girl." Fel pops up from behind the jewelry case when I walk in the front door.

Her wild red hair falls over her shoulders, and she smiles like someone who had plenty of fun on her honeymoon.

"You're back." I slide my sunglasses off and walk over to her, planting my hands on the display case and leaning forward. "How was Seattle?"

She's practically glowing. Her cheeks are as bright as her eyes, and it's more than just the shimmer she has coating her freckles.

"Incredible. Beautiful. Spectacular." She looks up, all smiles. "At least, I think so. We barely left the hotel room."

She bursts out laughing, and I shake my head.

"I did not need to know that."

And not only because Jude is like a brother to me. But the thought of what they spent the last week doing puts my feelings on display with everything I've been avoiding myself.

"Fine, fine. I'll share those details with Maren." Fel closes the display case, and her bracelets clatter against the metal as it snaps shut. "How have things been around here?"

"Good." I dip my thumbs in my jean pockets and shrug.

Fel scans me over, probably seeing straight through. "Good? Last time I saw everyone, Crew had a broken nose and two black eyes."

"We're past that."

Technically true.

Me punching him for being an asshole seems like a lifetime ago with everything that's happened since.

"Whatever you say." Fel circles the case. Her yellow sundress fluttering around her thighs as the wind kicks up with the shop door opening and Crew walking through it.

The sight of him is a form of sick torture. Dark jeans fitting him perfectly. His dark gray Lamb of God T-shirt revealing every sculpted inch of his tattooed arms. It's obscene.

Crew pauses, slipping his sunglasses off and raking his chestnut hair from his forehead. Our eyes meet, and we have the same silent conversation we've been repeating for a week. Secrets splayed out and neither of us is brave enough to face them.

The bruising around his eyes has all but faded, but he looks tired. Something is keeping him up at night, and my stomach's in knots considering what he's doing with that time. He isn't the kind of guy who gets lonely, and I've heard his conversations with Sage and Jude these past eight years. I have no doubt he's found plenty of ways to distract himself from my virginity.

Crew watches me as he walks past but doesn't say anything. He might be waiting for me to break the silence, but I won't.

I can't.

It isn't until his back is to me that I catch sight of the chain still around his neck. Even if he's started tucking my purity ring under his T-shirt, he's still wearing it.

Our secret.

I turn to busy myself by arranging the magazines on the front counter.

"What was that?" Fel spins the moment Crew disappears down the hallway.

"What was what?" I rearrange the stack again.

"Echo." Fel leans in close, planting a hand on the magazines to stop me from fidgeting. "Spill."

I look up at her and am reminded why I've been avoiding Maren these past few days. She didn't ask me what happened when Crew showed up at the bar last week, but I see the questions brewing in her eyes.

"Come on, we're friends. You can tell me." Fel cocks an eyebrow.

"Things have been weird."

"As in—him showing up at the bar and threatening some guy for touching you?"

I narrow my gaze. "Maren told you?"

Fel shrugs. I shouldn't be surprised, those two are tied at the hip.

"Okay, yes, he showed up. But that's it. We haven't really spoken since then."

"You work together."

"You know these guys." My gaze trails to the hallway that leads to our individual rooms at the shop. "I can avoid them if I want to. They keep to themselves, and when they don't, they're grumpy assholes."

"Fair enough. At least now there's two of us to try and balance them out." She smiles, and I'm thankful to have her hanging around the shop because she makes dealing with the guys more bearable.

"And I appreciate that, but I promise, I'm fine." I roll my shoulders back. "Crew was just checking on me for Rhett. That's all."

So many lies it's getting harder to keep track of them.

"Whatever you say." She winks, clearly not believing me. "Doesn't matter, I've got a solution to help you forget. We're having a housewarming party tonight, and you're invited."

"Jude's idea?" I joke.

She laughs. If it were up to him, the grumpy jerk would hide Fel away all to himself, and we'd never see either of them again.

"It will be fun." She reaches out and squeezes my hand. "Maren will be there with a couple of friends. You have to come."

"You know I'll be there."

"Good." She backs up and claps with excitement. "I'm going to find Jude and then take off, but let me know if you need anything?"

"Will do." I pop a piece of gum in my mouth. "I've got an appointment at ten, so I better set up."

At least tattooing is something to take my mind off the unresolved tension between me and Crew. A reason to hide behind a closed door and drown my thoughts in ink for a few hours. Because tonight is a collision waiting to happen. I haven't been to Jude and Fel's building since the night I knocked on the door across the hall. Since the night Crew sent my brain into a tailspin.

And I have a feeling going back will lead to nothing good.

I'm thankful Jude and Fel aren't *people* people because their party is small, consisting of the group that works at the shop and a few of Maren's friends. Add in the fact that there's plenty of weed to go around, and I'm floating until Crew finishes up with his last client for the night and arrives.

I knew he'd be here, there's no avoiding him, but it doesn't make it any less awkward when his eyes land on where Rhett's arm is draped around my shoulders. We're sitting on the couch directly in his line of vision when he walks through the door, and I don't miss that his jaw clenches as he takes in our closeness.

If only he could read my mind, he'd know I'm crawling out of my skin. Rhett might be my friend, but I don't like being touched by most people. It makes past trauma and insecurity blur. And I once more sink into that dark hole in my mind that's easier to exist in when I can't handle what's happening on the outside.

Crew doesn't stop and say anything as he walks past. Instead, he heads straight for the island and accepts a shot from one of Maren's beautiful blonde friends. Her hair's up in a high ponytail showing off her bare shoulders in her strapless top. And when her hand grazes Crew's arm as she leans her hip against the counter to talk to him, I'm surprised I don't vomit.

"Are you done with that yet?" Rhett unwraps his arm from around me, and his gaze falls to the joint pinched between my thumb and finger.

He doesn't like when I smoke pot. Something he made clear right after he told me he'd rather not be here at all.

At least he is.

Anything to prove to Crew there's a limit on whatever fucked up situation we're in. Lines I need to draw before they start blurring.

I pass the joint off to Sage, who's sitting a couple of cushions over. I've only had a couple of hits, so it's not enough to give me a buzz, but at least it'll get Rhett off my back when I need him to sit here and pretend to be boyfriend-of-the-year for five seconds.

"Happy?" I force a smile.

"Don't be like that, babe." He plants his hand on my thigh.

It's friendly. Appropriate given the relationship we're supposed to be in. And still it makes me want to shed my skin and escape.

Crew is the only man whose touch has had the opposite effect. And as his eyes move in my direction and drop to his brother's hand on my leg, I'm desperate for him to know that.

Not that I'll ever admit it. My body's reaction is just that—physical. What I feel for Crew doesn't change the fact that we spend more time bickering than getting along. He's wildfire in sagebrush, and I burn hot enough already to not need more fuel to my flame.

"I'm just looking out for you." Rhett smiles, and it's genuine, which makes me feel guilty for pouting over a joint.

"I know, I'm sorry." I force a smile.

He pats my knee before adjusting the collar on his polo shirt. He's out of place in this scene. A mess of band Tees, tattoos, pot, and booze. A metal mix playing in the background. He couldn't possibly fit less in this world.

It's the same way I don't fit in his.

At least he's here, establishing our middle ground and pretending we like each other. We need to get better at it if we're going to get married soon.

Married.

My stomach twists again, and I think I might be sick.

A laugh from across the room sparks like lightning, drawing me to the sound. Maren's blonde friend has her arms wrapped around Crew's, and she's whispering something in his ear. He maintains his hold on the island as he listens, but the entire scene makes my skin itch.

Just because I offered to sleep with him doesn't mean I like him as anything more than someone I wouldn't mind screwing me into oblivion. So why does the thought of another woman touching him make me want to peel her skin from her bones?

Rhett's phone buzzes, drawing my attention back to him, and I realize he's also staring at his brother, his eyes darting between us.

I wonder if he sees it—the tension—the change in the air.

I wonder if he cares, or if it's a relief to absolve him of guilt, because his face doesn't reveal anything.

His phone buzzes again, finally breaking him from his thoughts. And when he pulls it from his pocket, I catch the name *Angelina* on the screen before he turns it so I can't see what he's reading.

Angelina.

I bet she's pretty. Maybe she's even nice. She definitely doesn't have tattoos or dual-toned hair. I bet she would like whatever boring place Rhett would take her to for dinner. She's probably the girl he deserves, someone who won't have to force themself to be another person to make him happy.

I wonder if Rhett cares I'll never be that.

He's the one convinced marrying the preacher's daughter is the key to his own holy path. Right before I turned twenty-three, he helped set the plan in motion by asking me out. And even if he doesn't agree with how I look or my choice of profession, he's set on the fact that him marrying Ryan's daughter is the only way to win over the most devoted members of Eternal Light.

The faintest smirk climbs Rhett's cheeks as he types out a quick text, before shoving his phone back in his pocket.

"The church?" I pretend to sound interested since I probably should be.

"Sorry." He pats his pocket. "Things are hectic while we iron out the details for the move. And the camera crew just sent the schedule for the new docuseries."

"I thought they were only streaming one sermon."

"They were." Once more he drapes his arm over the couch behind me. "But after they came for the initial interview, they decided they need more."

His whole face might as well be glowing. No one cares what people think of Eternal Light more than Rhett—not even my father.

"That's good news then?"

"Echo, it's incredible." He rolls his eyes like he can't believe the question. "And speaking of, I've been meaning to talk to you because there are a couple of photo ops coming up."

"And you need me there." It's not a question, and now it's clear why he came to this party tonight willingly. Bargaining chips he's setting in place.

"They love the preacher's daughter angle."

"I'm sure they do." It comes out sarcastic.

Rhett's so lost in his own excitement he doesn't notice. "If we play this right, we might be looking at a full-time streaming platform. This could be huge. You'll be there, right?"

I nod.

His gaze drifts to the star tattoo on my shoulder. "And you'll—"

"I'll cover up."

When we get married, LA summers are going to be unbearable if Rhett insists on parading me around like his chaste bride in long sleeves and skirts.

"Thanks, babe." He leans in and kisses my temple. "You're the best."

His phone buzzes again, and he pulls it from his pocket, frowning at the screen.

"You can take off if you need to. You've made your appearance."

He did, and now I just want him gone. While I hoped he'd distract me from my unresolved tension with his brother, it's only intensified. Worse when all I can do is focus on Crew sitting in the kitchen talking to Maren's friend.

"If you don't mind." Rhett stands up, barely pausing at my offer. "There is something I should attend to."

I shake my head. "Not at all."

He leans down and plants a quick kiss on the top of my head before walking away. "Have fun and call me later."

I won't call, and he won't care.

"Hey." Sage nudges my arm.

Turning to him, his eyebrows are pinched, and I swear he reads every emotion on my face. There's something about his eyes that have an irritating way of cutting through all the bullshit. He holds my half-smoked joint up between us, offering it back, but I just shake my head and sink into the cushions.

"Everything all right with you and Preacher Boy?" Smoke curls from his lips at the question.

"Peachy." I force a smile.

Sage ticks up an eyebrow but doesn't ask. It's one of the reasons he gets along with everyone so well. He checks in but doesn't force a conversation.

Daring to look into the kitchen, Crew's eyes are on the door closing behind his brother before they find mine.

His steel-gray gaze cool and sending a shiver up my spine.

A chill that burns hot as I watch the blonde press closer and whisper again.

A familiar stutter in my breath as my heart tightens and my eyes burn.

"I'll catch you tomorrow," I say to Sage.

His gaze moves from me to Crew. "Sure thing."

I'm being obvious. I'm giving everything away.

It doesn't matter.

I need to get out—to breathe. I need to escape. People can whisper all they want—think what they want. I don't care.

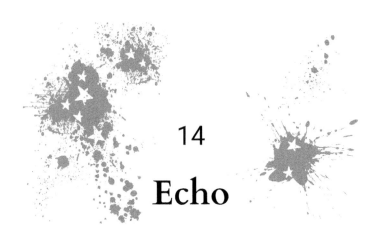

14

Echo

THE MOMENT THE DOOR to Jude and Fel's apartment closes behind me, I pin my back to the wall beside it and take a deep breath. I focus on every inhale and exhale as the roof shrinks down and my lungs push back.

I focus on my promises.

My happiness isn't worth going back to the unknown. A life with Rhett means I'll always be cared for. It means keeping up my end of the deal that saved my father's life. End of story. No matter what's happening, I have no choice but to see this through.

Sealing my eyes, I take in another deep inhale. I hold it until it burns my lungs, and I have no choice but to let it go, along with everything else. I blink my eyes open and peel myself from the wall.

Once I sleep, I'll feel better.

But just as I'm about to head home, the door opens again, and Crew slips out into the hallway behind me.

He's still wearing the same T-shirt he was earlier today, looking too good, even if a little tired. He shuts the door and rests his back against it, his hand still on the handle. An unspoken conversation passes between us.

Words when there aren't any.

Air.

Energy.

The lights flicker in the hallway—or maybe my brain circuits aren't firing properly. I watch him watching me with the same expression I've been faced with all week. Empty eyes instead of the familiar heat in his predatorial gaze.

After a long moment, he lifts off the door and walks past me, to his own door across the hall. And when he swings it open and steps inside, he waits for me to follow because he knows I will.

I can't help the destruction I cause both of us.

When he closes the door to his apartment, it's silent, and there's no sign of the small party across the hall. I follow him until he splits off to the kitchen to pour himself a drink, while I make my way to the couch.

"Strike out with blondie?" I ask, unable to help myself when he circles the couch and drops onto the cushion next to me.

"Not feeling it." He takes a drink of his whiskey, mulling my attack over with amusement. "Where'd your boyfriend disappear to?"

"Home."

"You sure?"

No.

He's probably with Angelina, but I don't need to give Crew any more ammunition.

"You've been avoiding me this week." I twist my legs beneath me and turn to face him on the couch.

"Could say the same for you." Crew sets his drink on the coffee table. One arm rests over the back of the couch, bringing us closer. "Scared you can't control yourself around me?"

"Says the guy still wearing my purity ring." I roll my eyes, before shooting him a hard glare. "And you think I'm obsessed? Don't flatter yourself."

"Don't need to." He shrugs. "You flatter me plenty with all your pretty little orgasms."

"That was a one-time thing and you know it."

"Really?" He leans in close, smelling faintly of bleach from spending all day at the shop. A hint of whiskey coating his tongue and making my head spin. "What about the bar?"

I lean in to meet him. "From what I recall, you were unsuccessful in getting me there that time."

"Only because you didn't earn it."

"Is that what you tell yourself when you fail to make a girl come, Crew? She didn't earn it? Are you sure it wasn't just for lack of trying?"

I'm so full of shit. I'm pissing him off just to see what he'll do about it. I want him to hate me as much as I hate him so I don't have to feel guilty about this.

He reaches up and cups my jaw in his hand, tipping my mouth just beneath his. "Careful, princess. Or I'll give that mouth something better to do than talk back to me."

Licking my lips, my core burns at how he watches it with intent.

"I'd like to see you try."

If fighting him is foreplay, my insides are molten hot. I grab his wrist and try to shove him away, but he grips tighter, grabbing my hair with his other hand and holding me in place.

"Now, now. You don't get to run when we're just starting to have fun."

I clench my teeth, and he grips my jaw tighter. His fingers threaded roughly in my hair as I narrow my gaze, eyes burning from his grip. My heart races in my chest and my nails dig into the flesh of his wrist.

His silvery-gray eyes brighten with the hint of a smirk, and my heart jumps to my throat.

He pulls me to him so fast, our lips connect before I can blink. Before I can assess the moment or have any regrets. He releases my jaw and hair, and grabs me by the hips, pulling me onto his lap so I'm straddling him.

I should fight.

Claw.

Run.

But I skim my hands up his firm chest, and over his sculpted shoulders instead. Along his neck, until I'm cupping the scruff dusting his jawline. And I kiss him like I hate him, and I need him.

He grinds my center over his lap, and I feel him hard between my legs. It's terrifying and intoxicating at the same time. My body throbs like he's the only home it knows, and I'm going to come apart without him.

He breaks our kiss and drags his lips down my jaw, down my neck. He bites at my flesh, and I burn for him.

"Tell me what I need to hear, Goldie." He sinks his teeth into the base of my neck again, harder this time, so I squirm, and he moves me over his hard length.

"I need you to fuck me, Crew." Words I've never meant more, no matter how much I shouldn't. "I need you. Only you."

He lifts to look at me, his pupils wild with excitement. Lifting his hand, he cups my jaw and brushes his thumb over my mouth. "That's it…"

His touch ghosts my jaw, down my neck. He brushes my hair back and let's his words fade in the silence of his apartment. His fingers clutch my hips, and he rocks me over him again.

"You're fucking beautiful, you know that?" he says before his smile turns wicked. "The darkest part of the universe and the brightest part of the sun. It's fucking irritating."

I can't tell whether he's complimenting me or pissed off.

If he hates me or wants me.

Maybe it's all those things—the same way I'm mixed paint when it comes to him.

"This is still a one-time thing." I'm not sure how I manage to lie to us both, but the words find their way out.

"Sure thing." He bites back his amusement. "Keep telling yourself that."

"Crew—" But he cuts me off with his lips. With his bruising kiss. With a rock of my hips, pulling my soul from my bones.

"You're perfect," he murmurs against my mouth as his hands move to my pants, and he unbuttons them. "You're a masterpiece. But if you're going to keep lying to me, I'm going to enjoy making you pay for it."

He kisses down my jaw again, to the stars tattooed on my shoulders. To the feather along my collarbone. He kisses my skin like he appreciates every inch of it. Every marking, every memory it holds.

Crew is the most violent, impulsive, ruthless man I know. But in his hands, he holds me so gently, I'm safer than I've ever felt. He touches me like he'd burn the world down to feel me against him.

He kisses me like I'm his.

I reach for the hem of his T-shirt and peel it off, trying not to lose my breath at the feel of his bare chest under my palms. I trace the demons on his pecs and the ink that laces up his neck, like I can burn the feel of me into him. I trace the chain hanging from his neck, down to my purity ring, loving the sight of it in this moment.

He strips me of my shirt, before tossing my bra to the side.

"Fuck, Echo." He holds my tits in his hands, and I almost burst at the sensitive way his thumbs brush my nipples.

Back and forth, before he dips his mouth to draw one between his teeth. His scruff rakes my soft skin. The roughness as overwhelming as his tongue rolls over me.

"Stunning." He leans back to look at me, rocking me over him again, watching my breasts like they're waves rolling just for him.

And I've never felt sexier than I do in this moment.

Climbing off him, I strip off my pants, dragging my underwear with them. And then it's just me, bare, before a man I shouldn't want in all the ways I do. Him seeing me in all the ways I've never allowed anyone to.

Kneeling between his legs, I reach for his jeans, and he doesn't stop me. His hands rest at his sides as I pop the button and slide down the zipper. A dark smirk crosses his cheeks as I peel them down in the front, and only then does he reach to help, stripping himself for me until I'm kneeling, staring at his hard cock in his hand.

I've only seen one when someone was getting theirs tattooed, but never like this. My stomach jumps to my throat at the sight. He's thick, and if the pressure from his finger at my entrance made me almost black out, I'm not sure I'll survive the size of him.

He drags his hand up and it pulls a bead from the tip, running his thumb over it and wiping the wet streak over the head of his dick.

My hearing pulses. It's so silent my heart hurts to listen to it as it races in my chest. Reaching for his wrist, I pull his hand away, and he lets me, releasing himself. I draw his thumb to my mouth and suck on the taste of him.

"Fuck." He plays with my tongue, rolling his thumb over it, before pulling it out and drawing the wetness over my lips.

I lift off my heels, but his grip on my jaw stops me from leaning forward.

"I'm going to stretch this pretty mouth of yours out until you're sobbing for me to stop. But not tonight, Echo. Tonight is about you."

He lifts me off the floor and pulls me back onto his lap. I'm slick as I glide over him, and he groans as his dick presses between my legs. Rolling my hips again, he moves me to a rhythm that makes the stars close in. And my inexperience floods my veins.

Wrapping my arms around his shoulders, I bury my face in his neck, moaning as he rocks me over him again.

"I don't know what I'm doing," I admit in a whisper. It must sound pathetic to a man with his level of experience, but it's the truth.

Crew grips my chin, forcing me to look at him. "It doesn't matter what you know, Echo. All that matters is how you feel."

He grazes the pads of his fingers down the center column of my throat, to my chest, down between my breasts. He grips my hips with both his hands and shifts me ever so slightly in his lap, just enough pressure that I'm almost ready to combust.

"Your body knows what feels good, doesn't it? It knows *this* feels good."

I nod as he rocks my hips again.

"All you have to do is chase that feeling, princess. Use me to make *you* feel good."

"And what about you?"

He draws my lips an inch from his, grazing his nose against mine. "You're all I need to feel good."

Leaning in, he plants the softest kiss on my lips. So quick, I miss it before I feel it. Then he's lifting my hips.

"Do you want me to get a condom?" He positions himself beneath me, rubbing the head of his cock where I need him.

The smart answer is *yes*. But I'm on the pill and Crew makes me anything but smart.

"Do you think you need one?"

"I already know I don't. It's been six months for me."

"Six months..." the words trail off as he puts pressure that makes me almost see stars.

That's the entire time I've been dating his brother.

"Mm-hmm." He hums. "Don't think too much about it."

And I can't. He doesn't give me the chance. One moment I'm floating, and the next he pushes my hips down over him. So quickly and with such force, he breaks through the resistance, and I'm fully seated on him, crying out in pain.

"Breathe for me." He brushes my hair off one side of my neck and kisses it, which is when I realize my body is wrapped tightly around him. I'm holding him like he's the only gravity left in the world. "Fuck you're tight, princess. You need to breathe for me."

I let out an exhale and will my body to relax. It burns as I feel him so deep, I didn't think it was possible to reach there. He's in the center of my soul, and his hands brush over my lower back in comfort.

"Breathe, Goldie."

He wills my steady breaths. I inhale slowly, and exhale again. And the pressure of his touch makes me ache for more, so I slowly start to rock back and forth.

"That's it." He runs his hands down my back and grabs my ass.

He kisses my shoulder, up to my neck, pausing at my pulse at the base of my throat.

"Chase what feels good, princess," he praises, grabbing me, kissing me, licking me, before pulling back and pinning me with his gray eyes. "Be a good girl and use my cock to make your virgin pussy come."

15

Crew

I MIGHT BLACK OUT, but I don't take back the dirty things I'm saying because it makes her squeeze my dick like she's trying to suffocate it.

Echo rolls her hips, and it sinks me deeper, bringing out my primal need to mark her so far, she'll never get me out of her system.

This was supposed to be a hate fuck after I was forced to watch her spend the night with my brother's arm wrapped around her. But the second I felt her body rip for me, open for me, let me in—there's nowhere else I belong. She can hate me all she wants, she's mine now. And it's a problem I'm going to have to solve.

"Crew." My name is a moan.

A gasp.

Salvation.

She chases it by rolling her hips over me. There's an edge to every breath, and I'm sure this hurts her, but she loves it when I hurt her as much as she despises it. And right now, she trusts me.

Gripping her ass, I lift us. "Hold on, princess."

She does, her pussy clenching around me with every step. I've never fucked a girl in my apartment, but if I'm going to have Echo here, I'm going to take her in my bed. I'm going to carve her innocence in the walls. I'm going to use her purity to bless this unholy ground.

Stopping at my bed, I lay her down with me kneeling between her legs. Our bodies still connected, and her tatted, naked flesh on display. I meant what I said. She's a masterpiece. Absolute perfection laced in ink.

Beauty that can't be defined or contained.

I pinch her rosy nipple, and she squirms for me.

"You like that?"

She nods, biting her lip and gripping the sheets above her head. Her black and blonde hair splays out across my navy sheets, painting the perfect picture of midnight and morning.

She circles her hips and adjusts, her face no longer pinching at her movements. Instead, her lips part in an exhale that takes my breath away.

I hold her hips and pull out just enough to see her blood streaking my dick. Her innocence bleeding for me. Like the chain holding her purity ring around my neck, I shove my hips forward, and I take that promise.

Her body is mine.

Her pleasure is mine.

Echo is mine.

My cock is drenched in her desire and blood as I pump into her again. I dig my nails into the soft flesh of her thighs. If I thought I got off on inflicting pain, this might be a whole new high. Watching her break for me is the most beautiful thing.

Her delicate fingers wrap my wrists, and she holds me through the movements. Her hips twist as I thrust myself in. And I love that she's listening to what I told her.

It doesn't matter what her mind is cluttered with. She might have been nervous, but her inexperience is irrelevant to me. She carves her name into my soul with every movement.

Pumping in again, she winces the slightest. As good as it might feel, I'm sure it still hurts. So I rub my thumb over her perfect clit, and her body shivers. I offer her the pleasure to chase the pain away.

She reaches up and grabs the chain hanging around my neck, pulling me to her. Magnetic force sealing us together as our bodies connect. Her lips on my lips, so I can taste the vibration of her moans.

I try to hold back for her sake, but her tight nipples raking my chest and her tongue slipping into my mouth draws out every animal instinct. I can't help but thrust harder. And as she screams for me, I give her more and more.

Her heels dig into the backs of my thighs, and her hips grind with my rhythm. This girl was cut from the stars and made for my galaxy. Custom built for me to orbit around, and I'm not sure how I'm just now seeing it.

I fuck her harder like it can stop whatever crawls through me.

Interest, ink, hesitation.

I fuck her with my soul as much as my body, and when her pussy clenches and her whole body shakes, I fuck her so hard she'll never feel anything but my dick making her come for me again.

She's so tight I almost black out. Her nails dig into my skin and rake it open. Blood and sweat as she pulses beneath me. My vision goes black as my balls pull up tight, and I mark her like I've never marked anyone. Shooting my release into her with the need to claim her with my cum.

I wasn't lying when I told her it's been six months, and the moment I sank into her I knew why. Echo was always supposed to be mine; it just took me too damn long to see it.

As we both relax, her body unwinds. I prop myself up on my elbows and look down at her. The most dangerous innocence brews in her eyes because I took her purity, but it still manages to bleed out.

"You okay?" I'm not sure why I care; I don't care about anyone but myself.

Except right now, all I need is to hear from her lips that I didn't destroy her.

She nods. "Perfect."

But there's hesitation. Darkness creeping like storm clouds rolling over her expression. A high she's coming down from, and it's not the good kind that can be chased with another hit. It's doubt—or guilt.

Because this is wrong, and we both know it.

And even if I don't give a shit, I know she does.

"Echo—"

"Don't, okay." She props herself up on her elbows, and I can almost see the gates closing off in her eyes one by one. "I told you that you didn't have to feel guilty about this. I knew what I was walking into."

Guilty?

I'm not the one who feels guilty, and I'm not sure what to make of her comment. But I'm not having this conversation with her like this. Because regardless of what kind of man I am, she makes me want to try and be better.

"Stay here." I climb off her and head into the bathroom to grab a wet rag. Cleaning myself off before walking back into the bedroom and spreading her legs.

Her pussy is pink and puffy from me fucking it. It's perfect, and I'd love to sink into her again if it wouldn't make her sorer than she already is. I press the cool rag to her inner thighs, cleaning her off, and to my surprise she lets me.

But unlike a moment ago when she held my soul with her own, she's closed off, and I don't like it.

My phone buzzes from the other side of the apartment, dragging her out of whatever trance she was lost in.

"Thanks." She takes the rag and walks out of the room with it, shutting herself in the bathroom.

I slide into a pair of sweats and sit at the edge of the bed. Staring at the bathroom door, wondering how she could so quickly flip the switch.

My phone buzzes again just as Echo walks out of the bathroom. She's still fully naked and a work of art in my otherwise boring bedroom.

From the other room, her phone starts to ring, and it takes me a second to process it's three in the morning and both our phones are going off as we stare at each other. Something she must realize too because she rushes to the other room as I follow her and dig my phone from the pile of clothes on the floor.

When I finally find it, I see my dad's name lighting up the screen. He never calls this late.

Never calls at all. The most I get are clipped texts with directions. Times. Places.

"Dad?" I answer, at the same time as Echo slips into her T-shirt and answers her own phone.

"Fuck, Crew, where have you been?" He's out of breath. Pissed.

But worse, he sounds almost scared.

"Home."

"Well get to Cedars-Sinai now." Something slams on the other end of the line. "Rhett's been shot."

At that, the line goes dead.

Down the hallway, something thumps. A solid sound that turns my insides hollow because it isn't right.

My feet patter toward it. I run through the maze of rooms and halls and whispers.

Mom. I need to find mom.

Down the hall there are voices, before a soul-piercing scream rips through every molecule of oxygen in my lungs. And I freeze in place instead of moving faster.

Whoever was here is leaving, but not out the front door, which would make sense. They're heading toward the back. And even if I can't put my finger on why, it makes my gut sink.

Feet moving.

Sounds changing.

Noises getting further away and then closer again.

Finally, I find my way forward.

Mom. I need to find Mom.

Bad things have a way of revealing themselves through instinct before your eyes see them. You can know before walking into a room that it holds the power to stain every good moment up until that point.

I know before turning the corner, I should walk in the other direction. I should get Dad or Adam. But I heard her scream like it was for my ears alone. It carved itself in my skull and it's rattling around there like her nails are clawing at the inside of me.

Scratching as they beg for answers.

Finally making it to the end of the hallway, I'm met with a room no one spends time in. If anything, this space is a trophy of everything our family isn't. Photos on the mantle—smiles that only exist within them.

A fire is burning, and for a moment, my senses are so overwhelmed, the flames seem to eat the whole room. They cover every inch, until my vision blinks into focus and puts them in their place.

It's quiet, except for the crackling of the flames, and Rhett is standing in the middle turning to me when he hears me enter.

"Crew it's—" But he doesn't finish his sentence with words. He doesn't need to.

My legs give out, and I drop down beside him, the hardwood floor bruising my knees at the force.

I kneel in front of the only person with a heart blind enough to love the evil that exists here.

I lay my hands over my mom's bloody throat, her empty, lifeless eyes staring back at me.

I failed.

We all did.

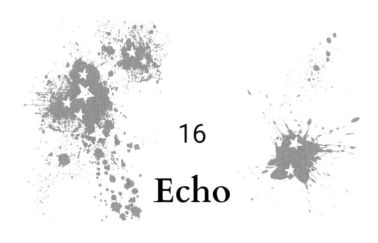

16

Echo

THERE'S ALWAYS A PRICE to pay for sin. Take a bite from the apple and a higher power will make you regret it. There is no escaping punishment. And I should know better than to try.

My hands are stained in blood.

In infidelity.

In transgressions.

Every last one of them coming full circle as the elevator doors slide open, and I'm met with my father's eyes.

Beside me, Crew is casually leaning against the back of the elevator wall with his hands tucked in his sweatpants pockets. We haven't spoken since hanging up with our parents, and I'm not sure if the silence is tension or regret as he pushes off the railing and waits for me to walk out of the elevator first. But he doesn't so much as glance in my direction when I pause in front of my dad.

Crew breaks off toward his father, and the room stretches with every step he takes—with every wrong thing we've done. And what's worse, I'm not ready to let it go.

I still smell him on me, feel him in me. Soreness and relaxation all at once.

While I told him it was a one-time thing, it hurts to think that as I glance over at him walking away.

"Echo, honey." Dad grips my shoulders, snapping my attention back to him. "Are you okay?"

"I'm fine." I swallow hard, hoping Dad didn't notice me staring. "What happened?"

Dad's face pales under the fluorescent hospital lights. "Max is still trying to figure that out. Rhett was heading home when he was shot in his driveway."

Both of us ignore the fact that he was heading home at three in the morning. And even if it should help me feel less guilty, the fact that he's my boyfriend and I have no idea what's going on with him only amplifies it.

"Who would do this?"

"We aren't one hundred percent sure." Dad straightens up, gripping my shoulders tighter, and I can't help but feel secrets in the current of his stare. "But there've been threats."

I shake my head. "People are threatening Rhett? Why?"

People love Rhett. He's the golden boy in the community. Church boy turned progressive preacher.

"Not everyone is on board with the direction he's taking the church. It's to be expected. You'll have your loyalists. But there will always be people who resist change."

Rhett mentioned something in passing after his sermon a month ago when he spoke about God loving all his
children without judgment. But I didn't think anything of
it. LA is progressive, and Rhett is determined to draw a
younger crowd. It made sense he shifted his stance to be
more inclusive, even if there has been some pushback.

"Who's sending them?"

"We don't know yet." Dad drops his hands and tucks
them in his pockets.

"But you know something..." More like—he's hiding
something.

Dad shuffles on his feet. Digs his hands deeper and
curls his shoulders up the slightest.

"You know about the protestors picketing the sight of
the new church."

I nod.

"They've been growing in numbers. And a few weeks
ago, they started leaving messages and sending letters."

I shake my head. "So why haven't you called the cops?"

"We have. Max and Rhett have been working with
them."

My stomach sinks at the fact that everyone is in the
loop except for me. Even if I don't involve myself in my
father's church as much as I should, they could at least
tell me they were in danger.

"Have they threatened you too?" My heart hammers at
the thought.

Rhett might be the new face, but it's still my father's
church for the time being. If these are the people who
did this, he's in as much danger as Rhett was.

"Don't worry. Max has security on me."

"So they have?"

He avoids my question, but his eyes reveal the host of secrets he's been keeping.

I've never liked the way Max Kingsley took my father under his wing after the deal we made, even if it was necessary. But for the first time since that moment, I wonder how deep his influence goes.

If Dad needs security, then things are worse than I realized, and he's kept me in the dark through all of it.

"It's going to be okay."

"Is it?" The question comes out louder than I mean for it to.

Down the hall, I'm aware of Crew's attention returning in my direction, but I try to ignore it. I brush my hair off my face and take a step back.

"Echo honey, I'll be okay. *Rhett* will be okay."

"None of this is okay, Dad."

And what's worse, there's nothing we can do about it. The protesters aren't going to stop. The church's stance isn't going to change.

Even if I believe in Rhett's cause, he's bringing this heat on my father. Signs and rallies are one thing. Threats and bullets are another.

"Max has this handled." Dad wipes his forehead, giving himself away whether he realizes it or not. "He'll deal with it."

I bite back my thoughts and nod. Dad's too trusting of Max Kingsley. He doesn't seem to realize the Kingsley men are nothing but trouble. But there's no convincing him of that. And even if I don't like it, at least Max is using his power to protect Dad right now.

The elevator pings behind me, and I look over my shoulder to see Adam walking out of it. Doesn't matter that it's four in the morning, he's in one of his ridiculously expensive suits, looking perfectly put together as always. At his side is his girlfriend, Lakeyn, looking more human than he does, even if she's still ridiculously pretty. Her blonde hair is in a messy bun and she's wearing jeans with her white cashmere sweater.

Adam and Lakeyn head straight for Crew and his father, which makes my stomach turn. It's rare to get all three Kingsley brothers under one roof, and the sight of them coming together has to be a bad omen.

Breaking my stare at them, I turn back to Dad, who's going through his phone and messaging someone.

"I'm going to go see Rhett."

"Of course." He nods, before jutting his chin to the left. "He's in room fifty-three. Down that hall."

Hopefully, he thinks I want to check in on my boyfriend and doesn't sense the real reason—I need to escape.

Dad steps close and plants a kiss on the top of my head. "It'll all be okay, Echo. Promise."

The problem with promises isn't the intention behind them. Most people make them to keep them. The issue is that some things are outside our control. And as Dad steps back to take a phone call, and I turn to walk away, I can't help but feel like this promise is one he has no control over.

The hospital is quiet at this time of night. Being in LA, I didn't think that was possible. But there are few people wandering the halls, and the nurses are gathered at their station talking over coffee.

Turning the corner, the lights are dimmer. Or maybe I'm blacking out. Each step stretches the space in front of me.

An inescapable tunnel.

My heart starts to race with my breath, and in my mind, I'm pulled back a decade, to when I walked through similar halls covered in blood.

She's crazy.

She's violent.

She almost killed him.

"Echo."

I jump at my name and realize I'm no longer walking. I'm standing frozen in the middle of the hallway outside Rhett's hospital room.

Crew steps around me, focusing on my cheeks, and I'm not sure what I look like, but his eyebrows pinch in worry.

"You all right?" His eyes scan me over.

I nod, rolling my shoulders back. "Why wouldn't I be?"

The last thing I need is someone sensing I'm falling apart. Especially Crew.

His eyes scan me once more, and the softness in his usually hard gaze tells me he sees through my lie, but I don't bother acknowledging it.

"We should talk about what happened." Crew takes a step closer, but I step back.

It's too much. The hallway's already a funhouse, stretching out with whatever occupies my brain. And being too close to Crew sends me to a dark place.

"There's nothing to talk about." I tip my chin up. "I need to go check on my boyfriend. *Your brother.*"

To anyone but Crew, the reminder might make them pause. But this is a man with fewer morals than his father, so I'm not surprised that my statement only ignites the flame in his gaze as he takes a step closer.

"Pushing me away already?"

"I told you it was a one-time thing."

He lets out a dark chuckle. "Is that what you're telling yourself to feel better about what we did? That it was a lapse of judgment? A *mistake*?"

I shrug, glancing away, not able to face those eyes that are bound to drag me straight to hell. But Crew notices, gripping my chin and forcing me to face him.

"I can still feel your virgin blood on my cock, Echo." He presses closer, his heat surrounding me. "I can still feel your virgin pussy tearing open for me. And do you know what? I'm the only man who can say that."

"Good for you."

"Better than good, Goldie." He grinds his teeth. "Best feeling in the fucking universe."

My words clump in my throat. I'm not sure if he's trying to taunt me or praise me for what happened, but I shouldn't be allowing any of it.

"It doesn't—"

"Change anything," he cuts me off, finishing my sentence. "Keep telling yourself that."

"Keep lying to yourself and thinking you know me better than I know myself."

Crew leans in closer, brushing my hair off my neck and trailing his fingers down the center of my throat. "Oh, but I do, Goldie. I know what makes you scream. What makes you beg. What makes you wet. Like right now, even if you're scared or worried, or I'm pissing you off, I bet if I slipped my hand in those panties, I'd find you soaking."

I squeeze my thighs tight, wishing he was wrong. I'm standing outside his brother's hospital room, and I'm supposed to be pretending to be the worried girlfriend, not his brother's plaything.

Rolling my shoulders back, I tip my chin up and force my confidence to the surface. "You wouldn't find panties at all, actually. So I guess you *don't* know everything."

I realize it was the wrong comeback the second his wicked smirk stretches his face, and he takes a step back. He toys with my purity ring hanging from his neck.

I hate that he has it. But more, I hate how much I love seeing him wear it. His trophy, giving my virginity importance, when I was the only one who seemed to feel like it was.

"That's my girl," he says, noticing me staring as he spins the ring between his fingers again.

Pushing past him, I head toward Rhett's hospital room. "I'm not your girl, Crew. I'm still your brother's. Remember?"

"This isn't over, Echo," he says behind me.

I walk into Rhett's room and somehow manage not to slam the door or scream. I close it softly and press my palms flat on the surface. Like it's enough to keep Crew on the other side of the walls I built to protect myself.

It does no good. I feel him out there, waiting for me. Amused he's getting to me. And every wicked bone in my body wants to let him in.

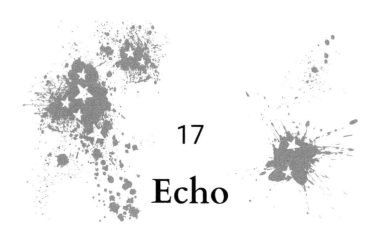

17

Echo

I REST MY FOREHEAD against the closed door and let out a breath as Crew's footsteps fade from the other side. There's no avoiding what we've done, but I'm not ready to face it and admit to myself that he's right. As much as this was supposed to be a simple means to an end of losing my virginity in a way I decided—to a man I chose—I made a mistake handing it to someone who can so easily crawl beneath my skin.

A lord of the underworld and the sick obsession I realize now I've been denying.

"Crew again?" Rhett's voice startles me.

I spin around and pin my back against the door. The room's lit only by a small lamp in the corner and Rhett's watching me from his hospital bed.

"You heard that?"

I didn't realize Rhett was awake, and I'm not sure how loud Crew and I were talking. Between my hammering heart and adrenaline, we were muted. But I doubt that's the case.

"Pieces." Rhett tips his head back and closes his eyes.

I've never seen Rhett like this—almost vulnerable. His expression is serene as he thinks over whatever's running through his head. He's in a hospital gown, far from the polos and jeans I'm used to, and his familiar confident smile is erased.

Walking over to the side of the bed, I drop onto the stool beside it.

"I'm sorry—"

"I'm seeing someone too," Rhett says, his eyes opening to look at me.

At first my mind tries to catch up, and then I'm sure I heard him right.

"Angelina."

"I figured you saw my phone tonight at the party." Rhett nods, pinching the bridge of his nose. The confession hanging heavy in the air, and an expression edging on guilt crossing his face. "It's not you..."

"I know."

Because it's not *him* either. This entire situation has nothing to do with either of us. But no matter how we feel about it, we can't absolve ourselves.

"Why are you telling me?"

We both agreed we were free to do what we wanted until we were legally husband and wife, but we don't openly go into depth about it. So something about how defeated he looks at his confession, bubbles my own guilt back up. A moment edging on friendship.

"Because I'm not blind." He rakes his nails through his hair, scratching his head. "You and my brother aren't as subtle as you think."

"Crew and I aren't anything."

At least, nothing more than sex. My body's reaction to him doesn't mean I'm dumb enough to believe Crew Kingsley is capable of caring about me on a deeper level.

"Keep reminding yourself of that, Echo." Rhett's gaze locks on mine. "Because Angelina, Crew—they change nothing."

"I'm aware." I shuffle in my seat. "I'm not backing out."

"I know you won't. You're smart." He shifts and his face winces from the pain of his wound.

I reach forward and help him adjust his pillow.

"Thanks." He sits back, and I do the same.

Rhett and I rarely spend time together, much less alone. And when we have, it's brief with little conversation. It's the opposite of whatever this is as we stare at each other now. The same oblivion in his eyes I spotted at Jude and Fel's apartment is once more present. We're both in this black hole and sinking.

"Do you care about her?" I ask, pretty sure we're past the point of pretending it's awkward.

"Not enough to make the wrong decision." His gaze drops to where my hands are twisting in my lap. "And you'd be wise to make sure you keep yours the same."

"You don't have to worry about that." I roll my eyes, leaning forward now and shaking my head. "But you aren't upset? Even if he's your brother?"

"Crew is Crew."

"What's that supposed to mean?"

Yes, *Crew is Crew*, that's the whole problem. He's unpredictable and sometimes downright mean. But for some reason, after last night, it hurts to hear Rhett validate it.

"Echo, I know my brother better than he gives me credit for. If you're looking for a good man, he's not it. And any bit of interest isn't what you think it is."

My stomach sinks. "Then what is it?"

"Crew doesn't get attached. At least, not for the long haul. He's like our father, interested in whatever serves his purpose. Chasing his obsessions and then dropping them the moment he's disinterested. Crew does whatever amuses him in any given moment, and it doesn't matter who gets in his crosshairs. Not even you."

"Maybe you don't give him enough credit."

"Or you give him too much." Rhett lifts an eyebrow. "When did Crew start showing interest? Be honest with yourself, when was the first time you saw him actually pretend to care?"

I swallow at the lump in my throat, but nothing can dislodge it. "Six months ago."

At least, that's when something shifted. His teasing became more frequent, and he found ways to be around me more often. I didn't think much of it until he said he hadn't been with anyone in the past six months, but once he did, the wheels started turning. He tried to act like nothing has changed. He maintained a facade for the guys at the shop, but there was no real confirmation he was doing anything with anyone, except for what he was telling us.

Six months ago, something changed, and that's when Rhett became my boyfriend.

"Exactly, when we started dating."

"So you're saying he only wants me right now because I'm with you?"

Rhett shrugs, but the hint of smugness is enough of an answer. "You and I both know this only ends one of two ways. We can chase our fantasies and walk out of this with nothing, or we can do what we always intended, build an empire."

I don't care about the empire, just the safety of it. The certainty and security of building a solid foundation with someone when I spent most of my life without one. Whether I like Rhett as more than a friend or not, he'll be a partner to me, and he won't hurt me.

"I made you a promise, Echo. This might have started with a deal over a heart, but it doesn't matter. All that does is that we're in this together now. And I'll always be here for you."

"And how do you justify what we're doing with God?" It's the one question I've never dared ask him because it felt like stepping over a line. But I have a right to know if we're going to be this open with each other.

Rhett's a man of faith on the outside, but underneath is murkier.

"I don't have to justify anything." Rhett schools his expression. "God accepts. God forgives. God loves. And that's why I'm in this hospital bed because not everyone understands that yet. But they will."

A shiver runs my spine at the firmness in his statement. At the surety in his gaze. I'm sure he means for it to sound comforting, but something darker plays in his statement, and I wonder if he's even aware of it.

Rhett plants his hand over mine on the bed as voices in the hallway kick up. For a moment, I hold my breath until they pass Rhett's door.

"Are you in this with me, Echo?" He squeezes my hand, once more pulling my attention.

I want to be in this.

"Yes."

I hope he doesn't sense the doubt when that word should be truth etched in stone by now. Our fate sealed for both our good.

I let myself be untethered once. I did what felt right over what was considered acceptable. And that girl found only darkness. She found blood. And they wanted to lock her away for it.

He squeezes my hand, and the faintest smile ticks up in the corner of his mouth. "I realize I've been less than ideal in this relationship, and I'm sorry about that. It's not because I don't care or because I won't commit when needed. It's just—"

"Not like that between us."

"Exactly." He nods. "But it needs to be."

He squeezes my hand again, but the tightness might as well wrap my heart with how the thought of it suffocates me. Once we get married, this needs to be more than what it is. The pretending will stop, and I'll officially be Rhett's wife.

"So are you saying you want to start trying now?"

No matter what I've said to Crew, I dread Rhett's response. I'm not ready to give up my last taste of freedom, and all I can hope is Rhett isn't either. If we'd had this conversation from the start, it might have been different. But we indulged, we chased.

We embraced each other as friends. And in this hospital room—everything fragile is on the verge of shattering—I feel it.

And I'm not sure what cuts deeper, that Rhett's asking me for the one thing I thought we'd try from the beginning, or if it's that he's asking *now*.

"Not necessarily." He shakes his head and pulls his hand back to my relief. "I'm just saying we need to start somewhere. I almost died tonight. If I'd have been one step to the left, I might have. But luckily the asshole had a crappy aim."

My throat tightens. Everyone around me has been downplaying the severity of what's going on. But if Rhett almost died, someone needs to start taking the threats more seriously.

"In less than a year you're going to be my wife."

That word rips me out of my thoughts. It might as well rip my soul out of my body. But I fight back the burning behind my eyes and the way my vision gets blurry on the edges.

"I'm saying we need to figure out what we're doing before then." He pinches the bridge of his nose. "At the very least we should learn to be proper friends."

Friends.

Like that's the end goal when the terms are marriage.

"And Angelina?" I ask, trying to gauge if that's why he looks torn in this moment.

"She knows my limits." Rhett's stare drops to my left hand, and I realize I'm once more rubbing the spot that used to be occupied by my purity ring. "Does he?"

I nod, hoping I'm right. But the truth is, Crew is a live wire who believes he can affect any situation. What it is and what he imagines might be two different things.

But I let that be my problem.

"Good." Rhett nods. "Because right now, we need to keep up appearances. And once we say I *do*..."

He trails off, but I feel it. Something between a warning and an order. Once we're married, it will be too dangerous to continue living separate lives. We're going to have to figure out how to actually make this real.

"I understand." Standing up, the room tilts, and it takes all my focus not to sink into the place my brain does.

"Echo." Rhett grabs my hand once more before I can turn and walk away. "Be careful. Crew doesn't know how to love, and I don't want you to get hurt by him. Regardless of what you think, I do care."

I'm not sure how to feel about his comment. He's right, his brother only cares about himself. And right now, Crew's probably only showing interest because he likes the idea of tainting his brother's possession.

"I've got this, Rhett." I nod, and he drops my hand. "Promise."

After all, I've been through worse. I've traveled to hell and come out the other side. I've sold my soul to the devil not once, but twice. And here I stand.

Crew Kingsley won't be the end of me. There's too much on the line.

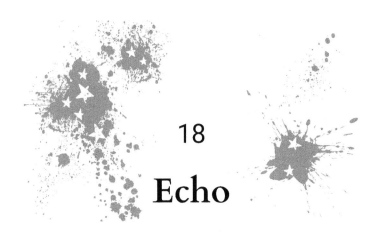

18

Echo

M<small>Y POORLY LIT APARTMENT</small> has never looked as good as it does this morning, returning from hours spent at the hospital. It's unimpressive and in a bad part of town, but at least it's mine.

Setting my purse down, I try to shake the energy from the hospital from my bones. I try to forget the feel of Crew on my skin.

The feel of his solid chest pressing down on mine. The soreness between my legs. The mark he made as he drove himself in.

It's addicting and wrong and I need more.

A chill shivers up my spine. The sealing around my windows is cracking and there's only so much the plastic film over them keeps the breeze of a fading winter out. I strip off my jacket and let the cool air in my apartment cut to the bone. Strip me of the day. I let it become the gravity I'm incapable of finding.

Especially when I sensed Crew the moment I walked into my apartment. Whispers of his cedar scent like a ghost hanging in the air.

All the guys at the shop have a key to my apartment because they're the closest people to me in my isolated life, but they've never used it. It was a *just in case* something happened.

Until now.

I make my way across the living room to my bedroom door and push it open.

"Stalker much?" I try to ignore how good he looks sitting on the edge of my bed waiting for me. Leaning back on his hands with his legs casually spread. He's relaxed, and I have to ignore how the sight of him makes my core clench. "How long have you been here?"

"About an hour." He doesn't flinch as he watches me circle my room.

"How sweet." I turn to face him, crossing my arms over my chest. "Are you always this worried about the girls you fuck?"

I can't help my survival instincts kicking in. My conversation with Rhett is still fresh in my mind, and no matter what I felt earlier tonight, I know what sex means to men like Crew. My virginity was a prize, and he won it.

Crew's jaw ticks. "No."

I'm not sure what to make of that, knowing I probably shouldn't focus on whatever it stirs up that he cared to check on me.

I nervously turn away from him before he can sense my hesitation. But I feel him watching me as I strip off my rings and bracelets.

"Well, I'm fine, if that's what you were worried about." I stack my bracelets. "You can go now."

"You don't seem fine."

"And why do you still care?" I spin around, throwing my hands up as insecurity swells. I might want him to care, but I don't understand why he's pretending to. "You got what you wanted, right? It's done now. You shouldn't be in your brother's girlfriend's apartment at six in the morning. It's a bad look."

"And you shouldn't fuck your boyfriend's brother. Guess we both have our vices."

I swallow hard, and he stands up, walking toward me. My skin prickling in anticipation with each step. If I thought my body responded to him before, right now I'm a live wire at the edge of water about to electrify every surface I contact.

I spent my life convinced losing my virginity would be like any other change to my body. Dying my hair, inking my skin. Something surface level that would leave me otherwise unaffected.

Only now the vibrations of what we've done skitter through me. The need he awoke that I didn't think could exist. His mark I feel branded so deep, I'm not sure I'll ever be the same again.

Crew stops directly in front of me, and I have to tip my chin up to face him. He's so close the heat of him lodges my breath in my lungs.

"I'm his." It's a whisper—a lie at its core. "It doesn't matter what we did. I'm still his. And you need to go."

He'll tire of me anyway, it's just a matter of time. Crew likes the chase, but now that I'm caught, he'll eventually move on.

I dip around him, like if I stay out of reach it'll make him easier to resist. But he doesn't leave, and he doesn't take his eyes off me as I strip out of my shirt and jeans and climb into bed.

"He doesn't deserve you," Crew says, an edge to his tone as he watches me bury myself in the blanket.

"Neither do you."

The asshole smirks like it's a challenge. One look that's so like him my belly flutters under his amused gaze. He steps forward, pausing at the foot of the bed. He's still wearing the sweatpants that show off everything I shouldn't be thinking about. His black T-shirt hugs his chest and his tattooed arms and hands flex. His dark hair falls just over the ridge of his eyes. Silver focus I can't escape.

Wrapping myself in my covers, I have to clench my thighs. The smallest tick of a wicked smile, and I know he's reading my lust all over me.

"You should leave before people get the wrong idea," I say, trying to find my confidence with him sucking the air from the room. His presence is gasoline, and he hands me the matches. I strike them each and every time.

"It's just us here, Echo." He leans forward. "I'm not even touching you. Is the fact that you still feel me inside you drawing out your guilt?"

"Asshole." I clench my fingers and narrow my gaze.

And he feeds on my reaction.

"Careful with that mouth. You know how much I love it when you hate me."

"That's your problem." And mine, even if I won't admit that to him. "But we can't. Not again. Not after..."

I can't finish the sentence. Tears sting my eyes as I'm being ripped down the middle inside. I belong to Rhett. He's safe. He's good. Crew is simply trying to prove a point, and I hate him for it.

My heart hammers like it's going to explode as Crew plants both palms on the foot of my bed and leans forward. The ink from his arms might as well crawl from his skin through the room. Black ink spreading this obsession we're feeding.

"He doesn't see you, Echo. I do." Crew's amusement fades. "He's incapable of it."

"And what is it you think you see?" I challenge him.

His fingers grip the blanket. "Every dark thing you try to bury. All the things you pretend don't exist. I see you."

"Just because you see my darkness doesn't mean it's all I am."

"What else are you, Goldie?" His fingers clench the blanket tighter, and in one swift pull, he tugs it straight off the bed, leaving me bare in my bra and underwear.

My skin prickles in the cold room as I'm exposed to him.

"The light? My brother's innocent, perfect angel?" He tilts his head. "Or does he already know I fucked that out of you?"

"I hate you."

He chuckles darkly. "You always hate me."

"You're *always* an asshole." I spit back at him, not that he flinches. If anything, he probably accepts it as a compliment.

"You like that about me."

"No, I don't."

He ticks his head to the side.

"Why are you here, Crew? You've already taken my virginity and had your fun. And we both know you don't care about the women you fuck the second you're done with them, so is this about work because, trust me, I won't tell anyone. And if it's about my virginity, I already told you I wasn't holding onto it because it was important. We're good."

It doesn't matter that I'm the one speaking, every word rakes my tongue on the way out. Bleeds my heart and burns my lips. Because I really want to believe all of it, but I don't anymore. My virginity wasn't important until Crew, and now it hurts that he took it when I can't be his.

Crew stands up tall, circling the bed. His lean body flexing with each step. The demons on his forearms taunting me the closer he gets.

"What are you doing?"

"Stop pushing me away and pretending you don't want me here." He stops right beside me, so close the heat of his body sets my skin on fire.

He sinks down onto my bed next to me, my body moving with the weight of him on the mattress. My heart skipping twice as fast at his nearness. Reaching down, he picks up my hand and holds it between us, his fingers grazing the spot where my purity band used to sit.

"And stop pretending you still belong to my brother."

I open my mouth to argue, but Crew leans in close, brushing my hair back, as his lips tickle the shell of my ear.

"Lie to yourself all you want. Hate me all you want. And tell yourself whatever you have to if it'll make you feel better about what we've done. But when you close your pretty, golden eyes at night, the truth will still be there—you'd rather be my slut than his wife."

Turning my face to his, he's so close our noses are nearly brushing.

Steel eyes drive daggers through me. Spears he uses to pin me to the center of the earth while he spins in circles.

I should be offended by the crude words and his demeaning tone, but all it does is make me more desperate.

"You only want me to prove a point to your brother."

His lips brush closer. "Does it matter?"

I don't know, does it?

It should.

Crew brushes his lips over mine, and I'm once more aware I'm sitting in bed in nothing more than my bra and underwear, exposed to him. Even if he's already seen it.

"Sweet dreams, Goldie." He pulls back, climbing off the bed and walking to my bedroom door. "This isn't over. Just say the word."

"What word?"

Why did I ask that? What's wrong with me?

Crew looks over his shoulder, the dark hallway cloaking anything more than his figure from my sight. It doesn't stop his stance from coating my body in a shiver.

"Please," he answers with a wicked grin, then he disappears.

19

Crew

TATTOOING IS MY CALM. The closest thing to peace for someone who barely believes in it.

When it's me and my needle, thoughts dissipate. Nothing but color bleeding into skin matters.

While Adam controlled the Kingsley empire and Rhett mastered the art of faith and manipulation, I chased what felt good.

Fighting.

Tattooing.

Carving a path for myself outside of my father's expectations.

As a kid, I'd fill blank sheets of paper with sketches. Mom hung them on the fridge, and it was the one thing that made our house look more like a home than whatever my father was projecting.

Until she died, and once more, stale darkness reclaimed those walls the way it reclaimed him.

But I never lost my passion for creating. On paper, I could control what was impossible on the outside. I could make art of my demons. And by the time I was eighteen, and I found Twisted Roses, I'd gotten pretty good at it.

Blaze brought me in, and Sage taught me how to translate what I could do on paper with skin. And I built up my client list one work of art at a time, until Blaze went back to his motorcycle club and left the shop to the four of us.

It was my first taste of real freedom—the moment I stopped accepting Dad's money and started making my own path. First as a part owner in the shop, then with the fight nights. I found what I'm good at when I didn't think there was anything.

And that was the singular thing I've cared about.

But now, as I drag my needle across Tatum's calf, for the first time since Mom died, I do care about something more than myself or my art—a girl who won't get out of my head since she left my bed last week and started spending every other day at the hospital with my brother.

I've given her space, but I'm getting impatient.

And tonight, there's no escape.

Fel convinced Echo to attend Blaze's bloody Valentine's party with her, and even if she thinks I wasn't listening, I heard every word. Echo's name has become some kind of beacon my mind targets.

My chest constricts just thinking about her.

I don't care if my brother almost died. She's not using him as an excuse to avoid me any longer. Just like my father isn't going to leverage Rhett's injury to try and drag me back into the Kingsley family mess. At least Adam is keeping Dad's focus on bigger problems because if I get one more text requesting a family meeting, I'm going to smash my phone.

Pulling back on the needle, I set it aside and clean off the fresh tattoo. It's a black and gray portrait of his kid's face, and when Tatum smiles, I accept the only validation I allow myself.

"Fuck, man, you've got talent."

I know.

Not that I say it.

There's a reason people pay stupid amounts of money to get inked here. And since I've always had a natural knack for realism and portraits, I've made it my specialty.

"You still planning out the half sleeve?" I stand.

Tatum nods. "Debating how bloody I want to make it."

"I'll sketch out a few ideas. Just drop off anything you've been eyeing, and I'll work on something you might like."

"You got it, man." Tatum stands up and walks over to the mirror, twisting his leg to get a better look at the tattoo.

"It's like a photograph. You seriously nailed it."

I lean against the counter and cross my arms over my chest, nodding, but not offering much more.

It's flawless, but lately, even that doesn't relieve the pressure between my temples.

"Hey, is Echo here?"

"Why?" And why do I instantly want to stab my tattoo needle through his eye for asking me that question?

"Oh shit." Tatum slaps a hand on his forehead. "I forgot she's still dating your brother, right?"

I nod.

"Well, if it doesn't work out..." He smirks, and I'm resisting the urge to hold his head under water until all he can think about is how his lungs are on fire and his eyes are going to explode.

"Sure thing," I say instead because no one needs to realize how unhinged I'm becoming over this chick, especially Tatum.

I've always been aware of the attention she gets from anyone who walks into the shop, but this past week it's mind-splitting. Every pair of eyes that dart in her direction makes me want to carve them out.

This girl is going to be the literal end of me, and she's avoiding me like the fucking plague.

"I'll see you up front." I snap my gloves off and lead Tatum out of the room.

We pass Echo's door, and even if it's closed, I hear her needle buzzing. I feel her mind thinking. I drown in the scent of lavender.

She's hiding, hoping it's enough to keep me away. It isn't.

Tonight, this ends.

The Twisted Kings compound is a shitshow. Bleeding with sex and drugs. The beat of the music vibrates the floors, and my boots stick to spilled booze.

If there's someone who knows how to throw a party, it's Kane. And tonight, him and Blaze, his Vice President, are at the bar enjoying every debauch perk of running the most ruthless motorcycle club in California.

The bar is decorated bloody for their annual Valentine's Day party. Bleeding hearts, naked cupids dancing around. It smells like pot, violence, and sex. All things that got me going a few months ago. Now, there's only one thing that does. And she's dressed up like pure fucking sin and talking to a biker who looks like he wants to get a taste of her.

Most of the time, Echo walks around in shorts and baggy T-shirts. Cute, edgy, simple. But every so often her dark side comes out. And tonight, the full force of it hits me when the crowd parts, and I spot her.

Her hair is tied up in pigtails, one blonde, one black. They're curled and flipping around like she's some twisted version of Harley Quinn. She's in a skintight leather dress that hits so high up her legs that the bows on the backs of them are on full display. In the front, it dips so low between her breasts it shows off the rose she has inked above her belly button. And at the top of the black leather is a lacy design that weaves up around her neck, tying to a thick black choker.

I'm tempted to chain this girl to a fucking leash just for testing my patience.

"You made it." Sage slaps me on the shoulder and hands me a beer, his eyes following my stare to Echo. "Nice outfit, right? Sometimes I forget Echo is actually hot. Too bad she's fucking your brother, or I'd be tempted to bend her over."

I punch him in the arm.

"What was that for?" He rubs it, grinning. "Something you'd like to share with the class, Crew?"

Fucking Sage.

I don't know how he does it, given the dude's incapable of caring about anyone but himself, but he has this way of reading through everyone's bullshit. And I have no doubt I've revealed too much with one glance as my gaze moves back to where Echo's standing too close to some guy I'm tempted to teach a lesson.

"So?" Sage knocks my arm. "Care to tell me what the fuck's going on with you and Echo? You care an awful lot about the chick dating your brother."

"Shut the fuck up." I take a sip of my beer.

Sage chuckles, taking a drink of his own, and thankfully letting it go. Even if I'm sure he sees that I can't take my eyes off her. Smiling, laughing, bubbling with every word and those damn pigtails flipping around.

"Crew." A voice pops up on my left, and I look to see Mandi and her Barbie-doll friend smiling at me. They're in matching red lace dresses with their tits practically spilling out the top. And the way Mandi's lips purse with her smile tells me I could probably have one—if not both—of them sucking my cock.

The thought has never been less appealing.

I tip my chin up, acknowledging them and taking another sip of my beer. But Sage doesn't hesitate.

"Ladies." He steps around me.

Usually, the fact that he can be a major cock block bothers me, but tonight, it's welcome. At least if Mandi and her friend are distracted by whatever it is chicks find appealing about Sage, they won't notice I'm not the least bit interested.

But while Mandi's friend takes the bait and wraps herself around Sage's arm, Mandi doesn't take her eyes off me.

"You dipped out too soon the other night." Her red claws graze my forearm. "I tried to find you after the fight, and they said you were already gone."

"I had shit to do." I chug my beer now, my skin crawling at her touch.

Over Mandi's shoulder, Echo's eyes meet mine with jealousy raging in her sparkly, golden ones. She schools her expression and tries to bury it, but her cheeks get rosy, giving her away.

Too bad the girl doesn't bow down when challenged. Instead, Echo leans closer to the biker, giving him her full attention just to piss me off.

Perfect.

All I need is one excuse.

And it doesn't have to be a good one. I'd like to see him do anything so I can justify the sick rage desperate to get out.

Toying with the ring dangling around my neck, I watch the two of them. Echo wants me angry, so she's standing close. But every time the biker leans in, she recoils.

Because she's mine.

"Well, now you're free." Mandi steps in closer, and I get a hit of her too-strong perfume. "Want to go somewhere a little quieter and talk?"

Maybe if she'd asked me a year ago, I'd have been dumb enough to take her up on it. Now, I can barely hear what she's asking me because Echo Slater's brushing her hair off one shoulder and stealing all my attention.

"Not tonight." Not ever.

Echo rolls her shoulders back, standing up taller as her eyes once more flick in my direction. Her gaze moves between me and Mandi, then to the ring spinning between my fingers. She's trying to appear strong, but her endless eyes show me all her cards with one blink.

"If you like that girl, she can join us." Mandi lifts onto her toes and gets really close. "I wouldn't mind."

She smiles, and for the briefest moment, my attention is drawn back to her. How desperate she is and how the old me might have fallen for that shit, but now it's just fucking sad. I don't want Mandi, and her perfume that makes me want to hurl.

I want golden eyes that sparkle when I look back up at them.

The biker talking to Echo grabs her chin to steal her attention, and that's it. My excuse. My reason.

My world.

Brushing past Mandi, I don't let her red claws stop me. I shove through the crowd and ignore anything I've denied up to this point.

The biker wraps an arm around Echo's waist, and like the feisty girl she is, she shoves him off her, flipping him off and taking a step back. Echo can hold her own. She was forced to the way she was raised. But it doesn't matter because I'm going to do something about this rage that's been buried for too long.

Echo might tell herself what we did was a means to an end but fuck that shit.

This Goldilocks with her Cruella De Ville hair is my darkness. My light. My other half. And the only one who has ever made me feel weak, whether she sees it or not.

Biker dude brushes her jaw with his hand like she belongs to him, and she swats it away, taking another step back.

I've seen this before, and any other night I'd watch with amusement as Echo would kick him in the balls and tell him to fuck off. But that was then. Now she's mine, and he dared to fucking touch her.

He made the mistake of waking up the beast that lives in my dark, sadistic soul.

When I finally reach them, I shove the biker back.

"Crew." Echo tries to warn me, but there's no stopping this.

After all, she's the one who does this to me.

"Hey, man." The guy pushes his dark hair back and straightens his cut. "We were having a little chat. Go find your own bitch to fuck."

The room might as well go silent.

Rage is my element. It's who I am, and where I belong. It's the only emotion I've ever understood, so I embrace it.

And as Echo tenses at what this guy just said about her, it fuels me.

Nothing feels better than inflicting pain, and I'll snap every bone in his body to write her a love song with the sound of his screams.

I grab the biker by the throat and hit him over the side of the head with my beer bottle, leaving a gash in his forehead, even if the force alone isn't enough to break it. So I smash the bottle on the bar top behind him instead, making jagged edges of one end.

People around us step back and start cheering. And off in the distance, I spot a couple of Twisted Kings making their way through the group to get to us.

Lucky for me, this asshole isn't a Twisted King, or they'd probably slit my throat for what I'm about to do. Even that wouldn't be enough to stop me when he had the nerve to call Echo a bitch.

Blood pours from the gash in the biker's forehead, down his cheek and over my hand. His gaze is hazy as I pull him close so we're face to face. And I shove the shattered beer bottle into his side, feeding on the scream that rips out of him.

Beside me, Echo's hands fly to her mouth as Blaze appears between us and pulls me back.

"What the fuck, Crew?"

The guy slumps to the ground with the beer bottle sticking out of him, blood pooling out. He's not dead yet, unfortunately.

Kane makes it to us next, looking from me to the guy on the ground.

"I've got this," Blaze says to him. "Bones has been testing the guys all night."

Bones. Fitting, I'd like to break all of them.

"I'll deal with this." Kane walks past me and Blaze, nodding.

They should probably be pissed I'm starting shit at their bar, but it's not the worst this place has seen given how they use the empty horse stalls out back. And even if I'm not patched in, I've helped them with enough favors to have their trust.

"What was that?" Blaze asks, turning back to me.

I look over at Echo, whose wide eyes are fixed on the man bleeding on the ground as she bites her lip.

"Did he do something to her?" Blaze's jaw clenches, and I sense he wants to continue what I started.

Echo shakes her head.

"Didn't get the chance." I reach out and grab her hand, those golden eyes connecting with mine, before I look back at Blaze. "We good to take off?"

"Probably best you do." He looks over his shoulder as Bones screams. "We'll deal with this."

"Thanks, man." I tug Echo's hand. "Let's go."

She tries to shake me off, but I ignore her. I'm over this push and pull shit that's got me on edge. She's going to learn once and for all to fucking listen.

Blaze lets us pass, ignoring that Echo's trying to fight her hand free from my grip.

"I'm not going anywhere with you." She pushes my arm as I pull her through the crowd. The force of it nearly sends her toppling in her five-inch heels, and I have to wrap an arm around her waist to steady her.

Holding her to my side, I pause, dropping my mouth to her ear.

"Outside, Echo. Don't fucking test me right now."

When I pull back, she's given up her fight. Blood streaks her arms from where my fingers gripped her. I reach for her hand again and she doesn't pull back this time. Instead, she allows me to lead her out of the bar.

The night air is a relief with all the pot that was clouding the atmosphere inside, and I take a deep breath, trying to clear my head. A few bikers sitting on the porch pass glances at Echo in her ridiculously short dress, so I move her to block their view as I walk us around the outside.

Once we turn the corner, she shakes free of my hand, and this time, I let her.

"What was that?" She crosses her arms over her chest, smearing the blood on them as she does. "I was dealing with him. I don't need you protecting me."

"I'm aware." Doesn't mean it will stop me.

"Then stop using me as an excuse to let out your aggression." Her eyes narrow, and she looks once more at the ring around my neck that has her constant attention. "And stop wearing that."

"No."

"No?" She reaches for it.

But I grab her hand, shoving her back against the side of the bar and pinning her wrist overhead, while pushing my knee between her legs.

"That's what I said. No."

She grits her teeth, but her legs clench around my thigh. She can hate me all she wants; it turns her on when I piss her off.

"Don't you have some sleazy cupid to get back to?" Venom and jealousy lace her tone. "Mandi, I think her name is."

I reach up and rub my thumb over her lip, peeling her mouth open. "There you go again with that bratty little tongue of yours."

"You're an asshole." She turns her head.

I dip my mouth by her ear. "You like it."

"You're sick."

"Yep."

"Violent."

"Mm-hmm." I release her wrist and wrap my hand around her throat to pin her to the wall, forcing her to face me. "And you're the dirty fucking girl who loves that about me."

"I don't."

But her breath hitches when I drag my other hand down her side, over her hip, teasing the line of her short dress.

"You sure about that?"

"I'm your brother's girlfriend." This threat is nearly a whisper. The last weapon in her arsenal, even if she knows it won't make an impact.

"I appreciate the reminder." I shove my knee forward, which draws her thighs further apart, the heat of her pussy making my dick rock hard. "You seem to have forgotten how much I enjoy taking what's his."

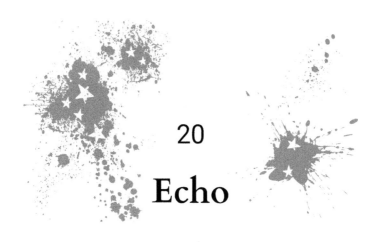

20

Echo

I TIP MY HEAD back and look Crew in his evil eyes. "You're obscene."

The sick thoughts no doubt running through his head are clear in his wicked expression. But what's sicker is I don't mind it.

I want it.

I *need* it.

I feed on the way my morals break for him.

"Only because I know you like it." He dips down and brushes his lips over my jaw, pressing his leg harder between my own, and I have to fight every urge to not grind against him.

"How very *nice* of you," I tease. "Don't tell me you're going to be sweet with me now, Crew. That wasn't why I asked you to be the first man to fuck me."

"*First*, huh?" His pupils blow wide with his gritted tone, and his fingers grip my throat tighter, blurring my vision.

I'm pushing him on purpose. I love the feel of his flames. How one touch of his palms on my skin sets my entire body ablaze.

Deny it all I want, I'm desperate to do this twisted dance with him.

I knew Crew would be here tonight, which is why I wore this ridiculous dress and thigh-high stiletto boots. I wanted to prove that he isn't the only one in control and that I can fuck with him just like he does to me—walking in tonight in his pale blue jeans and dark gray band tee. Always casual, and ridiculously hot.

I was tempted to break the silent treatment I'd been giving him for the past week, until Mandi walked over to him in her skimpy Cupid outfit and started pawing at his arm.

Then all I saw was the hate, and I was desperate to inflict that same pain.

Not that I thought he's stab someone over it.

It should have scared me that Crew went to those lengths over one comment. But as I stood there watching Crew with his hand around the guy's throat, spilling blood because he called me a bitch, deep inside I thrived on it.

I'm not sure who's sicker anymore, just that we're both losing this inevitable battle.

"You think you can handle someone else, when you can't even handle the things I've still got planned for you?" Crew sinks his teeth into my neck and covers my mouth when I let out a strangled scream. "Tempting me like you're not still sore from the first time."

He pulls back and smirks.

"Sore?" I tip my chin up, challenging him because I can't help it. "Was that supposed to hurt? Gotta tell you, Crew, I thought you were better at inflicting pain after hearing all the rumors. I'm a little disappointed."

"Testing me like you can handle it." His grip on my throat tightens, and my vision starts to darken now.

"Think I can't?"

"Guess we'll see."

Crew releases my throat and spins me around as air rushes back to my lungs. He uses one hand to pin my chest to the side of the bar while he pulls my dress up over my hips with the other, exposing me to anyone who might walk by.

"Out here?" I'm not sure if it's excitement or fear that prickles my skin with my question.

Crew rips off my underwear, chuckling. "Thought you could handle it, Echo? That's why you were teasing me with your bratty little mouth, wasn't it?"

He wraps an arm around my waist, pulling my back to him, and it's so rough and sudden I clutch the wall for balance. One of his hands works his belt, his knuckles brushing my bare ass as he releases himself.

"Let them walk by and see you like this." He pulls himself out, rubbing the head of his dick between my legs, coating himself in my excitement. "Let them all see who you really belong to."

Crew shoves himself inside me in one brutal thrust. He hits me so deep at this angle, I almost black out from the intensity of him filling me. His arm wraps my waist, while the other one grabs the back of my head, holding me hard against the side of the bar as he fucks me.

"You want to be fucked like a whore?" His fingers tighten their grip on my hair, and he slams in harder. "Then take me like one. Out here where anyone can see you begging for my cock."

I've pissed him off, either with my actions tonight or the reminder that at the end of this I still belong to his brother. But right now, I don't care. Because I want him to punish me for all the wrongs I'm committing.

Light me up in flames and send me to hell with my sins because I need this.

I need the pain to remind me there's still a reason to keep fighting.

He pounds into me with such force, I can't keep my balance, but his arm holds me in place. Thrusting into me until my legs are shaking and the threat of being caught makes my entire body shiver.

"Crew." My nails dig into the building, and I'm clenching so hard, he grunts like he's in pain.

"That's right, Goldie." He hits me deeper, pressing me into the wall as he fucks me, leaning in so his lips brush my ear. "Take this cock like my good little slut. Lie to yourself and say you still belong to my brother. I fucking dare you."

"I—" But he hits me so deep it takes the words from my lips; my body quivers, and I start to clench around him.

"Exactly." He thrusts. "Whose cock is inside you right now? The *only one* that's ever been inside you?"

"Yours." I think I say it. I'm halfway between coming and blacking out as dots spot my vision.

"This pussy knows who it belongs to, even when your bratty mouth tries to deny it. Squeezing me, desperate for my cum. This pussy is mine, Echo." He releases my hair and reaches around to wrap his hand at the base of my throat. "Your sassy tongue, your body, your soul, the air in your fucking lungs. You shouldn't hand yourself to the devil if you aren't prepared to belong to him."

Crew pulls out and spins me around. My focus zoning in on his dark steely eyes. My climax has barely faded as he shoves me to my knees.

"Open." He squeezes my jaw.

In my pleasure-induced haze, I can't help but comply. My lips part, and Crew shoves himself in.

"Relax your throat, Goldie." He holds my hair, and even if his words are encouraging, he fucks my mouth like he fucked my body. Like he needs me, and he hates me. "Hollow your cheeks and breathe through your nose."

I do as I'm told, not able to move when his grip holds my head in place as he fucks it.

"That's it." He tips his head back, and the sight of how I'm pleasing him has me desperate to come again. When he looks back down at me, his gaze is heated. "Taste that, princess? Your cum all over my dick. I want you to choke on the taste of us, Echo."

He shoves in so far, he hits the back of my throat, and I can't help the tears pouring out of my eyes at the sheer force. My fingers dig into his thighs, but he doesn't let me go. He fucks my mouth harder.

"I want you to taste how insane you make me. I'm going to be the first man to ruin every part of you, and if you still think there's any escaping this, you're wrong."

I'm crying and coming as he hits the back of my throat harder, and his fingers tighten in my hair. His jaw clenches, and he might as well be the devil himself.

"Swallow me like a good little slut."

It's the only warning I get before his cum hits my tongue.

Crew fucks my mouth through his release, and I swallow what I can while the rest drips between my lips and down my chin. I'm a mess, and my legs quiver at the recklessness of this. At how I want him to use me until there's nothing left.

When he finally relaxes, he pulls out, releasing me, and I slump back onto my heels, into the dirt outside this disgusting bar. My cheeks are stained in tears, and there's cum on my chin and chest. Blood is dried on my neck and arms from where it rubbed off his hands. But as Crew tucks himself back into his pants and looks down at me, I've somehow never felt more perfect.

The hard, angry edge in his gaze slips, and he reaches down to help me up. Once I'm standing, he adjusts my dress back down my hips and wipes himself from my chest. I brush under my eyes, but I know I'm a mess.

I shiver, even if there's no breeze, coming down from a high that has my insides plummeting.

"Here." Crew peels his leather jacket off and wraps it around me, pulling me to his side. "We're leaving."

"My car—"

"I'll deal with it." He pulls out his phone and shoots off a text.

If I wasn't shivering and on the verge of passing out from excitement and exhaustion, I'd ask questions. But right now, I don't care. I sink into his side and let him hold me. I soak in the moment that would be sweet if he hadn't just fucked me in the dirt like he hates me for being his brother's girlfriend.

I pretend we're not people who feed on this kind of twisted behavior.

Crew guides me to his car, and he holds the door open while I climb in. My eyes drift, and I'm not sure what to make of his expression as he pauses outside it for a moment, watching me through the window before walking around the other side.

I'm too tired to analyze it. If I do, I'll want it to be what it isn't. So instead, I close my eyes and disappear into the darkness while Crew drives us home.

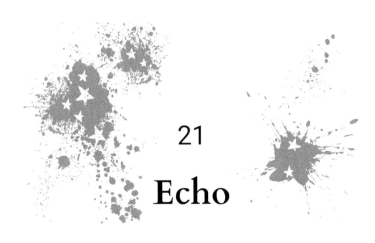

21

Echo

"SO PRETTY. SO SWEET."

In the darkness, hands find me. Climbing like ants up a tree, but the bark is my legs and my skin prickles.

Jumping upright, I try to make sense of the shadow. Of the figure looming over me. I reach for the blanket, but it's no longer there, pulled down on this stripped bed.

"It's okay, sweet girl."

His voice crawls my skin, my ears. Stale cigarettes and cat urine flood my nose.

"Go away. Why are you in here?"

He chuckles, those ants—his fingers—climbing up again.

"Shh, sweet girl. It's okay. Stay quiet, and you and your mom will be fine."

"Echo."

I startle at Crew's voice. My eyes fly open, and I shove his hand from my leg, fighting for breath.

The familiar nightmare once more sitting on the edge of my mind, reminding me what I've done. Why I'm sick. Where I went wrong.

Why I can't back out on my commitments.

Crew is crouched down outside my car door with a pinched expression. I slept the entire drive to his apartment. And between the ledge I'm resting on from my memories, and my exhaustion from the night, I don't have the energy to ask him why he didn't drop me off at mine.

"Sorry." I brush my pigtails off my shoulders and take a deep breath. "Nightmare."

He nods, his dark hair falling just over his eyes as the gray orbs watch me.

I've always recognized a familiar darkness in him, even when I hate him. Something deep that rots Crew's soul, the same way memories rot mine. Witnessing death at a young age will do that to you.

My mom.

His.

It shouldn't settle me that he understands the pain from my past, but it does. It carved us into the misshapen creatures we are. Wounded in ways that can't quite be understood.

We're pieces.

Yet somehow, mine fit with his. If only they could make me whole.

Crew reaches out his hand, letting it hover.

As cruel as he is at times, he pauses, not touching me as I adjust to my fading nightmare. It's safety I shouldn't feel as I slip my hand into his palm and let him help me from the car. Things he can't ever be in the long run because it's not who he is.

It messes with my head. Because understanding his aggression and expecting his volatile nature is one thing, but care is another.

That's not his role, it's supposed to be his brother's.

But tonight, Crew was the one there standing up for me when I've always been left to fight my own battles. He was there making someone bleed for their lack of respect.

What does it say that he wants me safe to such an extreme extent?

Rhett's warnings blare as Crew guides me out of the car, watching me tug his leather jacket closed over my chest. If Rhett is right, and Crew's only using me until he loses interest, when will it happen?

How much is enough?

There's already so little of me left.

Crew wraps his arm around my shoulders and guides me into his building. He blocks the doorman's view of me, and I'm thankful, given I'm a mess of dirt, tears, and so much more. He holds me at his side in the elevator and doesn't lose his grip on me.

"Better now?" he asks, looking down at me.

I nod.

"Do you get the nightmares often?"

"Some months more than others."

And lately, they're more frequent. Little triggers and I'm flooded with evil I'm not sure I'll ever escape. Hands on me when I didn't welcome them—thinking they deserve to take what they want without asking.

Tonight, at the bar, when the biker closed in on me, for a moment I froze. Bile rising and needles prickling my skin. It doesn't matter how strong I am, or how quickly I slipped out of it, for a moment I was that twelve-year-old girl again, waking up in bed with an unfamiliar man sitting on it.

Fear splitting me in half.

Crew stops us at his apartment door and unlocks it, waiting for me to walk in first. It's dark, with a woodsy, warm scent hanging in the air, even if the room is cool.

I shouldn't be here, but instead, I let Crew guide me to his bedroom.

I'm not sure what to make of the fact that he's being caring after fucking me outside of the bar and calling me a whore. But I want that push and pull. The give and take. The hot and cold. He's my balance.

With Crew, I'm more than a puppet on strings. I'm feeling—living. I'm me.

Crew leads me all the way to the bathroom and strips his leather jacket off my shoulders. Walking over to the shower, he turns it on, and a hot fog fills the room. He grabs the back of his T-shirt and tugs it off, pausing.

I want to read his mind. Take a walk in that tangled forest and see what he's wrestling in there. Angry, broken. All the sides he never lets anyone see, as I'm just now learning they exist.

Reaching up, I unclasp the choker that secures my dress around my neck. And when I undo the zipper, my dress puddles to my feet. I slip out of my boots and walk to Crew like he's my magnet, planting my hands on his back.

His breath hitches with the contact.

Electricity.

And I wonder—even if this is just for his amusement, and if he'll discard me once he's done—if he still feels it. Sparks that light when we touch. Circuits that fire no matter how much either of us fights it.

He can fuck me like I'm worthless, but he can't deny whatever plays in his eyes each time they connect with mine. Secrets we try to hide and truths we're scared to admit.

"Why are you marrying him, Echo?" Crew tips his head back, taking in a deep breath.

I rest my forehead on the center of his back, between where my hands are planted, and soak in the rise and fall of his body like waves crashing.

"Because it's for the best." I press my lips together and inhale through my nose. "Because I made a promise."

One I wish I hadn't, and even if I could, I'm a coward and can't take it back now.

"Why do you ask?" I know better than to push for answers I won't like, but I'm not able to help myself as steam cloaks my fears in this bathroom. "Isn't it easier when there's no risk I'll want more from this?"

Crew turns around, catching my wrists when I try to pull them away, planting my hands on his chest. He pushes my chin up with his thumb and forces me to look in the broken depths of his eyes.

"None of this is fucking easy." He grinds his jaw. "Why can't you see that? You deserve so much more than you're giving yourself."

"You don't know what I deserve."

My soul is damned to hell.

"But I do." He releases my wrists and reaches up to undo my hair, letting it pool over my shoulders. "You deserve to be with someone better than my righteous brother. You deserve to be with someone who will worship *you*, not God."

"And who would that be?"

We both know it's not him. Crew's words might be sweet, but it doesn't mean that's something he can offer. Which is why he says nothing to answer my question.

"Exactly." I shake my head. "Just admit you only care because you're going to have to spend every family gathering for the rest of your life sitting across from me, reminiscing on how you fucked me out of boredom and revenge. And you won't be able to do what you normally do with girls, and just escape them."

Crew's jaw ticks with his smirk as he rakes my hair off my face. "You're beautiful when you're being vicious, Goldie. But that's not going to happen."

"You might be a good fuck, but you're not changing my mind."

Now I am being mean. *Vicious.*

Cruel like him.

"We'll see." Crew releases me, reaching down and stripping off his pants.

Naked, tattooed muscle bare in front of me, and I have to clench my thighs to hold back what the sight of him does. Not a scrap of clothing on him, besides the single chain holding my purity ring around his neck.

The one piece he doesn't seem to ever take off.

A taunt and a promise twisted together.

Stepping to me, we're skin to skin. We might as well melt in the heat of the steam in this bathroom. Crew's hand finds my jaw and his thumb presses my lower lip as he dips his face to mine.

"You're going to tell me the truth no matter how hard you try to run from it." He rubs his thumb over my lip, my chin. "Maybe not tonight. But you will."

"What makes you so sure?"

My heart is racing with every graze of his thumb.

"Because I *see* you. Even if you're not ready to admit it to yourself yet."

Crew drags his hands down my arms and laces our fingers together, leading the way around the shower until we're stepping inside.

I hate that he ignores how cruel I'm being in an effort to push him away and holds me close instead. It breaks through all my defenses.

Hot water floods my skin as he pulls me under it with him. And I close my eyes as his hands roam my body. I soak in the feel of the only man I've trusted to touch me. A man I said I was handing my virginity to because it would mean nothing. Because he's incapable of caring about anyone but himself.

But as I open my eyes and am met with his gray gaze, I'm well aware I've been lying to myself. I gave my body to Crew because I wanted him to have the last piece that felt like mine. I trusted a monster because it's a reflection of what I am inside.

"Crew."

His soapy hands rub my arms. Water runs in rivers down his face, over the demons carved into his flesh.

"What, princess?" He cups my jaw in both his hands, and I wrap my arms around his neck.

"I wish things were different."

He tips his forehead down to mine and takes in a deep breath. "Me too, Echo. Me too."

I lift onto my toes, and he captures my mouth. Soft, tender. The sides of him he never shows me as he wipes my wet hair off my shoulders and over my naked body. He presses his hips against me, his cock firm between us, and my entire body aches.

Spinning us around, he presses my back to the shower wall. The cool contrast of the tile against the hot water has my senses on overdrive.

I tip my head back, and he leans down to kiss the path along my neck.

"Fuck me." I rake my hands through his wet hair. "Make me forget."

Crew doesn't ask questions. He doesn't need to know what problem he's solving. And I appreciate the silence as he hitches one of my legs up around his hips and drives himself in.

He hits me deep enough that my soul leaves my body. Floats in the steam and melts into him. Crew tips his head down to press our foreheads together, and he fucks me slow and deep. I'm still sore from earlier tonight outside the bar, but I want that pain.

I grab the chain around his neck and hold onto my ring. My purity. Something he keeps safe when it no longer exists. He cherishes it like it was worth something it wasn't.

He kisses my forehead. My temple. My cheek. He claims my mouth and our tongues dance. Our bodies mold. He shapes my heart and brings it to life again.

"What do you need, Echo?" he murmurs against my mouth, hitting me deeper.

He could be talking about this moment or in general. Either way, I only have one answer.

"You." I cling to him tighter as he lifts my other leg and wraps it around him, pinning me to the shower wall. "Just you, Crew."

"You have me." He thrusts in again as his teeth sink into my lower lip. "You're mine. All mine..."

He trails off, fucking me as the words reverberate through my being with every thrust. As he hits me until I'm coming hard, and he's jerking inside me.

"You're mine."

He says it again and again. So many times, I almost believe it could be possible.

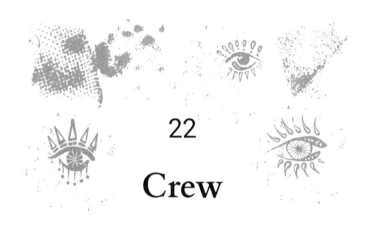

22

Crew

WALKING INTO THE SHOP, I stop at the wall on my left and slap another pair of eyes on it. These ones are gold, cut from the magazine Echo was flipping through this morning as she ate breakfast.

No one understands this wall, or why I continue to add to it. But something about the way it sees around every corner, around every secret. I can't help it. It started when Blaze first sold the shop to the four of us, and we decided to renovate the lobby. No one could decide what to do with this wall, so I started what was meant to be a collage but ended up being a wall of eyes instead.

Some are photographs, some magazine cutouts, some art. A collection of all colors, expressions, feelings. The eyes tell a lot about a person. You might think the mouth is how to read a smile, but it's not. Lips lie, but you can't hide from the truth in a person's eyes.

And Echo's show me everything I need to know.

She didn't say much this morning when she woke up, but unlike last night, she seemed at peace. And I appreciated that I was awake before her so she didn't have a chance to disappear from my bed like she's so good at. Instead, I forced her to sit and eat some toast with her coffee before she inevitably found an excuse to get to work early.

But she left the magazine open on the counter when she left, and the golden eyes on the page were familiar. Warm like the sun, even if they still lack the sparkle only hers hold. And now they're on this wall like every other thing inside me I can't escape.

"I like it."

Turning, I spot Fel standing behind the counter, sorting through a new collection of barbells.

She tips her chin up at the wall behind me. "I used to think that wall was kind of creepy, but it's growing on me. I think I like them."

She might be the first person to share that feeling. Everyone else says the wall makes them feel uncomfortable. Which is the point when people are always trying to hide shit. But something about Fel and her innocence, with no more secrets—it doesn't scare her.

When she first started coming here, and I noticed Jude becoming more and more obsessed, I didn't get it. But now, seeing how she balances out his darkness, I might.

"It's all right." I shrug, walking over to the counter and glancing down at the new collection of barbells. "Wicked shit you've got here."

I pick up a barbell with a skull on either side. One has roses in its eyes and the other has a dagger in its mouth.

"Testing out a few new things."

Lucky for us because her shit has been selling like crazy at the shop. And Jude's in a better mood when she's here, so it's a bonus for all of us.

Jude walks around the corner and Fel straightens up, smiling as he walks over to her. He glares at me, and I can't help but smirk. I might have teased him a few times about trying to steal his girl, but it was just to piss him off. Besides, if he could have read my mind, he'd know it was all total bullshit. A mask I was using to hide the fact that I had my own wicked little Goldilocks on my brain.

"You giving my girl shit?" Jude tips his chin up.

Fel playfully slaps him on the chest. "We were just talking. Leave him alone."

Jude glares at me because he's protective to the point of edging on insane. I guess I'm not one to talk after what I did to the biker last night.

Blaze texted me this morning to say Bones was still breathing, but barely. And part of me was tempted to drive to the hospital to finish what I started.

"You dipped early last night," Jude says.

"Yeah." I scratch the back of my neck. "Shit got awkward."

"I heard." He doesn't offer much more.

Jude is as cold and impossible to read as I am. But right now, his eyebrows pinch, and I'm not sure what he's thinking about my actions, but I don't like it. The guys are starting to suspect shit with me and Echo, and until she stops lying to herself about whatever the fuck we're doing, I'm not ready to answer questions about it.

Luckily, if he was going to ask anything, he doesn't get the chance. The shop door swings open, drawing his attention.

Turning, I can't help but chuckle. If I thought Rhett visiting Echo here was amusing, Adam in his suit in the middle of a tattoo shop in downtown LA has me actually laughing.

He's so out of place it's ridiculous.

"Did Lakeyn leave your ass already?" I can't help but chuckle. "If you needed a place to stay you could have called instead of risking the rims on your Ferrari to beg me to sleep on my couch."

Adam doesn't so much as frown, unaffected as always. "You done?"

"No fucking fun." I shake my head. "Fine. This way."

He follows me to my room at the shop, and I shut the door behind him.

"You lose your phone?" Adam doesn't small talk. Which I guess is better than Rhett always talking in circles around everything.

At least with Adam you know what you're getting.

Each of the three of us brothers dealt with our mother's death differently. While I became impulsive, indulging in anything and everything that felt good, bad, or otherwise, Adam did the opposite, shutting down almost entirely.

Until he met Lakeyn, I was convinced he was morphing into a full-on robot.

Now, at least he acts like there's something that makes life worth living, even if he's still cold to anyone who isn't her.

Then there's Rhett—I'm still not sure what to make of how he processed Mom's death. Ever since I saw him standing over her body, with an unreadable expression, I knew something changed, I just didn't know what.

He called it a religious awakening, but I was in that room. There was no God.

Only evil.

"Nope, got my phone right here." I pull it out of my pocket and place it on the counter before I begin sorting through my sketches.

"Dad's been texting you."

"I'm aware."

"You're ignoring him."

I shrug.

Adam lets out an annoyed huff.

While I've done everything to separate myself from the Kingsley name, Adam plays the role of my father's son well. He's a driven, more powerful version of him, amassing the family fortune and feeding our power. And while it used to be my father people feared, Adam has slowly taken over that role. Which is why he's here now. Adam has the influence, in the community and in our family.

"There are some things you can't avoid, Crew."

"Like Rhett's bullshit?"

"Like family."

I can't help but laugh. "When's the last time I saw you at Sunday dinner, brother? If you want to preach family, why don't you start there."

"My time's limited. Don't question what I do with it."

"That's the point, I don't care what you do with it." I flip through a stack of sketches and find what I'm looking for, trying to ignore the fact that Adam won't leave me the fuck alone. "It's not my fault Rhett's pissing off religious zealots. You guys handle your shit, and I'll handle mine. Like it's always been done."

Adam leans against the counter, crossing his arms over his chest. "And what about Echo?"

I loosen my grip on the sketch before I set it down and turn to him. One look—the smallest tick of a smile—he knows he's got me.

"What about her?"

"You've been spending quite a few late nights with Rhett's girlfriend." He lifts off, pacing the room now and scanning the artwork.

"Stalking me now?"

"You're family, like it or not." Adam stops in front of a picture of heaven and hell, and I wish it wasn't how I feel inside. "Just because you don't understand the risk in that, doesn't mean Dad or I will let anything happen."

"How very *big brother* of you." I shake my head.

Adam ignores the sarcasm in my tone, turning to face me again. "What are your plans with her?"

"Is Dad asking or Rhett?"

"I am."

He sounds like he actually means it, and it makes me wonder what, if anything, he's told my father about my forbidden obsession.

"We both know her relationship with Rhett is bullshit. So what does it matter?"

Adam hums, running his hand over the bottom edge of a framed photo of one of the first tattoos I ever did. "Appearances, Crew. Not that I should expect you to care about those."

"Why do you?"

Adam straightens the frame, fixing his stormy gray gaze on me.

"You think you're free from your obligations because you walked away and got distracted with this little shop of yours. But you can't deny the truth. You're a Kingsley whether you like it or not. And with that name comes responsibilities. Like pretending to care that your brother just got shot, or that someone's been funneling money from the church."

"What do you mean someone's funneling money?"

"Exactly what I said." His jaw ticks. "If you'd have answered your phone, you would know that. This isn't just about Rhett and his relationship with his girlfriend. Someone is after what our family has been building. And if you don't care about that, maybe you'll care about this—they're after what Echo's father's been building. Think she'll be happy about that?"

I clench my fists at my sides.

"Didn't think so." Adam huffs. "The last thing this family needs right now is more heat, especially from the inside.

So if you're fucking her just to give the middle finger to Rhett, knock it off and find someone else to distract yourself with."

"And what if that's not why?"

I'm not sure what compels me to ask. The question tells Adam way too much. But the fact that he's here means he already suspects something more, so there's no real use in trying to hide it.

Adam walks toward me, stopping a few feet away. "If that's the case, then you need to be smart and learn how to play the fucking game."

It almost sounds like he's encouraging me, which would be odd considering Adam is the careful brother.

"What are you saying?"

Adam brushes his hands over the front of his suit jacket. "Everything comes to light eventually. If you keep this up, it will hurt Rhett. And worse, it will hurt her. She's sweet, innocent, *the preacher's daughter*."

He's right, and my stomach sinks at his reasoning.

"Unless..." Adam lets out a long exhale. "You both face it before that happens. Make the decision and cut the ties that make this messy."

"She's staying with him."

"I'm aware." Adam's gaze narrows. "But is that what she really wants?"

"No." Doesn't matter what she tells me, I know I'm right.

"Then do something about it, Crew, before this spirals more out of control. I have enough to clean up right now between Rhett and the family business, without you adding fuel to the fire."

He turns to walk away.

"Adam."

He pauses.

"Why aren't you just telling me to stay the fuck away from her?"

It's no secret Adam likes things clean. And once a line is drawn, he expects it to stay there.

"Because I get it now." He looks back at me. "Lakeyn broke all my rules. And dragging her into our family is the worst thing I could have done to her. But it didn't matter. She's mine, and when something is yours, you don't let it go. No matter the price."

Not even if it costs a brother.

He doesn't say that, but we both know it would. Even if Rhett suspects something is happening between me and Echo, he likely doesn't care right now because he's distracted himself. And he thinks I'll get tired of her soon.

If she were anyone else, I would.

"If she means something real to you, then you need to make a decision." He opens the door to the room and pauses. "You're good at resisting, Crew. Denying your part in this family. But have you ever stopped to think that's also what got you in this situation? Freedom is still an option. But it might require playing a few hands to get it."

He turns and walks away, leaving me with a pit in my stomach. Adam is suggesting I fight for something I shouldn't, and I'm tempted to do it.

My phone buzzes, and I look down to see Paul's name lighting up the screen. Opening the text, I can't help but smirk at the karma.

Paul: Oakland ring is ready for your eyes boss, when do you want to head out?

Crew: Tonight

Paul: Damn, that's fast. I'll get my shit.

Crew: It's fine, you stay here and take care of the week-end madness. I'll make this trip alone

Paul: Sure thing, boss, see you when you get back

Just what I need, a few days away. A little space. And some uninterrupted time with my devious golden-eyed girl to fuck some sense into her once and for all.

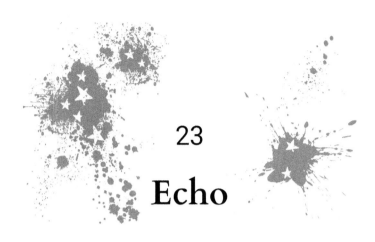

23

Echo

"HEADS OR TAILS." CREW is leaning against his car outside the shop with a quarter in his hand, smirking at me.

"What are we playing for?" I cross my arms over my chest and narrow my gaze.

"Pick one and find out."

"Tell me, and I'll pick one."

He lifts off the car, stepping right in front of me. Static electricity running like a current through the air. My breath catches in my throat as he closes in. Leaning so close his lips almost graze mine.

"Crew..." I step back, glancing around, worried about who could be watching.

There are always eyes looking for a scandal. Someone hoping to catch the preacher's daughter in her fall from grace. It's something I wouldn't care about if it only affected me. But Rhett... my father.

I take a step back, and Crew just smirks.

"Scared?"

"We could get caught." I pop my gum between my teeth and look around again, knowing that's probably why Crew is doing this, so I'm not sure why I'm trying to use it as a threat.

He shrugs one shoulder. "Heads or tails. Choose and I'll stop."

I narrow my gaze and pause with my gum clenched between my teeth.

"Okay—" He steps toward me again.

"Tails." I step back, my gaze darting around again.

Crew pauses a foot away from me, and flips the coin into the air, grabbing it and flipping it on the back of his hand. "Heads."

Of course. I should have known there's no winning against the devil.

"What do you want?" I pop a bubble.

"Get in the car, Goldie."

He turns and walks back to his car, opening the passenger door.

"Where are we going?"

"It's a surprise."

"I have an appointment."

"I rescheduled it."

"You can't just reschedule my appointments." I storm over to him. "You didn't even know if you would win."

Crew leans in, and I realize I've placed myself in his bubble. "I always win."

My hands clench at my sides, and I wish I didn't notice how good he smells when he's skipped the cologne today, and it's just his shampoo clouding my judgment.

"Now get in the car, or I'll pick you up and throw you in myself."

My core shouldn't clench when he's being an asshole, but I can't help how my body reacts to hating him.

"Fine." I grit my teeth and climb in, crossing my arms over my chest as he slams the car door shut behind me.

At this point, it's the path of least resistance. And the one that will draw the least amount of attention to anyone passing on the street.

Crew gets in and starts the engine, his expression's passive as he pulls out onto the road.

"So where are you taking me?"

"Oakland."

"What?" I spin to face him in my seat. "I'm not going to Oakland with you."

"You sitting beside me right now says the contrary." He plants a tattooed hand on my thigh and my skin prickles. "Besides, *heads*, remember?"

"You didn't tell me what we were playing for. Manipulation isn't winning."

He squeezes my thigh, lighting a path of heat all the way up to my core. "It's cute you still think I have limits on how low I'll go to get to you, Goldie."

"Oh please." I roll my eyes, popping my gum. "And what about Rhett? I was supposed to go see him later."

"Your boyfriend's busy planning his holy comeback, I'm sure he won't mind." Crew grits his jaw, pulling his hand away. "Not to mention... he's still healing from his bullet wound."

I rub my palms over my thighs, guilt creeping through. My boyfriend's barely a day out of the hospital, and I'm being kidnapped to Oakland by his brother. And as much as I know I should probably jump out each time we hit a stoplight, I don't. Because I want this, whether I should or not.

"How long are we going to be gone for?" I cross my arms over my chest, giving in to the fact that I'm not even fighting this.

"A day." He shrugs. "Two max."

"Don't I at least get to pack? I need a toothbrush at the very least."

Crew tips his chin to the backseat. "Already done."

Turning, I see a familiar black duffle bag in the backseat. Red roses and skulls decorate it. Until recently, Crew never used the key to my apartment. Apparently, now he has no problem letting himself in whenever he pleases.

"Of course you did." I roll my eyes as Crew's phone starts ringing through the car speakers.

"What?" he answers.

"Have you seen Echo?" Rhett's voice comes through, and my insides are in knots.

"No, why?" He glances over at me and smirks.

Asshole.

"Just checking." He pauses, clicking his tongue. "I heard Adam came to see you."

"Mm-hmm."

He looks away now, his jaw clenching. Crew rarely sees Adam, so I'm not sure what to make of the tension that welled at Rhett's comment.

"Everything good then?" Rhett asks.

"Fucking peachy as always." But Crew sounds the opposite of it.

"All right. You coming to dinner tonight?"

"I had to take a quick trip out of town. Sorry."

Now I can't help but wonder if this wasn't planned specifically to avoid something.

"I'll be back in a day or two," Crew says, gripping the steering wheel.

"Let me know if you hear from Echo." Rhett's tongue clicks with the word, and the tension is palpable in the car—in all the things being left unsaid.

"Sure thing."

"And Crew..." Rhett pauses. Silence so thick you could slice it. "Never mind, we'll chat when you're back."

Crew ends the call, and we sit in silence for a minute. I'm not sure if he's waiting for me to call Rhett or jump out of the car, but I don't do either. Crew's avoiding something by taking me to Oakland, and I need the escape right now.

As if he reads my mood, he reaches over, planting his hand on my bare thigh. "It'll be all right."

I'm not sure he can make that kind of promise, but it feels good to hear it from him, so I lace my fingers through his and tip my head back.

"You can pick the music if you want." He tips his chin to the stereo feeding music through the car speakers.

Someone is screaming while the drums go wild.

"It's fine."

"You don't like this music."

"Doesn't matter." I close my eyes and lose myself in the screams. "I don't want to think right now."

He releases my leg to turn the music up. It's terrible. Loud.

It's Crew.

But instead of grabbing the wheel, he takes my hand again. And all I can do is hope the screams and the road help me escape whatever feeling wells up when he does.

The car turns and my neck jerks, waking me up. Crew squeezes my hand, and I glance over at him.

"You're cute when you sleep. Almost sweet."

"Deceiving right?" I squeeze his hand, and he smirks.

"No nightmares?"

I shake my head.

"Good."

I'm not sure if it's that Crew grounds me, but the nightmares fade when I'm in his arms, or when he's holding my hand. His touch puts my mind at ease.

His fingers graze the inside of my thigh, brushing the edge of where my shorts ride up high where I'm seated.

My body ignites at the simplest touch when I spent my life thinking it was impossible. I was convinced I just wasn't a sexual person. My indulgences were in ink, pot, booze. But when it came to sex, I didn't feel that interest girls always talked about.

As Crew's feather-light touch sends my insides fluttering, I realize I just hadn't felt the man with the power to wake me up. One brush of his fingertips on my inner thigh, and I can't help that my knees widen for him.

He smirks, his eyes darting briefly to my lap, telling me he didn't miss it. He grips my thigh tighter, drawing his hand further up my leg.

"We shouldn't," I say as he runs his hands between my legs, setting me on fire with his touch.

"That's never stopped us before."

He's right.

"Undo your shorts, Goldie." He drags his hand down my thigh, and even if I shouldn't, I can't help but obey.

This far outside the city, the road is empty enough that no one will see us, but the thrill of possibly getting caught is what excites me more. Ever since Crew fucked me outside the bar, I can't deny how much the risk turned me on.

Undoing my shorts, I peel them open in the front and widen my legs.

"Happy now?"

"Not yet." He skates his hand up and into my shorts, cupping my pussy, but not taking his eyes off the road.

I grip the sides of my seat, my fingernails digging into the leather as he pulls my panties to the side and slides his fingers through my slickness.

"Now I'm happy." He shoves two fingers in, and I lose all thoughts on my exhale.

Crew grinds the heel of his hand against my clit, and I can't help but ride it. I need that wrong feeling he gives me. The depravity only he offers.

I close my eyes and tip my head back, and Crew rocks my center with the road. He shoves his fingers deeper and sets every urge on edge. My legs start shaking, and I can't help but grab his wrist. I clutch him like I'm trying to hold on as I start to float, and my skin prickles.

But he pauses.

"Crew." I groan, tipping my face to him.

"You want to come, Echo?" He pushes his fingers in deeper once more, stopping there.

"Yes."

He hums, grinding his palm over me. "Then tell me the truth."

"What truth?" I tip my hips up, barely hanging on.

I thought we were past this when I admitted I wanted him the night he took my virginity.

"Why are you marrying my brother, Echo?" He grinds his hand again, holding me on the ledge.

"You're—" I rake my fingers through my hair. "Why are we talking about that right now? Is it because he called?"

"No." Crew starts fucking me with his fingers again, and I grab his wrist, teetering on the line between making him stop and forcing him to keep going.

I need him as much as I hate that I do.

"I'm not going to be your weapon. I'm not your excuse. Tell me the truth." He doesn't let up and I'm shaking. He's ruptured every wall I've built and burst through.

"Because your dad saved my father's life." I'm nearly yelling, so close to coming I can't handle it.

Crew pulls his hand away, and I slump in my seat while he grips my thigh again.

"Explain."

"When my dad found me, he was dying." I fight back the emotions that threaten to spill out with the reminder. "He needed a heart, but he was at the bottom of the list. Or so far down he'd never live to get one. Doesn't really matter. Technicalities."

Crew glances over at me. The setting sun shading his features.

"Your dad found out somehow and came to him with an offer. He'd help him get his heart if my dad did something for him in return. Rhett was looking for a mentor, and my dad could be that to him."

"So he made a deal with the devil?" Crew's gaze narrows.

"No one wants to die."

Crew nods, listening intently, but keeping his grip on my thigh and his eyes on the road. "What does this have to do with you?"

"You know how it works in that world, Crew. Don't pretend you're blind to it. Nothing looks better than a man of God and the preacher's daughter."

"So you agreed to marry him?"

I nod.

"To save your dad?"

"Right." I bite the inside of my cheek. "I made a promise."

"So fucking break it then."

I shake my head, running my hands through my hair. "It's not that simple."

"Why not?"

"Because I don't want to." The admission burns, and I'm sure it hurts Crew, but I can't lie to him. "I get that it sounds extreme, but I made a deal for my father's life, and I'm going to keep it. You can hate your brother all you want, but he's nice to me. He's... safe."

Crew's fingers tighten on the steering wheel. "And me?"

Two words so gritted it hurts to hear them. Because I'd love to tell him what I'm feeling is enough for me, but it wouldn't matter when I'll never be enough for him.

"You're what I need, Crew," I say, nearly a whisper. "But it doesn't change who you are. And I accept that."

He nods his head, but I'm not sure what he's thinking. And even if I wish he'd tell me I'm wrong, he doesn't.

"So that's it then?" Crew says, glancing in my direction. "You've got us both all figured out, and you've made your decision."

I nod, the lump in my throat hardening.

"Okay." Crew slides his hand back up my leg and slips between them again.

"Okay?"

"Yep, we'll do this on your terms, Goldie." He drags his fingers over my pussy, and my core clenches. "I'll play this little game of chicken you think you'll win, and we'll see who caves first."

This time, when he shoves his fingers inside me, it's brutal, and he doesn't relent. I have to grip the seat and bite my lip to keep from screaming. He grinds my clit and fucks my pussy, all while sitting in the driver's seat, relaxed.

At peace.

He shoves in deeper and reaches the places that pull me out of my body.

My skin prickles and my vision darkens. I'm not sure if I'm coming down or high because I'm fraying apart at the seams.

"Come for me, Echo."

My nails dig into his skin, and blood heats my core as I start to shake with my climax. My senses flood with every sensation. Crew shoves his fingers in again, and I'm so sensitive that my entire body shakes at the pressure of his touch. I'm not sure how long an orgasm can last, but I'm riding the feeling as the tires glide over the pavement.

When I finally relax, my eyes flutter open and Crew pulls his hand out. But instead of gripping my thigh again, he brings them to his lips, sucking me off them.

"That's one," he says, glancing at me and grinning. "Next one will be on my tongue. Then my cock. Let's see how long you can continue resisting us."

There is no *us*. But as his hand slides on my thigh once more and he squeezes, I don't know how much resistance I have left.

24

Crew

T<small>HE WAREHOUSE IS DARK</small>.

Empty.

Perfect.

"This is horrible." Echo's gaze darts around.

She's so pretty when she's surprised. Her wide eyes sink into me. Knives slicing through barriers I didn't think had breaching points.

"So..." James doesn't know what to make of Echo's comment since Paul already gave him the green light, and I'm just here to sign the paperwork.

He straightens his tie and runs a hand through his dark hair, looking at me for guidance.

"It's perfect. Draw it up."

"Excellent." He relaxes. "I'll have everything ready to sign in the morning."

I nod, and he passes a glance at Echo before walking away.

Girl's too fucking magnetic. Everyone wants a piece of her, and it's driving me more out of my mind by the day.

"Perfect? Are we even standing in the same building right now? There are rats running around, and mold growing from leaks in the ceiling." She points overhead, where there's a gnarly piece of the roof missing. "Why are we here?"

Echo moves in front of me, crossing her arms over her Namaste T-shirt, clearly missing the irony. She's incapable of chilling the fuck out as she chews her gum and taps her toe on the ground.

"I'm buying it."

"What?" Confusion knits her eyebrows. "Why?"

I lean in and kiss her temple because I can't help myself. I should be hate fucking her against a wall after what she said to me on the car ride here, but instead, she makes me soft in ways I'm not.

Gravity pulls me forward, and I clutch her arms. "It's a business expansion."

"The shop isn't adding a location in Oakland."

She clacks her gum between her teeth, and even if I shouldn't tell her, I can't help it as she looks up at me with innocence that bleeds my soul dry. Gentleness that reveals all the shit I normally hide from people. Her bright eyes, a balance of the goodness she forgets exists within her.

"Crew..." Her eyes narrow. "What's going on?"

"I'm expanding the fighting ring."

"What do you have to do with that?" Her eyebrows pinch and her nose scrunches.

"Everything. I started them." I brush her hair back off her face.

"You…" But she doesn't finish her sentence. The wheels behind her eyes clearly spinning in circles. "You're the owner?"

I nod.

"Do the guys know?"

"No one knows except the people who work for me." I spin a blonde lock of her hair around my finger. "And now you."

"Not even Jude?"

I shake my head.

"Sage?"

"No one."

It's cute she can't put the pieces together, but she keeps trying. She can't connect why I'd tell her and not them because she still doesn't understand she's becoming an exception.

She breathes out her surprise. "Why?"

"It's none of their business," I say honestly.

"Is it really that hard for you?" She takes a step back, looking me over.

"What?"

"Letting people know you're capable of more?"

After our conversation in the car, I'm surprised she has to ask. Of anyone, she obviously thinks the least of me, and still, I can't take my fucking attention off her.

"You tell me. Is it?"

Me returning her question makes her pause. Her shoulders tense, and she must realize she hit a nerve.

"I'm sorry about what I said." She frowns.

"It's fine."

"It's not."

I grip her chin. "Echo, I've given you no reason to think I give a shit about anything. Don't worry. I get it."

"But now you told me this." She bites her bottom lip. "You clearly don't want anyone knowing you run the fight nights, but now I do. Why let me in?"

Her eyebrows scrunch, and I know what she wants my answer to be—it's the same thing she was begging me to tell her on the car ride here. That I'm the right choice. That my brother is the mistake. That I can offer her the safety she's desperate for after surviving the way she was raised.

She wants me to tell her this is real, and I won't get bored and toss her away.

But I don't. And it's not because I wouldn't mean it. But Echo needs to come to that realization herself, without my direct influence or Rhett's. Anything else will just be her playing into what someone else wants from her. Pieces she needs to stop handing out.

No matter how much I crave them.

I'll sit back, let her sort this out. I'll wait until she wakes up and feels me in her fucking bones. But until that moment, I'm not going to battle with my brother for her heart.

When she hands it to me, it'll be her choice.

Mine without question.

"I trust you." I shrug, trying to play it off like she's not the center of my world, and I want her to know all of it.

"I'm expanding a business opportunity, and we needed a break from LA. Two birds, one stone. You know how it goes."

Her expression falls with her disappointment, so I can't help but soften the blow.

"It doesn't mean I'm not still happy to share it with you."

"I get that." She relaxes with the ounce of hope I want her to feel until she's ready to acknowledge it. "It's just surprising. A whole other side of you. You do all this in secret because it's more important to you that people believe you don't give a shit."

"I don't."

She pins me with her wicked little gaze. "You pretend not to, especially at the shop. But all this..." Her stare moves around the room once more before landing back on me. "You're running a whole other business outside of Twisted Roses."

"One where people beat the shit out of each other."

She shrugs. "Even so. What made you want to?"

Big questions that should probably have easier answers, but I settle on, "I like to fight."

"That would explain what you do in the ring, Crew," Echo continues pushing. "But not the rest of it."

"Why does it matter?"

She glares at me, and I can't help but wipe my palms over my face because this girl never lets anything go.

"I'm not my brothers, that's why." I rake my hair back off my forehead.

"What do they have to do with it?"

"Adam runs the family business, and Rhett's chasing his holy calling, but at the end of the day, they're both still tied to him."

"Your father?"

"Yeah." I nod. "They might not mind, but that's not what I wanted. Sure, he helped me out, and considering worse things, he gave me a good life. It's not like I'm blind to the opportunities he's afforded me. But my end goal wasn't to do it to further the Kingsley name. I don't give a crap about that. I wanted to forge my own path. Do something I enjoyed. And if it failed, at least I'd give a shit."

Echo watches me, and I swear she picks apart every word looking for the truths and lies.

"It's—"

"A hobby that happened to work out."

"That's not what I was going to say." She frowns. "It's impressive, Crew. I didn't think you had it in you."

I'm not sure if that's a slight or a compliment. I've given her no reason to think I'm capable of anything other than beating the shit out of people. But for some reason, hearing her doubt cuts a little deeper than I expected.

Just because I don't want people seeing I'm capable of more than they read on the surface, doesn't mean I want her to be one of them.

"Come on, Goldie." I take her hand, and she reluctantly unclenches her arms and laces her fingers through mine so I can guide us out of the warehouse.

"My hair hasn't been its natural color in years, so why do you still call me Goldie?"

It's a question she hasn't asked in a long time, and it drags me back to the vision I met standing in the darkest room in my father's house. I should have known in that moment there was no escaping her. But I was young and in denial.

Dumb enough to think there would always be time when my father had promised her to Rhett.

"Two reasons." I look down at her. "First, you're fucking havoc, just like Goldilocks. Walking into the bears' house and messing it all up."

Her lips part like she's about to argue, so I stop and spin her to face me, planting my finger over her mouth to silence her.

"You are, trust me. In my head. My bones. You rip shit to shreds. You walked in eight years ago and made a mess I didn't see coming, and every moment since, you might as well have just played in it because I can't escape you."

Her eyes go wide, and I've probably said too much, but I can't help it.

"And the other reason?" she asks.

"The real reason..." I grip the back of her head, pulling my forehead to hers. "Your eyes."

"So, not my hair?"

I shake my head. "Your hair is your darkness, your light. You can change that like you ink your skin and make it whatever version you want them to see. But your eyes..." I can't help but run my hands down her cheeks. "They're your truth. You can't hide from me in them. They tell me everything."

Echo blinks at me, sparkling gold orbs that reveal my destiny.

"What are they telling you now?"

Dangerous questions when she probably doesn't realize it. Just like her offer that hangs around my neck. Promises I won't let her escape now that she's made them.

"That you're the end of me."

She presses her lips together and takes a quick breath through her nose. And when her lashes flutter again, a sheen coats them. Sadness creates distance between the girl I'm falling for and the hard exterior she projects to the world.

"Why aren't you sick of me yet, Crew?"

"Sick of you?" My eyebrows pinch.

"Why didn't you get over me after that first time? You already took what I asked you to. Why aren't you tired of me now?"

If only she could read my mind, she'd have all the answers she needs to rock her wild mind to sleep at night.

"Because it's not possible."

"Because I'm with Rhett, right?" Her words catch in her throat. "Or because you still see innocence in me you'd like to ruin? Because I'm not special or interesting. And I've been a bitch to you the majority of our friendship—the car ride being a prime example. So why are you still holding on?"

Something hot boils up. For all the confidence this girl displays, her insecurity makes me mad as hell.

Gripping her chin, I tilt her face up. "Don't talk about yourself like that."

"I will when you stop lying to yourself, Crew." She rolls her shoulders back, the bit of flare that burns bright still shining, even when she's revealing a weakness. "You don't hold onto things, especially women. How long until I'm just like them—disposable? Rhett said—"

"I don't give a fuck what Rhett said," I cut her off, realizing where this is really coming from.

While Echo might be fooled like most people are by my brother, there are sides to him she'll never understand. And he's feeding whatever doubt swirls in her pretty little head.

"Trust me. You don't want the answer to these questions right now."

"Why not?"

"You aren't ready for them."

Her expression falls. Light might as well leave her eyes, and the loss of it sinks something inside me.

Before she can ask more, I grab her hand. "Let's go. This trip is supposed to be fun."

Surprisingly, she doesn't pull away from me. She doesn't even ask me to answer her, and it's for the better. Her silence might be defeat but it's for the best in this moment. She's not ready for what her rant has stirred up.

Too bad I'm going to make her face it anyway.

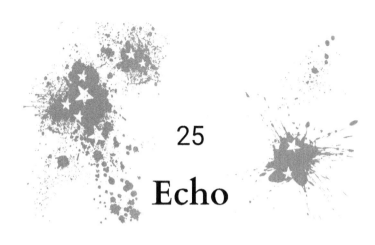

25

Echo

THE MOMENT I STEP out of the hotel room bathroom, Crew's gaze drags my body.

"Are you trying to fucking kill me?" he asks, drawing his joint to his lips and taking another hit. Looking too damn good in dark gray jeans and a solid black T-shirt.

He pauses at the short hem of my dress.

Even if I usually wear casual shorts and nostalgic Tees, I know how to get attention when I want it. And here, in Oakland, far away from eyes that could catch us, I want Crew's full attention no matter how bad it is.

Which is why, when he said we're going out tonight, I stopped by a little shop on the corner and bought this outfit.

The dress is short, made entirely of black lace. The hem barely covers my ass, leaving a gap of bare thigh between my thigh-high nylons and leather boots. The dress is a halter, which wraps my neck with a leather choker.

"You deserve it for being an asshole."

I walk over to Crew, and the moment I'm within reach, he snakes an arm around my hip and pulls me to straddle his lap.

"Careful." He brushes his lips over mine. "Pissing me off makes me hard."

He grinds me down on his lap, and he's not lying.

"You ready?" He skates his fingers over the back of my neck, watching me.

I nod but can't help biting my lip. As much as I want him to fuck me right now, the idea of walking around the city with Crew at my side, and not having to pretend his brother's in the picture, is far more enticing.

Climbing off him, he helps straighten the hem of my dress before running his thumb and forefinger along the edge of the front of it.

"You and your fucking outfits." He shakes his head, putting out his joint and standing up. "I'm going to enjoy making you pay for this later."

I can't help the shiver that climbs my spine. Anticipation he inflicts like a form of punishment. While he knows I'd gladly let him fuck me right now for testing him, he won't. Crew would rather have me begging before he gives me what he knows I want.

Like he's reading my mind, he smirks at me, grabbing a jacket off the chair and shrugging it on.

"Where are you taking me?" I ask as he opens the door to the room and waves me through it.

He catches my wrist as I pass him and draws his hand to my jaw. "To Hell, Goldilocks. Where your destructive little soul belongs."

I figured Crew was joking.

He wasn't.

Hell is actually a place, and the booze is flowing as sex practically bleeds from the walls.

The bouncer lets us skip the long line, nodding at Crew like they know each other. And Crew leads me into a crowd so thick, their bodies throb with the screaming coming from the band performing.

I don't recognize them, but they sound like all of Crew's favorite music—angry, unhinged. I can't make out a word, and my ears are already nearly numb.

Crew leads me into the madness, zipped to his side. His grip tightens on my hand the more people there are, and it's protective—comforting even—from a man who should probably scare me.

The dance floor is packed with people, elevating the temperature in the room as they pulse to the beat. For a moment I think Crew's taking me to the center of it. Instead, he tightens his hold on my hand and continues to weave through.

He glances back at me over his shoulder, and for a moment the light catches his gray eyes. A shimmer that holds the line between devious and downright wicked.

When we make it past the dance floor to the bar, he props himself against a stool and slips out of his jacket, widening his legs so he can cage me between them. One tattooed arm is wrapped around my waist while he waves for a bartender.

It's a small protective gesture that feels bigger than it probably looks. Possessive when he knows he has to share me with his brother. And as we wait to place our order, I can't help but toy with my ring hanging from his neck.

The truth that I'm all his where it actually matters. That in the deepest pit of my soul I'll never be anyone else's. Even when this inevitably has to end, I'll live in this spot beside his heart.

"What do you want to drink?" He tips my chin up and forces my gaze to his.

"Vodka soda."

Crew leans toward the bar when the bartender stops at us, yelling our drink order, before returning his attention to me. He holds his arms around my waist and watches me. Almost like he can read the music in my eyes. His gaze only dipping to see my fingers spinning around the ring.

The song ends as our drinks arrive, and he hands me mine so he can keep hold of my free hand as he leads me to a row of booths in the very back of the club. They're secluded and roped off, but Crew hands a stack of cash to a security guard to get us past.

Guiding me with his fingers on the center of my back, he leads us to a booth near the end. From here you can still see the stage—and certainly hear them—but we're nearly in our own world. It's dark apart from the occasional throbbing light, and couples in the booths as we pass are using it to their advantage.

Crew slides in first, but when I scoot in next to him, he grabs me by the waist and plants me in his lap, forcing me to straddle him like we did in our hotel room.

"Crew."

He wraps his jacket around my waist to hide my ass from being on display.

"Like I said, Goldie." He leans back and watches me with amusement. "You and that fucking outfit are going to pay."

Reaching into his pocket, he pulls out a joint and lights it. There's so much booze and pot in here, no one will notice. He takes a long drag, before tipping his head back and letting it curl out from between his lips. And when he draws the joint to his mouth again, the smallest smirk flicks at the corner of his lips as he inhales.

Crew pulls me close, stamping his mouth over mine and sealing our lips together. He feeds me the smoke, and it goes straight to my head.

His tongue tangles with mine, and I can't help but drown in the intimacy of it. My head floating to the stars while his fingers grip my lower body.

On my inhale, Crew tilts his mouth and grips the back of my head, melting into a kiss. So sweet and gentle it's unlike everything about him. So I wrap my arms around his neck and hold onto it. Sink into the peace of this quiet moment when my mind stops, and the world is so loud it's white noise.

When Crew pulls back, he holds the joint up for me and helps me take the hit. He watches my mouth wrap around it like it might as well be his dick. His pupils blown wide and focused as he stares.

My bones soften the longer I hold my breath, and my body gets waxy with relaxation. Somewhere in the distance, my thoughts skitter away, and it's just me and Crew—his steel eyes honed in on me—as the pressure escapes with the smoke curling from my lips between us.

"That's good shit." I smile.

"Blaze only sells the best."

Hence his nickname.

Marijuana smoke clouds the room. Fogs my head. Makes a mess of my already distorted thoughts. And sitting in Crew's lap, with his arms around me, I can't help but fight the urge to float away with him. To pretend we're far enough from our problems that they don't exist.

Crew takes another drag, and I smooth my fingers over the back of his head, unable to help that my hips circle in his lap.

I need his heat. His friction.

I need to let go of whatever tethers me back.

Crew grins, the smoke filtering out from between his lips with it. "Careful what you start, Echo. I have no problem fucking you in front of everyone in this room."

Why does that make my insides flutter?

In LA, I'm his brother's girlfriend. I can't be caught walking too close to Crew, much less holding his hand or sitting in his lap. But here, in the shadows of Oakland, we bleed into the background of this club like anyone else. We hide in the screams of the music. We look like any other couple, not running from our secrets.

I circle my hips again and lean close, burying my face near his neck. "What was it you said outside the bar? Let them watch?"

That night he unlocked something I didn't realize lived within me. Something almost as forbidden as he is. And when he shoved me to the ground and stuck his cock down my throat, the risk of being caught was what nearly sent me over the ledge.

The fact that he empowered me to not be embarrassed or ashamed woke me up inside.

Rhett wants me to hide my ink. He wants me to dye my hair back to its natural blonde and give up the leather and studs.

Not Crew.

He wants me raw and messed up.

He wants me as is, and he doesn't care who sees it.

"Is that a challenge?" Crew wraps my hair around his fist and pulls my head back so he can look me in the eyes.

"Maybe."

The tilt of his lips goes straight between my thighs. He drags his hand around my throat and grips the collar there.

"I'd like to put a leash on this and watch you crawl for me." He tugs it, drawing my face to his and biting my lower lip, eating the little moan he elicits.

When he releases the collar, he drags his hand down between my breasts, over my stomach, until his knuckles sneak under the short hem of my dress and brush my pussy.

"Can we get kicked out?" I'm not sure why I'm suddenly nervous when I'm the one who tempted him.

"Probably." He slides my panties aside and shoves two fingers in. "Seems you don't mind though. You're so fucking wet."

I glance around. The club is dark enough that no one is paying attention. And our particular spot in the booth makes it difficult for anyone to see what's happening unless they get really close.

Besides, couples on the dance floor are doing worse.

Crew leans his mouth by my ear. "Take me out, princess."

The way I want to follow this man's orders to the end of the earth is going to be my destruction.

Snaking my hands down his hard chest, I slip my fingers through his belt and unbuckle it, before undoing his pants. I have to shift back to undo his zipper all the way.

Reaching in, I pull out his hard cock, and my heart is hammering.

Anyone could see us, and for some sick reason, it just makes me want it more.

Crew pulls his fingers out of me on an exhale, grinning, and once more brings his mouth to my ear.

"It's cute... you pretending you're innocent by dating my preacher brother, when we both know you're not." He wraps his hands around my waist, holding his jacket in place. "Be my good little slut and sit on my cock in front of all these people. Show them who you really belong to."

There's an edge to his tone, but I can't process it as he sinks his teeth into my neck.

Lifting up, I get in position, and he shoves me down on him.

I'm not sure how I went from being a virgin to having sex in a packed club, but I can't seem to care as Crew wraps his arms around me and pulls us chest to chest.

"Circle your hips for me, Echo." He kisses the side of my neck, my cheek, my temple. "Chase what feels good."

I move, and I'm so full it makes my head spin. At this angle, his pelvic bone grinds against my clit with each roll of my hips, and the friction building intensifies it. He controls my movements, keeping them small so they aren't obvious, while still striking every nerve that nearly sets me off.

It doesn't matter how subtle. I'm so full and connected I can't catch my breath as I start to climb.

Crew lifts his hand, still holding the joint. He brings it to my lips, and I take in a long drag.

It's impossible to hold it with the pressure building, but it doesn't matter. Crew seals our mouths together and steals the smoke like he does everything else. Directly from the source, leaving nothing but ash behind.

Our tongues tangle and my mind floats. My body quivers. I tighten around him, and he digs his nails into my hip, so I imagine the way I'm squeezing is hurting him.

But like I enjoy his punishment, he thrives on my pain.

When he breaks the kiss, I turn my face, and he continues kissing a path down my jaw. My throat. The peak of my shoulder.

And from the corner of my eye, I catch someone staring.

A man standing nearby has his eyes locked on me. He whispers something to the woman in his arms, and she passes a glance at us.

Her cheeks flush and our eyes connect.

"We're caught." Crew chuckles in my ear, noticing them like I do. "And my dirty fucking girl loves it. You're so tight with them watching me fuck you like a little slut in public. Watching me claim you. They wish they could have this sweet pussy, but it's mine. My virgin cunt. My virgin lips..." He grabs my ass. "I'll take that too soon enough."

My eyes flutter, and my attention returns to Crew, even if I still feel stares on me. I tip my forehead to his, and my breaths begin to stutter.

"I'm the only man to fuck you." Crew kisses my lips. "The only man who is ever going to."

I'm not sure why he's making promises he won't keep, but I try to ignore it. In this moment, the lie is enough to make my entire body tense.

He holds me close and circles my hips over him, and when his lips once more find mine, I detonate.

I'm shrapnel.

Fragments.

Floating in space where the pot sent my mind.

And as my pussy squeezes him, he lifts his hips to shove himself in deeper as he comes inside me. He holds me tight and fills me up. Our mouths connected and our bodies in sync as we ride a wave so close to crashing down around us.

When I stop shivering, he relaxes, kissing my lips once more.

"We should take off." He smirks, glancing to where the couple was, except now they're gone. "Just in case."

I lift off him, and he pulls my panties to the side, tucking himself away.

And I can't help but giggle as he sneaks us past security and out of the club. Because Crew sets me free when everything else in life is a weight holding me down.

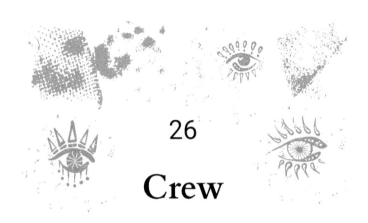

26

Crew

My eyes open to the sun. It's blinding and bright as it shines through an open window.

I take a moment to adjust to where I am.

My bedroom is dark, with blackout curtains and dark gray walls. The opposite of this hotel room. Glancing over, I stretch my arm out and find an empty spot where Echo slept. If we weren't in Oakland, I'd think she disappeared again, but as I look through the balcony door, I spot her.

Rolling over to watch her, I wrap my arms around her pillow and inhale her lavender scent. If she were here, I'd be tempted to sink back into her, but the sight of her tightens my heart in my chest.

She's wrapped in a blanket, sitting on the balcony watching the sunrise. The warm glow brightens even the dark half of her hair, and there's no better sight to wake up to.

Climbing out of bed, I slip into my sweats and walk toward her.

She's a gravitational force.

Uncontainable energy.

And the girl surprises me at every turn.

Like last night at the club. I wasn't actually planning to fuck her in public, even if I know the forbidden nature of it turns her on. But something about how she sat on my lap and offered the challenge. How she trusts me to take her as far as we can go without getting caught. And something about knowing I could make her mine in front of anyone who might be watching was a temptation I couldn't resist.

"About time you woke up." Echo smiles up at me.

It's bright. Stunning. Not a splash of makeup on her face, and she might as well be glowing.

I glance over my shoulder at the clock on the nightstand. "It's seven."

She shrugs when I look back at her. "I've been up since six."

"Nightmares?"

"No." She shakes her head, pulling her lips between her teeth like whatever kept her up wasn't any better.

Walking over to her, I pick her up.

"Crew," she shrieks, holding the blanket tighter against her chest as I sit in her chair with her in my lap. "I'm not wearing anything under this."

"Interesting." I try to peel the blanket off her chest, but she swats my hand away, and I can't help but laugh. "What are you doing out here? Watching the sunrise?"

The light of day does nothing to make this part of downtown easier on the eyes when all it does is reveal a concrete city.

"I was, but then I couldn't stop thinking about that tree over there."

"What about it?"

We're only three stories up, and through the balcony slats, she has a perfect view of a tree swaying in the breeze. It's still hibernating from winter and looks out of place on the city sidewalk.

"It has no bones."

I tip my head back and laugh.

"I'm serious." She nudges me with her elbow.

"Okay, Goldie." I squeeze her when she tries to wiggle away. "And here I thought we smoked all the weed last night."

"Very funny, but I'm not high."

A piece of black hair falls from her messy ponytail, and I brush it aside. "I'm just messing with you. Tell me more about the tree."

"So you can make fun of me?"

"Nope. Now I'm genuinely curious."

It's not a lie. I love how her wild mind works. Wheels spinning so fast I'm not sure how her thoughts don't all cave in on themselves. She rarely says what I expect her to, and it's fascinating.

"Well, like I was saying..." She rolls her eyes. "That tree moves like it has no bones."

"Trees don't have bones."

"Says you." Echo shrugs. "A tree has a spine stronger than either of us. Have you ever seen a forest after a wildfire's moved through it? Even black and charred you'll still find the trees standing. And it might look dead and desolate, but it doesn't mean the forest is gone. Eventually, everything regrows. It just takes time."

It's so random and adorable; I can't help that I'm lost in her words.

"But you're saying that tree has no bones."

"Not anymore." She looks almost sad about it. "I'm sure it did once when it was just planted, or back in the forest where it belongs. But it doesn't belong here."

Her lips turn down, and I can't help but think we aren't talking about the tree anymore. She's seeing herself in the branches—the roots. Her obligations.

"Who says a forest is where it belongs?" I challenge her. "Just because you come from one place doesn't mean you aren't really meant for another."

"It's nature." She looks at me like my question is ridiculous.

"But in a forest, a tree is just like anything else around it. It's nothing special or unique. It's one in thousands of the same thing. But here in this city, it's different."

"Being different isn't always good."

"It's not always bad either." I tuck a piece of hair behind her ear. "What's really on your mind, Echo? Because I know this single tree in the middle of Oakland isn't what's stressing you out."

She tugs the blanket tighter around her chest and curls against me. Whatever kept her up last night has her obsessing over anything and everything.

"You remember how I told you I was locked in a psych ward when my dad came and got me?"

I nod, and the reminder of the story has my fingers once more itching for the blood of a man who tried to force his hands on Echo.

"When I was there, they put me in a tiny room by myself because they said I was violent. And I was—"

"You were defending yourself."

"I guess."

"You were." I squeeze her. "Don't let whatever they said make you question that. There's nothing wrong with standing up for yourself when someone's trying to hurt you."

"I suppose," she whispers, twisting the blanket in her lap.

I wish I could say more to make her believe it.

"Well, like I said, I was in this room, and it wasn't white and bright like movies make you think. It was gray and cold. And outside the window, all I could see was a single tree in the middle of a field, watching over me."

She takes a deep breath, and I hold her tighter. She's mentioned the hospital to me briefly before, but this is the most she's said since. And I can't help but appreciate that she trusts me enough to open up to me in this moment.

"The tree reminds you of that place?"

"Yes and no." She sighs. "It reminds me of how I felt back then. Lost, wondering where I belonged. I thought about—"

She chokes on her words, cutting herself off.

"What did you think about?"

Something heavy sits in the air between us, even if the city breeze tries to sweep it away.

"I thought about ending it." She wipes the underside of her lashes, and it streaks her eyes with a wet path from her unfallen tear.

"I'm glad you didn't."

She shrugs. "I was trying to be strong."

"You are strong."

"I'm not."

My eyebrows pinch. "Why do you say that?"

"Because it doesn't matter that I'm still here. I'm still lost."

She shivers, and I pull the blanket up over her shoulders, wrapping my arms around her, even if I'm cold myself. I can't help but try to contain whatever nervous energy she's radiating as she sits in my lap.

"There's nothing wrong with being lost, you learn a lot that way. Who you are, who you aren't. What you want. What you don't." I glance out at the city as it starts to wake up. Streets slowly filling with cars. Sidewalks with people. "But I still get what you're saying. I was lost for a long time after my mom was killed, and I was too young to know what to do with that."

"You were five, right?"

I nod.

"Losing her made me sick in ways there's no reversing."

"There's nothing wrong with you, Crew."

It's sweet she thinks that—innocent. Seeing the best in people who don't deserve it.

"No." I shake my head. "There's nothing wrong with *you*."

She tips her head back and sinks into my arms.

"I might not know where I belong, but I like it here," she says, nearly a whisper.

"In Oakland?"

"No." She doesn't elaborate but she squeezes my arms tighter, where they're wrapped around her, and that stupid, hopeful piece of me I don't usually feed wants to think she's talking about me.

I kiss her temple and pretend she doesn't break everything inside me as her eyes flutter closed with the trust she places in my hands.

"I'm not ready to go home."

"We can stay."

She sighs. "We can't."

"Well, I wish we could."

And it pisses me off because tonight, I'll be back in LA, where she's still resisting the fact that she's meant to be mine, and I'd rather just hide us both from that truth forever.

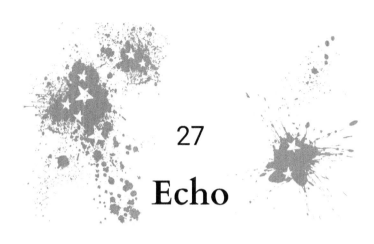

27

Echo

DAD IS ALREADY AT the café when I arrive.

"Hi, sweetie." He stands and gives me a quick kiss on the cheek before sitting back down.

The waitress is quick to circle around as she refills Dad's tea, and I order a coffee—black. There's not enough caffeine in the world to wake me from the haze I'm in.

Crew and I stayed in Oakland for two days. Doing nothing and everything. Fucking, sleeping, walking around the city hand in hand. And now that I'm back in LA, I'm not ready to wake up from the fantasy.

After the initial bumps in our journey, we managed to set aside our reality for twenty-four hours, and in that time, I almost felt like his. Like our lives back in LA didn't need to exist and we could disappear in whatever we were feeling.

If only that were possible.

My gaze moves to the four not-so-subtle bodyguards seated a table away, and I'm reminded reality always finds a way to come crashing back.

"Everything okay?" I ask.

Last time I saw Dad he had two guys following him, and now they've doubled in numbers.

"I'm fine. Max is just being careful."

"At least someone is," I grumble, not liking that Dad's putting himself in danger through whatever situation he and the church are in.

The waitress sets my coffee in front of me before disappearing once more, and I take a quick sip. It burns my lips and makes my heart race. The harsh reality of everything I've been avoiding for two days is flooding back in full force.

"What have you been up to? I haven't spoken to you these past couple of days." Dad pats the table, ignoring my irritation with his situation and focusing on me instead.

I shrug. "I've been busy."

It's not odd to go a week without seeing him, but we usually text daily. Except these past forty-eight hours when I lost all sense of time and space.

Setting down my coffee, my fingertips burn from the hot liquid heating up the mug, but I pause there. Feeling it. Begging for punishment from the universe for giving in to the magnetic pull I feel towards Crew when I should know better.

"Seems Crew was busy too."

My gaze flicks up to Dad, and I try to bury the fact that his comment catches me off guard.

"Oh?" I'm not sure it comes out genuine, but I try.

Dad nods. "Max was hoping he'd come around with Rhett getting out of the hospital, but he was tied up with other things."

I curl my fingers in my lap and play with the hem of my T-shirt.

"Rhett's doing fine though, right?"

"You haven't seen him?" Dad's brows scrunch.

"Busy, remember." I force a smile that constricts my heart.

Dad and I grabbing coffee after church on Sunday has been a weekly ritual for years. Somewhere these past few months it's started to fade away. My guilt over how I'm feeling and what I'm dreading bleeds out, and I've never been more terrified for him to sense it.

"He's doing much better. The doctors said he'll make a full recovery."

"Good."

The last thing I need is more guilt thrown on this dumpster fire.

"So how is the new church?" I grab my coffee once more and let it burn my tongue.

Sear the lies living there as I divert the subject.

"It's beautiful. It's too much... I don't know." Dad pats his hand on the table. "I'm not sure we're ready to scale, but Rhett has a vision."

"And you trust him?" I set my cup down. "With the church, I mean."

Dad nods. "He's young. He's got the energy. So who knows, maybe he'll be able to pull off what I couldn't and actually make a mark in the community with Eternal Light."

"They love you."

"It's not about me, Echo." Dad leans forward, resting his weight on his elbows. "This is for them."

Always the humble one. Dad is the opposite of Rhett. While his focus has always been on the people he serves, sometimes I worry Rhett is letting his pedestal go to his head.

"Rhett will do good things," Dad decides. "He just has a little more growing up to do."

Something about how Dad leans back and pauses. How his stare drifts off and the corners of his lips turn down. He loves Rhett, but he's hesitant to hand over the one thing he cares about as much as his daughter.

"He'll be fine. Promise." I reach across the table and plant my hand on one of my fathers, forcing a smile.

I slip into the girl Rhett needs me to be to get us all through this transition.

"And if his ideas get a little too wild, I'll help him tamp them down."

I'll be the good girlfriend. And then I'll be the good wife.

A role I shouldn't be able to play so well. But if my dark past taught me anything, it's how to mold to a situation, no matter the self-sacrifice.

Dad places his other hand over mine and smiles. "You're too good for all of us."

"You're only saying that because you love me."

"Maybe." Dad laughs, and I can't help but smile. "But I'm also saying it because I'm right. You're special, sweetie. Unique. It's what draws people to you."

"That and Rhett standing at my side."

Dad frowns, patting the back of my hand. "They love him for what he promises, but they love you for who you are. Doesn't matter how well they know you. They see it."

I wish he was right. I wish I was still that girl he thinks I am. Pure, holy. Deserving of a place in his church when I feel the flames of Hell nip at me each time I step inside.

"Maybe your expectations of me are too high." I pull my hands back and plant them in my lap. "What if I can't live up to that?"

"That's not something you need to worry about." Dad shakes his head. "I expect nothing from you, Echo, except for you to be who you really are. And who you are is a girl her father is proud of. More than anything I've done in my life, watching you succeed is my greatest gift."

"Even with my tattoos and hair?" I wave up at the black and blonde.

"Especially with those." He smiles. "It's your differences that make you who you are. I know Rhett gives you a hard time about it, but he'll understand someday. Like I said, he still has some growing up to do. In life—and in his role."

"I hope so."

I really do. If I'm going to be stuck with him, one of us needs to begin to like the other as more than friends.

"I know so."

The waitress drops off the check and Dad pulls some cash from his pocket as he stands. His bodyguards take the cue and make their way to the door, while Dad helps me with my chair.

"You'll be there tomorrow night to celebrate the official opening day announcement for Eternal Light's new location, right?"

I nod. "Wouldn't miss it."

"It's all going to work out for the best, Echo." Dad plants his hands on my shoulders and gives them a gentle squeeze. "Rhett will love you second to none but the Lord."

I'm sure he will. Just like I know Crew in all his evil intent would put me first.

But Rhett is perfect. He'll be the golden beacon for the church and the cookie-cutter husband. Rhett is everything a girl could ask for, and more.

If only I wasn't falling in love with his brother.

28

Crew

DOESN'T MATTER HOW MANY times I shower. I smell her on me.

Lavender, innocence, darkness, and sex. The perfect blend of unholy temptation. And in Oakland, I had her in my arms, on my lap, in my bed.

She was *mine*.

Except now, we're back in LA, and she's standing next to my brother pretending to be his.

An itch crawls my skin.

Before Echo, I never felt truly attached to anything, not even this world. But she's the cord. The sole being breathing life through my otherwise cold veins. She's got me thinking dangerous shit like *'til death*. And she has the fucking nerve to tell me she thinks I lack commitment.

I spin her promise ring around between my fingers as I watch her through the crowd.

She's avoiding looking in my direction, but I know she senses me. Feels me lingering in the air around her. The same way she's encompassing my head. Ever since I first got a taste of her electric heat, it's all I ever want to spark me to life again.

Tonight, Echo's hair is pulled back in a perfect ponytail. I want to grab it and bend her over. Fuck her in front of everyone in this room to prove to them who she really belongs to. But I need to be patient and let this play out.

She's wild; she'll claw if she feels cornered. So when she decides to be mine, it needs to be from her lips.

And she *will* choose me, whether she realizes it right now or not.

"Thank you all for being here." Rhett snakes an arm around her lower back, and I clutch the ring tighter.

Finally, her eyes do dare to find me. Locking where they belong. Her wild mind can deny it all she wants, but her body instinctually knows where her calm is—in my chaos. She doesn't want him touching her any more than I do, and I'm her anchor in whatever this mess is that our fathers have made.

Echo clutches the bottom of her long-sleeved sweater. Her clothes strategically hide every beautiful inch of her tattooed flesh because she's pretending to be perfect for *him*. I'm tempted to take a knife to the entire outfit.

Rhett pulls Echo closer to him, and she flinches.

That tiny fucking flinch sets my nerves on edge. He doesn't see it or care—or know why she does it. But if I thought it bothered me before, once I learned about her past, it has me seeing red.

After she told me about what her mom did, I tried tracking down her mom's dealer. But in those circles, everyone's too high to remember things clearly, and the closest I could get to finding a guy who might have fit the bill overdosed around the same time as her mom.

If it was him, he's lucky. That's a nice way to die compared to what I was prepared to do to him.

The good thing about money is the ease at which I can get away with certain shit.

"We're so happy you could make it." Rhett holds up his glass of water, projecting exactly what he wants everyone to see. "My beautiful girlfriend, Echo, and I are thrilled for you to share in this celebration with us."

My stomach flips at the forced smile crossing Echo's cheeks.

She's so far outside herself even her eyes dim, and I have to take another sip of my beer to ignore the shit brewing inside.

I probably shouldn't even be here.

Six months ago, I wouldn't care if Rhett and my father were celebrating whatever plans they had to expand the church with their congregation. Six months ago, it didn't matter. Because back then, Echo wasn't at the center of their plans—of my fucking universe.

But now that she is, I couldn't help showing up tonight just to see how this would play out.

"We've been blessed with good news, and the new church will be opening in just over three weeks." Rhett smiles wide and claps fill the room. "And I can think of no better way to celebrate this glorious occasion than to also celebrate with the woman at my side, who will take this journey with me."

The darkness that coats Echo's eyes makes my gut sink. This was supposed to be a church gathering. An excuse to bleed people for money to ensure their plans stayed on track. But something about how Rhett hands my father his water glass and turns to Echo has my insides turning to cement.

"Echo, my love." Rhett kneels and my beer bottle nearly shatters from my grip. "My partner. My friend. There is no one I'd rather share my life with than you. You are the light in my life, and with His blessing, I ask you to make me the happiest, humblest man. Marry me."

It's not even a question. Arrogant prick. He's flipping open a box as gasps cloud every thought in my head. Her eyes are wide, and she's frozen as he takes her hand and slips the ring on her finger.

And when he stands up, he pulls her body close and presses his lips to hers.

My sight goes black as I watch him take it.

Her mouth is *my* mouth.

She's fucking mine.

I can still feel her pussy squeezing me as I fucked her in every corner of the hotel room, and my brother dares to think she's his.

Echo is my destiny.

My fate if I have one.

The darkness deep enough to make me feel like there actually might be light inside. It reaches for her now. It needs her now. Without her, I'm just empty, and I can't handle it.

If I thought there was a point we could turn back, we passed it. Long before Oakland, or even the bloody Valentine's party.

It was her standing in front of me eight years ago, in the spot where I found my mom's bloody body.

It was her finding a man beneath the sickness I thought had fully taken hold.

Her palms press to Rhett's chest and curl on his shirt. I don't know if she's pushing or pulling, only that the whole scene rips me apart.

She's choosing him while I've been waiting for her to make the right decision.

"Cute couple, right?" Some chick stops beside me.

She's tapping a water glass with her long red nails that match her lips.

Her nearly black hair is in long waves over her shoulders, and her eyes are dark, focused on Echo and Rhett.

"That's not what I'd call it." I take a drink of my nearly finished beer.

The girl hums, continuing the tapping on her glass, as the crowd cheers. Her eyes narrow as she watches Rhett hold my girl.

My fucking girl.

And while everyone else seems excited for the happy couple, this chick seems to share my feelings.

She's probably one of the girls screwing my brother. Her dark hair, wicked eyes, and polished perfection are his type. And the way she clenches her drink until Rhett and Echo break apart tells me everything.

"On that note." She downs her water and glances up at me. "Good luck to you too."

Then she disappears into the crowd, leaving me with an unsettling feeling. This entire night has me twitching like a raw nerve, and that's not who I am. I'm the one who inflicts pain so I don't have to feel it. But right now, Echo's stabbing me in the heart.

Looking up, I've lost sight of her and Rhett. They've molded into the crowd and are probably basking in congratulations.

Some stupid part of me thought I could fix this for her. That I could be enough for her. That she'd choose me, and this entire thing would never happen.

Now she's wearing his ring, while hers burns through my fucking chest.

I hand my beer to a passing waiter and fight through the crowd. I can't be here anymore where the walls are closing in. Where I'm forced to face the fact that I'm losing her, and I don't know how to fix it.

In the ring, I'll win every time. But here—Rhett's pulled one I didn't see coming.

Stepping into the empty foyer, a hand wraps my arm, stopping me.

"Crew, wait." Echo's voice sounds so small in this big, dark house.

I stop but don't turn around. I'm not sure I can look at her when she's the mirror that forces me to face myself.

But it doesn't stop her from circling until she's standing in front of me.

"You're leaving?"

It's either that or I walk over to my brother and shove a knife in his throat.

"Bothered I didn't stay and say congratulations? Please give my brother my apologies." I try to step around her, but she just moves, blocking my path.

"Not right now, Echo."

"You're upset." It's not a question, more of a realization. Something that surprises her, like she wouldn't have guessed it.

"What do you expect me to be? Happy the girl I'm losing my fucking mind over just said she'd marry my brother?"

"You knew this was coming." She crosses her arms over her chest. "And I didn't actually say yes."

"Really? You're going to go with technicalities right now?" I can't help but laugh as I try to walk around her. But she gets in my path.

"I'm sorry, okay?" She grabs my arm. "You knew I had to do this. When I offered—"

I grip her chin between my thumb and forefinger to cut her off. "Don't you dare say what's on the tip of your tongue until you're ready to admit why you really came to me. This wasn't about your virginity, and you fucking know it. You and me, we're bigger than this bullshit, but it won't stop you from making a mess of it anyway."

"I was clear about this."

"Clear as fucking mud." I let her go.

I've hated Echo for a lot of things. For how she's tempting and annoying. For how I can't get her out of my orbit like I can't get her out of my head. But the lies spilling out of her right now make me hate her more than anything else.

"I don't understand why you care." Her shoulders deflate, and I think as tough as she is, she genuinely means it. "Crew—"

"It's fine." I step back, putting some distance between us like it'll help. "Go back to your party. You've got an engagement to celebrate."

"It's not real."

"Neither is this, apparently." And it fucking hurts.

Her fingers tighten their hold, and I wish it meant something. "I made a promise. I'm doing what's right. I don't know how to do this any differently."

"Then come to me. Not him. *Me.*" I step toward her. "Let me fucking help you. But you won't. Either because you don't trust me or some other reason. This back and forth is fucking with both of us. Just when I think..."

But I can't finish that sentence. I can't admit it to her and open myself up to that.

"I need some air." I step back, and she releases me. "Figure out what it is you want. But I'm not doing this shit right now."

She's Goldilocks. My Goldilocks. But in this moment, I have to walk away from her before she sees what she's doing to me. Even if nothing can clean up the mess she's made.

29

Crew

CREW: FUCK YOU

    Paul: What crawled up your ass and died?

    Crew: Why am I getting blasted with texts of Mandi's tits

    Paul: Fail to see the issue

    Crew: She's my employee

    Paul: And? This have anything to do with Oakland?

    Crew: No

    Paul: Whatever you say, boss

    Crew: Just do your job. I'm blocking Mandi. She's your problem again

    Paul: You say that like it's a problem

I toss my phone onto the counter and pour myself a shot. Then I double it and drain it down my throat like it can solve my problems.

If distractions could get rid of this knot in my gut, I'd be jacking off to pictures of Mandi's fake tits right now. One look, and I deleted them because I couldn't care less. She's not Echo. No one is. And I'm the idiot who let this happen.

I lift the whiskey bottle, considering another shot, and draining it straight from the bottle instead. I'd like to take a bath in it. Drown in it. Let it either eliminate my thoughts or kill me. At least then I wouldn't have to keep seeing the image of Rhett's lips on Echo's mouth.

Sealing my eyes shut, I try to take a match to that image. In the six months they've been together, they've held hands. He's put his arm around her. Kept her at his side. But it was fake—nothing. Until tonight.

Until he kissed what's mine.

A knock comes at the door, and my eyes fly open. I'm frozen, losing my grip on reality like I've done only once in my life. My palm is imprinted with Echo's promise ring from my firm grip, and my muscles are so tense they hurt.

Everything fucking hurts.

I don't feel pain.

I don't feel anything.

I'm steel.

Except for her.

The knock comes again, and I release the ring.

Destiny is knocking. I know it's Echo without checking my phone. I feel her through these walls like fate calling out to me. And when I swing the door open, there she stands.

"Hey." She pops her gum, digging her toe against the wooden floor.

She's changed since the party. No longer buttoned-up. Instead, she's in her baggy jeans and a skintight, black long-sleeved shirt. The boat neck shows off the stars on her shoulders. Ones that escaped her eyes and marked her body like the galaxy reaching out to me.

"Can I come in?" She pushes her fingers through her straight hair.

She ticks, moves, fidgets.

Pop rocks on the tongue that find it impossible to sit still.

I step aside and hold the door open, watching her pass. The cloud of lavender that follows her demolishes my senses.

"Party over?" I walk past her into the room, stopping at the counter and once more drawing the whiskey to my lips.

"Rhett had to get some sleep." She rubs her arms.

No one is sleeping tonight. Not Rhett. Not her. Not me.

We're all too busy lying to ourselves.

"And you?" I set the bottle down.

Echo's gaze moves to my windows, where the city shines through them. The slightest glassy sheen coating her expression. "I'm scared."

That's not what I expected her to say.

"Of what?"

She bites her lip, glancing back at me with a broken frown. "The outcome of this."

The one unknown. While I manage to maintain control over most situations, she's the wild card.

"Why do you wear my purity ring?" Her gaze falls to the chain around my neck, and I realize I'm gripping it again.

"Because it's mine." I hold it in my palm like it's the center of my gravity. "Just like you are."

"I'm not supposed to be, Crew. None of this was supposed to happen." She pauses her chewing, holding the gum between her teeth.

I walk over to her. Can't help that my hands need to hold her. That no matter how much she rips me to shreds, I'm nothing without the feel of her teeth on my flesh tearing me to pieces.

"Doesn't matter what's supposed to be. This just *is*."

"And what is it? Your current form of entertainment?" She grits her teeth.

I grab her jaw in my hand and force her to look up at me. "I'm getting really sick and tired of you saying that shit."

"I know you." Her shoulder shrugs up in the slightest movement that makes me tighten my grip. "I'm just stating facts. You only play along until you lose interest."

"Echo, if I was in this for the fun then why am I still here? Because that ended a long time ago."

Her eyebrows pinch. "Sorry I'm only a virgin once."

"I'm not talking about your fucking virginity." I tip her chin up farther and bring my mouth right over hers, kissing the puffy mound of her lip. "I'm talking about you, Echo Gwendolyn Slater, and what you do to me. I don't feel pain. I don't feel anything. It's something I learned when I found my mom with her throat split open in my living room."

Her eyes sheen at my harsh comment.

"But do you know what *you* make me do?"

She nods—barely. The smallest movement.

"You make me feel *everything*. You hurt so bad I can barely stand it. You're my worst nightmare and my best dream. I hate you. And I fucking love you. And everything in between."

Echo's eyes widen, and I realize what slipped out.

"You're incapable of love."

I can't help but chuckle because she's right. At least, I thought I was until her golden eyes burned a hole through my chest.

"Doesn't matter what you want to call it. Love is a worthless word anyway. Especially given your love is already promised to someone else. I'm just trying to make you understand this isn't fun. And it isn't entertainment. Whatever you do is violent and rips me to pieces. But now that I've felt it, I can't live without it. So I hope you're happy."

Echo's breath hitches as pools form in her lashes.

"I'm not." She blinks and a single tear rolls down her cheek.

A girl who doesn't break in front of people, who pretends she can't be harmed, splitting open and leaking out for me.

"I thought I could do this." Her words are nearly a whisper, but it's so quiet, and we're so close, I hear every crack in her tone. "I thought if I was making the safe decision, eventually it would feel right. I thought if I could just get you out of my system, I'd get over it. You weren't supposed to be so persistent and mess all that up."

"From what I recall, you're the one who came to me." Not that it matters.

Whether I realized it or not, I was circling. Waiting.

"You could have just fucked me and walked away." Her voice cracks at the end.

"You're lying to yourself if you think that." Releasing her jaw, I skate my hand along it, into her blonde hair and brush it back. "There is no walking away from you."

"I'm a mess," she whispers.

"I know."

"I've stabbed someone."

"I've done worse."

Her eyes narrow and the littlest smirk ticks up in the corner of her mouth. "We're terrible people."

"Or we're just not full of shit like everyone else." I shrug.

"I can't marry him."

She spins the ring my brother gave her around her finger. The sight of it where her purity ring lived is wrong.

"I'm only going to ask you this one more time, Echo..." I lock our gazes, her golden eyes spearing through my chest. "What do you want?"

She bites her lip, and her eyes are glassy. "I can't answer that."

"Why?" I pull her lip out from between her teeth when she moves to bite it again.

"I promised him my future."

I'm not sure if she's referring to my brother or father. Or maybe hers. It doesn't matter. I might not play their games, but I know how to fight.

I shake my head, dropping my hands to hers and wrapping them in my palms. She stands still in the silence for a long moment. Her mind waging a battle with her heart. The aftermath playing out in her stare.

"Stop lying. Stop fighting. Stop with the survival instincts and just talk to me. Tell me what you want."

"I want you, Crew." It's so quiet I barely hear it. "Even if you're going to make me regret it."

I can't help but smirk because she's right to fear me the way she does. I might never let anyone hurt her, but it doesn't make what we are a pretty picture either.

We're messy. Disastrous. A galaxy caving in on itself and impossible to stop.

"You'll only regret it when I refuse to let you go."

Feathering my hands down her side, I snake them around the backs of her thighs and pick her up. She wraps her legs around me and catches my neck with her arms. Foreheads pressed together as I spin us around and sit her on the counter.

My mouth finds hers and our tongues tangle, until I steal her gum like I plan on stealing every part of her.

Pulling back, I pop it between my teeth, and she glares at me.

"That was mine."

"You belong to me." I reach down and grab her hand, pulling off the ring my brother gave her and tossing it somewhere in the apartment.

For a moment, I expect her to argue, but she's quiet as she watches my finger graze the once more empty spot.

"No one marks you but me, Echo." I drag a hand up the center of her throat, still rubbing her hand. "And when I replace that piece of trash he gave you, it will be with ink. Because there is no backing out of us."

The column of her throat moves with her swallow.

"And in the meantime, I'll mark you with my cum. Because I'm the only man allowed to do that."

Her breath hitches. Catches in her throat as I squeeze her neck. And her body melts at the pressure. No flinch, no fear, no resistance. She trusts me, and it's my responsibility to make sure she always can.

"Who do you belong to?" I tighten my grip and her stare gets hazy.

"You." She chokes out, her fingers gripping the counter where she sits.

I release her, and she gulps in a breath as I take a step back. "Then prove it."

30

Crew

Echo holds onto the counter as I inch back, walking away from her. She's been fighting this like she has a chance. She doesn't, and I need her to finally accept it.

Sitting in the chair across the living room, I watch her tap her heels against the island.

I've been chasing her, while she's been his. And I need her to be mine, to prove she wants to be. There's no more denying this.

"Come here," I say, and her feet pause.

Echo bites her puffy lip and her eyes light up. They shimmer. Flecks of gold that might as well be the sun.

She slides off the island and takes one step, pausing only when she sees me shake my head.

"You have some things to make up to me, Goldie." I lean forward, resting my elbows on my thighs. "On your knees, princess. I want to see you beg for it."

The fighter in her might hate when I'm demeaning, but her dark side thrives on it—lights up for it.

Proven by the wicked hint of a smirk that crawls the corner of her mouth. "Yes, my lord."

Fuck, this girl.

She drops down to her knees, and I'm tempted to rush her just so I can shove my cock down her beautiful throat so hard she'll regret ever considering saying yes to my brother. Instead, I sit patiently with my elbows digging into my thighs as she plants her hands on the floor in front of her and slowly crawls over to me.

Wetting her lips, she doesn't break her stare, even as she stops in front of me and sits back on her heels, waiting for what she knows is coming.

I want to hate her. Love her. Make her pay for all of it.

Reaching out, I grip her chin and tip her to face me fully. "You lied to me earlier."

"When?" Her eyebrows pinch, and there's a nervous edge to her tone.

"When you said you're only a virgin once." I brush my thumb over her lip. "Because I've taken yours twice already. And there's still one more for me to claim."

Her breath hitches. Gold eyes wide and innocent.

"You mean..."

I rub my thumb over her lip again. "Don't worry, I'll prepare you first."

She swallows hard, likely sensing I'm not joking. I'm going to take every sweet thing Echo has, and I'm going to claim it. I'm going to make her mine until there isn't one part of her that could possibly be tainted by anyone else.

When she handed me her virginity, I don't think she realized at the time she was feeding a monster. One taste and something pure had never been so good.

Leaning back in my chair, I plant my hands on the armrests, not sure how a damned man ends up blessed, but realizing the universe fucked up placing Echo at my feet.

"You let my brother put his lips on you tonight."

She must sense the edge to my tone because she sits silently waiting.

"So when I fuck all traces of him off your pretty little mouth, I want you to remember why I'm not going to be sweet about it. Now take me out like a good little whore and wrap that mouth around me. You need to learn what happens when you let someone touch what's *mine*."

Her thighs clench. It's faint, barely noticeable, but I see it. Because I see *everything* when it comes to her. How her throat bobs at my statement, but she leans forward. Gravity, and she can't resist me.

Unlike the first time, when I brutally fucked her face, I sit back and wait for her to undo my belt. For her to take me out and wrap her delicate hands around me. It's so pure and sweet I could blow my load in her pretty little face.

"Don't play, princess. I want you to suck it. Choke on it and make me come. Remind me who your mouth belongs to."

Echo lifts off her heels, brushing her hair to the side, planting her lips on my cock, and making me see the universe closing in. I planned to be nice, but she makes me unhinged. And she let him kiss her. So I can't help that I grip her hair and shove her down onto me until I hit the back of her throat, and she's drooling and gagging.

"That's it." She might not have any experience, but she's a quick learner, taking me deep like she's desperate for it. Her innocent lips wrap around the base of my cock as her eyes widen.

She pulls back for a breath, tears leaking from her eyes, and her spit streaks my dick, but her air's cut off by me shoving her back down over me.

Because she let him touch her.

"You're mine, Echo." I hold her against me while she chokes around my cock. "These lips will never touch another man again. Learn your lesson and take me like I want you to."

She's crying, gagging. But she hollows her cheeks and swallows me further. I hit the back of her throat again, and she steadies her breaths through her nose. She sucks me hard and wet. Stroking my cock where it's too much for her.

"There you go." My balls pull tight, and I'm burning up inside.

She snakes a hand up to my wrist and grips, helping me force her deeper.

"Fuck."

Echo is messy. Dangerous. Perfect.

Mine.

Tears and spit spill over me, and it's the most beautiful sight. I want this girl to hurt for me as much as I hurt for her, and I'll chase every bit of pain with pleasure.

"Swallow." Our eyes connect, smeared mascara running down her cheeks as my release shoots down her throat.

Some spills out the corners of her lips, but she fights to take in all she can. Her mouth slides over me, sucking me down. And when she pulls back, I wipe her mouth and shove in the cum that's trying to spill out.

"Good girl." I paint her lips with my release. "Such a pretty little whore taking every drop."

She wraps her lips around my thumb, sucking me in.

"You're fucking perfect." I smear my thumb over her mouth when she releases it again. Her messy face flushed and glowing. "I can't get enough of you."

"You sure that wasn't enough?" She pulls back with a wicked little smile. Slowly, she stands and strips off her jeans before crawling up into my lap. She reaches for the hem of her shirt and strips it overhead, revealing a see-through black bra that shows off her perfect tits and matches her thong. "Because I can give you more, my lord. Unless... you're tapping out already."

I grab her hips, shoving her harder onto my lap and circling her center over my dick. Grinding her pussy over my cock, which is still wet from her sucking it. The friction is already pumping blood back to all the right places.

"I don't tap out, princess." I circle her hips again, and it digs her underwear into her. "But you will. I'll fuck you until you're begging me to stop. And when your pussy can't handle it anymore, I'll shove my dick in your ass and fuck you harder."

Echo leans in. Her tits brushing my chest, her lips grazing over mine. "I'd like you to prove it."

Sweet as she pretends to be, the dark side of Echo is coming out. Her other half speaks to mine. The parts of her she fears exist, but I feed it because I can't get enough of her.

She drags her mouth back and forth over mine, a fraction away from a kiss. "Show me I'm yours, Crew."

Vulnerability.

It's halfway between a plea and a beg. Her body wants to be broken like her mind has been. And this girl who hasn't belonged to anyone her whole life wants to be mine. She trusts me to take care of what's left of her.

Nearly everyone in her life has hurt her, betrayed her, but she doesn't want me to.

I draw my hands up to her face and cup her cheeks. "I love you, Echo. The good in you. The bad in you. All of you."

My fight fades, and it's just her in my hands. A soul where it belongs. Trusting me to keep it safe. Doesn't matter how many terrible things I say to keep the distance between us, she trusts my actions.

"I'm going to figure this out for us."

I don't make people promises, but I won't break this. I can't. Not now that I have her.

"I know, Crew." She wraps her arms around the back of my neck and sinks her lips to mine.

Drinks my heart from my chest. Blinks my soul from existence.

Echo is endgame.

I pick her up and carry her to the couch, laying her down on it and stripping off my shirt as I kneel between her legs.

Heaven between them as I peel her underwear off and spread her thighs for me. I thumb her clit, and she shivers. Her body reacting to the only man who has ever come inside it.

I kiss her pussy, and she clenches her thighs around my head. She can suffocate me all she wants. I'll die between her legs a happy man.

"Crew." Her nails dig into my scalp, and I love how my name sounds in a moan from her lips.

I shove my tongue inside her, and she holds hard enough she might draw blood. I don't care as I bury myself deeper. She's shaking and climbing. Chasing her release like the good girl she tries not to be around me.

Sucking her clit into my mouth, she detonates. Her screams filling every inch of my apartment.

I'm the only man who has ever heard Echo scream like that.

Her legs are still shaking as I lift and pull my pants down. I lean in, and she's so slick I slide into her. Shove myself as far as I can go as I grab her throat and hold her down beneath me.

"You're mine now, Goldilocks. I'm going to clean up this mess you made, and you're going to be *mine*."

I thrust into her again. Harder. Faster.

Her legs wrap around my waist while her nails score my chest, streaking them with blood.

"Mine."

My grip on her throat tightens, and her eyes are wide. Her lips part, but there's no use as she tries for breath. Instead, I lean down and release her throat to offer her my own air. I feed her lungs with my exhale and melt into her.

She might still be coming; she's squeezing me so tight.

"Crew," she moans, wrapping me closer.

Holding my mouth to hers. She's breathing me to life.

"Yes, Goldie?" I kiss her. "Do you need to come?"

She nods, holding me tighter as her pussy squeezes. "Yes."

"Come on my cock, princess. Let me feel how much you want my cum inside you." I thrust in, and she loses her breath. She shakes as her pussy grips me.

Her tight cunt pulls out my release, and I fuck her through it, giving her as much as she can handle, and more.

I fuck her until there's nothing but us fused on this couch. A mess of sweat and cum and hearts ripped out.

I fuck her until she's only mine.

When we finally relax, I carry her to the shower, and we rinse off before heading to my bed. A place that was only mine before her, and now I don't want her anywhere else ever again.

Echo falls asleep the moment her head rests on the pillow. Her light and darkness spilling out across the navy pillowcase. But I don't climb in beside her. I slip into a pair of sweats and walk back into the living room, grabbing my phone off the counter.

I can't sleep, not now.

Not until I do what needs to be done.

Crew: We need to finish the conversation we started at the shop

Adam: I was wondering when you'd say that...

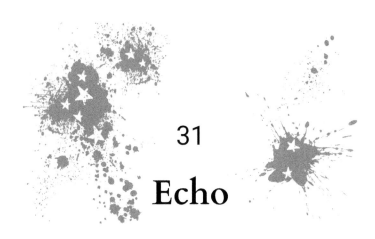

31

Echo

I STOP IN THE doorway between the bedroom and the living room, not sure if I'm sleepwalking or if Crew is actually setting down two plates of pancakes on the coffee table before he sits on the couch.

"Breakfast?"

"Don't tell me you aren't hungry after being fucked awake this morning."

The dirty smirk he offers brings heat to my cheeks. The first time I slept in Crew's bed, I disappeared before he woke up. This morning, he beat me to it, waking me up with his tongue between my legs.

"I didn't say I wasn't hungry." I walk into the room, pulling down the bottom of the oversized Iron Maiden T-shirt he left for me to wear. "I just didn't know you could cook."

I tug the hem of his T-shirt again out of habit. Even if I know Crew loves every inch of my marked skin, Rhett's been slowly training my mind to be more self-conscious.

"Fuck no, I can't cook." Crew laughs.

The sound is so unlike him, I can't help but fall for him a little harder. Last night when he said he loved me, and I didn't say it back, it wasn't because I don't feel the same. I'm just scared of what it means for me. I don't know how to choose myself and what I want over the promises I've made.

I drop down onto the couch beside him. "Where did you get these then?"

"Fel brings me food." He shrugs. "The one and only perk of living across the hall from those two."

"You're kidding?" I can't help but laugh. "And Jude doesn't mind?"

"I'm sure he does, but that chick loves pissing him off."

He's not wrong. Fel's favorite hobby is pushing Jude to his limit just so he can make her pay for it. Something I didn't understand until I involved myself with Crew Kingsley. Because pushing his buttons might be my favorite form of foreplay.

"So does she know I'm here then?"

"Nah, she doesn't come in."

His mood shifts, but I pretend not to notice. Facing this with him is one thing, but I still don't know how we'll navigate it outside these walls. Instead, I grab my fork and take a bite of my pancakes.

"So if you never cook, what do you eat?" I try to cut through the tension now palpable in the room.

"Anything that comes made and packaged." Crew shrugs. "Or I order out."

"Of course you do."

"Something wrong with that?"

I roll my eyes. "It's just a waste, that's all."

"Of what?"

"Money."

I freeze, fork halfway to my mouth. I didn't mean to say that. Crew makes me too comfortable. I don't let anyone see my insecurities, especially men who clearly don't share in them.

Everything about Crew's apartment is expensive. And even if I know it's because he worked hard for it, I also know he was raised with certain advantages. We didn't experience the same struggles, and I don't like anyone knowing I'm still affected by mine.

Crew sets down his fork, watching me as I shove another bite in my mouth.

"Sore subject?"

"No." I stuff more food in, but even chewing doesn't help dislodge the knot in my throat.

My blush burns hot on my cheeks, and when Crew won't stop watching me, I finally set my fork down and lean back against the couch, swallowing my bite and combing my fingers through my hair.

"You wouldn't get it."

"Try me." His expression softens with his tone, and I hate it.

He's easier to deal with when he's evil and devious. But right now, when he's looking too closely at all my scars, he's digging into wounds I don't like to think about.

Tucking my legs up under me, I turn on the couch to face him, leaning with my back against one of the arms. He isn't going to let this go, and I can't expect him to continue opening up to me if I'm not going to do the same.

"I didn't grow up with money."

"I know."

"No." It comes out snappier than I mean, so I try to reel it back. "Sorry, it's just you don't know."

I fidget my fingers in the hem of his T-shirt, wishing any reminder of my past didn't make me feel like I'm crawling out of my skin.

"Until my dad came along, I'd never had a home. Mom bounced between friend's houses—hopping around from one couch to another. Sometimes we stayed in a shelter. And those were the good days."

I bite my bottom lip, trying to bury the choked lump that's lodged in my throat.

"And the bad days?" Crew asks, watching me. Not a flicker of judgment in his gaze.

My past isn't a secret, but I also don't talk about it. And even if Crew knows I came from nothing, I'm sure he can't picture the extent of what that really means.

"On bad days we'd find a bus stop, a park bench, or an abandoned building." My eyes glance around his apartment, at all the clean lines and polished surfaces. "Anything that resembled a roof over our heads."

He nods, his jaw clenched.

"I survived. That's all that matters." I brush my hands over my lap. "And I didn't have to become her to do it. I figured it out without having to sell my body, so that's got to mean something. Even when she tried to force it. I survived her."

My forced smile hurts, and the way Crew's teeth clench means he sees it.

"Echo, come here." He holds out his hand, and only then do I realize I'm curled in on myself at the other end of the couch.

My safe space.

It's easier to hold myself together when I'm closed off. And how Crew reaches out now bridges that gap I maintain between myself and everyone else. But he doesn't drop it, he waits for me to plant my palm in his, and when I do, he pulls me to him.

I straddle his lap, but unlike any other time I've done this, it isn't sexual how he holds me. His arms wrap around my waist while he draws circles with his thumbs on my lower back. His eyes meet me like a cool ocean, rocking my wicked nightmares to sleep.

"You did more than survive it, Echo," he says, rubbing my back. "You're so fucking strong it's incredible. And I'm sorry."

"For what?" Tears burn in my eyes, but I don't let them fall.

"I'm sorry if I made you feel like there was something wrong with you for being a virgin for so long. For all the things I've said. The fact that you saved yourself because of what happened to you, and then for some fucked up reason decided to give yourself to me..."

I shake my head, cupping his jaw in my hands. "I'm not sorry for any of it."

He closes his eyes, and I tip my forehead to his.

"I wanted it to be you." I sigh. "It had to be you."

"Why?"

"Because..." I pull back as he blinks open his eyes. "It doesn't matter where I come from. Just like it doesn't matter where you come from. Money, no money. Drugs, death. There are broken pieces inside both of us, Crew. And you're the only one I'd trust with mine."

He wraps his arms tighter around me, holding me close. My heartbeat is in my throat at the way his warmth settles me.

"I didn't tell you this so you'd feel guilty. I told you because I want you to know. I want you to understand why I was scared for so long. But I'm not scared with you. Of all the things I fear, you aren't one of them. That's why I tried to tell myself I hated you, then I could try to deny the fact that you were the only person really seeing me."

"I do see you."

"I know."

"And you're perfect."

I roll my eyes. "Not quite. Not even close."

"You're too good for me."

I can't help the broken laugh that breaks free. "Okay, maybe you don't see me then."

He shakes his head. "I'm serious."

"So am I." I pull back, looking at him. "Did you not hear anything I just said? How could you think I'm too good for you? I'm a broken mess with mommy issues and nightmares that still live rent-free in my head."

"And I'm a sick fuck who gets off on hurting people."

I bite my lower lip, wrapping my arms around the back of his neck and tilting my head to examine him. "Why is that?"

"Because if you're the one inflicting pain then you're not the one receiving it." The circles he's drawing on my back stop, and he freezes at what he said.

"Who says it's all a fight, Crew?"

He shakes his head. "It's dangerous to think it isn't."

"Why?"

His teeth clench, and I know he's holding back. He doesn't want to open up to me, but I don't care. Because that's what he made me do, and I need it in return. We're going to rip ourselves open until we're raw nerves, on fire with every little touch.

"You can tell me." I rub the back of his neck. "You can trust me."

"I know." He tips his head back and lets out a long breath, before once more looking at me. "I grew up with money, Echo. Sickening amounts of it."

"I'm aware."

"The problem with having something like that is that other people will always want it. And you can have all the money in the world, but it doesn't replace certain things. It couldn't replace her."

"Your mom?"

Crew nods once.

"Money was my father's sickness. Still is. It's all he cares about, and she paid the price for it. He let his guard down because he was getting what he wanted, and he forgot about the sacrifices you have to make when you make trades with the devil."

"Is that what you think?" My eyebrows pinch. "That if you get something good, you're going to have to pay for it some other way."

"I know it." He squeezes me tighter.

"And it scares you."

It's not a question, because it's all over his face. Fear beneath the surface. Something he hides behind his façade of being a sadistic asshole.

"You want to know what scares me?" Crew rubs his hands up my back. "That I have all the money you could ever want, Echo. I could give you anything your heart desires. But it means nothing."

"I don't want any of it."

"I know you don't. And that terrifies me more. Because you're a force that can't be contained. And if I take my eye off the prize for one second, I'm worried I'll lose you again."

"Again?" My eyebrows pinch. "What are you talking about?"

"You should have been mine from the moment we met."

"When? Eight years ago?"

He nods. "I knew something was off that night, I just didn't know what it was. My father's always had a soft spot for his favorite son, so I should have guessed it had to do with Rhett's religious obsession. But instead of trying to figure it out, I did what I'm best at and ignored my family's mess. Back then, I didn't realize they were dragging you into all their shit. You didn't deserve that."

"It's not all on them. I was always going to do what I had to for my father. I owed him. He's the reason I got out of the hospital."

The last word is nearly a whisper. Embarrassment, fear. It doesn't matter if I did the right thing protecting myself from what my mother's dealer tried to do, I don't want Crew thinking that broken girl is all I am.

Like he senses my energy shift, he leans forward and cups my cheeks in his hands.

"You don't need to hide your darkness from me. I'm not scared of it. It's beautiful. You're my destiny, Echo. Always have been."

"Even when I said I'd be his?"

"Especially then. Because you forced me to finally stop being a fucking idiot always convincing myself I wasn't obsessed with you."

"You acted like you hated me."

"It was easier than dealing with the fact that you liked my brother instead."

I shake my head. "Technically you can't *like* a Kingsley. It's an impossible task. They're all too stubborn and diffi-cult."

He tries to fight the smile at my comment but fails miserably.

"But I never liked him anyway—at least not as anything more than a friend—if that makes you feel better." I ghost my fingers along the back of his neck. "You're the only man for me. The only one my body's ever responded to. And that's not an exaggeration."

Crew rubs his thumb over my lower lip. "I don't deserve you, Echo."

"Keep me anyway." I wrap my fingers around his wrists and drag his hands lower, and he pauses them at my throat, gripping it.

"Don't worry." He pulls my face to his. "I will."

He tugs me to his mouth—to his kiss. He sinks himself against me, and there's no world outside this moment. No city to judge us. Nothing we can't face.

Crew holds me in his arms, and this might as well be the first home I've known. Because I'm safe, and in my mind, three words play in a dangerous loop.

I love you.

32

Crew

DOESN'T MATTER HOW MUCH distance I put between me and
Echo, she's in my veins. Her ink's carved like a memory
into my bones. She's my ghost of all good and bad things.

Watching her leave this morning with still-wet hair,
tied up in a messy bun, wearing nothing more than short
shorts and a simple T-shirt, was almost enough to have
me following her to the shop on my day off.

Not a drop of makeup, and she's a sculpture.

If there is a God, they spent centuries crafting creatures until they carved perfection with her. Gold eyes
that drag me to hell, and a delicate face like a porcelain
doll. The way I want to smear my cum all over it to
mess her up almost had me dragging her back into my
apartment this morning.

Only today, I can't.

After texting Adam last night, I didn't sleep. Echo might
think she's done with Rhett, but in the light of day, there's

a risk she'll change her mind. She doesn't come from a safe life like I did, and even if I'm haunted by my ghosts, they're nothing like hers.

She needs security she's still not sure I can offer.

I'm not used to caring enough about anything to try to prove myself. But for her, I will.

For her, I need to stop hiding my potential. Chaos might be our foreplay, but what she needs from me right now is to feel safe.

Not with my brother.

With me.

After last night, Rhett isn't getting near Echo again. When I stole his ring from her finger, it was my promise to her. To protect her, to keep her. She's mine now and forever.

The way she hands herself to me is a level of trust I've never known. Partially because I don't give people reasons to trust me, but mostly because when they do, I use it against them.

Echo pushed past that barrier. She used her golden eyes to see right through. She witnessed every rotten inch of my soul and asked me for more.

She hasn't said she loves me yet, but I hold onto that hope in her eyes. The softness she only ever shows me. How she hands me her body because she doesn't know how to say the words out loud.

It's terrifying, I get it. I'm scared of loving her too. It's a weakness, and those are dangerous. If there's one thing I learned from my father, it's to not let anyone hold something over you. That's how enemies win. How empires fall.

But I'd burn to the ground for that girl.

I walk into my father's house, and each time I do, it feels emptier. This place is as hollow as his soul.

His staff bustles around, cleaning and polishing unused tables and furniture. There are so many of them and only one of him, so I can't imagine how they keep busy, but they're good at pretending. My father is a lot of things, but he's not cheap. And he pays them well.

A few nod at me as I walk past, while the others pretend not to notice. Some faces are familiar, others aren't.

I make my way to his office and find Adam standing beside the desk with his arms around Lakeyn. Her blonde hair is nearly white in this dark room, much like the shade of Echo's on one side.

Every sight.

Every thought.

I circle back to *her*.

Lakeyn is smiling, and I'm not sure what my grumpy brother could have possibly said to draw that reaction, but it lights her up from her cheeks to her eyes.

She's too sweet for him. Nice in the kind of way that others use against them. It's no wonder he's overly possessive and practically a stalker. Sometimes its necessary.

Darkness drinks light.

Purity is chased by ruin.

It doesn't matter that I'm not religious. I read enough of the Bible to be clear on temptation. The forbidden things are what we want the most. And all it takes is one taste to be lost forever.

One kiss from Echo's lips.

One moan vibrating in her chest.

One statement—I *want you*.

When Adam spots me, he relaxes his grip on Lakeyn and gives her a kiss on the temple.

She glances over, her honey eyes darting between us, before she tips up and kisses him on the lips.

Adam isn't an affectionate person. He doesn't even shake hands unless it's a necessary part of a business transaction. But Lakeyn brings out another side of him. And something about how she trusts him makes me hope I can too.

Rhett might be Dad's favorite in some regards, but Adam holds influence over his finances, and nothing means more to dear old Dad than money.

"I'll see you at lunch." Adam squeezes Lakeyn a final time, before letting her go.

There might as well be an invisible cord pulling as she walks away from him because his entire demeanor changes. Any warmth snuffed out the moment his girlfriend disappears through the door.

Girlfriend.

I've never wanted one. Never understood the point of committing myself to a single person. But fuck, I would love to make Echo mine.

Adam circles the desk and drops into the large leather chair, sitting back, relaxed as ever. "You wanted to talk."

The confidence I wear when I'm standing in the ring before a fight is the same he projects in his five-thousand-dollar suit. Miles apart but common ground. Calmness in our own element.

Ruthless in our own ways.

Every Kingsley has spilled blood—apart from Rhett. It might as well be stained on the family crest. Dad's path for revenge after Mom's death led us down some dark roads. And something about taking a soul out of a person sticks with you. There's no shaking those demons.

Echo might have stabbed a man, but she's never taken a life. While she thinks she understands her dark side, it's nothing compared to mine. And even if I want the man who tried to touch her dead, I'm glad she wasn't the one to do it. There's no erasing the vision of life leaving someone's eyes.

I sit across from Adam and kick my feet up on the desk, which he frowns at. It's no secret he thinks I'm unruly and disrespectful, but it's better than being a kiss-ass.

We don't understand each other. I doubt we ever will. Three brothers bred from the same fucked up family, and somehow we all ended up different.

"How's the hunt for Rhett's shooter?"

Adam taps the desk. "Nothing new yet."

"Losing your touch, brother?"

Adam smirks, crossing one ankle up on his opposite knee. "Of course not. Things have calmed down. I think whoever did it might have given up. At least, for now."

"So what's with all the extra security then? You think I don't notice the cars tailing me?"

"Not that it's changed how you're approaching any-thing." He's not the least bit guilty about the fact that he's got surveillance on his entire family.

If anything, he's proud of it.

"You're lucky it's me watching, not Dad."

"God forbid he sees his favorite son can't keep his girlfriend satisfied."

"Because that's all this is..." Adam narrows his gaze.

"That's between her and me." I lean back. "So you have no idea who targeted Rhett?"

Nothing is more annoying than when Adam avoids an-swering questions. It's the one and only trait he picked up from our father. He can dodge anything he wants, and it's why he's so successful.

Me, on the other hand—I prefer more brutal, specific methods.

I'm straight to the point. Leaving no confusion for any-one involved.

"Didn't say that." Adam taps his thumb on his thigh, clearly not happy about something the way his jaw tight-ens the slightest. "But it's more complicated than we thought."

"Meaning?" I swear if I have to punch my brother in his billion-dollar face it will at least move this conversation along.

"I think it was personal."

I can't help but laugh. "You're saying someone doesn't love our saint of a brother?"

Adam smirks because he knows Rhett as well as I do. The show he puts on for his church is just that—make believe. It feeds his ego, his mommy issues, and his need to be loved. But it isn't for them. And it isn't for God.

"So who wants Rhett dead then?" I lace my fingers together behind my head and lean back.

"Long list apparently."

I can't help but smirk. "Maybe look into one of his many girlfriends. You know he's fucking around on Echo, right?"

"And what she's doing with you is any different?"

Adam doesn't operate in the gray area. Everything with him is black or white. Right or wrong. Yes or no. Which is why he doesn't understand what I'm doing with Echo. And also why he came to the shop the other day and tried to convince me to make a decision.

He stands up, straightening his suit jacket and finishing up the buttons as he circles the desk and stops to lean on the edge of it in front of me. I can't remember the last time I've seen Adam wear anything other than a suit.

"This isn't a game, Crew."

"I'm aware."

"Good. Because while I don't know who shot our brother yet, I did find something else."

"What?"

Adam doesn't ever look nervous. He doesn't hesitate. Right now, I sense both those things as he stares at me.

"Things that are going to make this a lot more complicated for all of us." Adam crosses his arms over his chest, and his jaw clenches. "Seems Ryan has been getting into trouble, and he's using the church to cover it up."

"Echo's dad?"

Adam nods.

"What could a preacher possibly be getting into?"

He makes the rest of us sinners by simple comparison. Ryan doesn't swear or get involved in any of my father's bad shit. It's annoying as fuck because I watch him get constantly walked all over because of it.

"He's funneling money from the church."

That can't be right. Her father wouldn't.

"Why would he do that?"

Adam relaxes his posture and grips the desk. "I'm still figuring that out."

"Does Dad know?"

He nods.

"Rhett?"

"Not yet."

A lead weight drops in my stomach. "Echo?"

Adam shakes his head, his expression tense. Echo worships the ground her father walks on. He saved her from a mother who deserves to burn in Hell. But if he's been hiding this, what other secrets is he burying?

"You're the one who texted me." Adam taps the desk. "But are you really prepared to face what's about to happen? Because when Echo finds out what's going on, things are going to get a lot worse, and she doesn't need someone who is going to waver on her. Rhett might be a prick, but he'll take care of her."

"And I won't?"

This conversation isn't about Ryan or what he's doing to pad his pockets. Adam's genuinely worried about me. And it's so unlike him, Lakeyn must be to blame.

"I need to hear you say you won't back out of this, Crew. You might care about her, but if you're going to break them up, then you need to hold up your end of it. If there's a fallout with her father, we're all she's got left."

"Since when do you care?"

He barely knows Echo. He never comes to family dinners. And this lecture is so unlike him I can't find my bearings.

"Because I've recently learned that there are in fact things more important than money. And I'd hate to see you fuck this up like you do everything else. Just because you're destructive or bored or pissed at our father. Are you really ready for this?"

"Were you?" I stand in front of him, looking him dead in the eyes. "Because if you really understand how I feel, you'll know there is no *being ready*. There's nothing to prepare for. One look in her fucking eyes, and she drags my ugly, bloody soul straight out of me. She empties me until there is nothing left but how I feel for her. Ready or not means nothing when she's *everything*, Adam. And I'm not letting her go."

Adam crosses his arms over his chest, and if he were the type of man who would be caught smiling, I'm pretty sure that would be what lights his eyes.

"Very well then."

He's so fucking proper and uptight, I can't help but chuckle. If it weren't for our dad's cheekbones and Mom's dark hair, Adam and I wouldn't even look like brothers. Him in his suit and styled hair, me fresh out of the shower in faded jeans and the Iron Maiden T-shirt Echo wore all morning so I can spend the day drowning in her scent.

"So what's the plan? Because she's not marrying him. And I need to know what the fuck is going on with her father."

"Same." Adam walks back around the desk. "And I'm drawing him out as we speak."

"And here I thought you called me in for a brotherly brainstorming session." I don't bother trying to bury my sarcasm.

Adam smirks, clicking away at something on the computer. "How do you think I run five multi-billion-dollar corporations, Crew? I don't walk into meetings unprepared. I just needed to verify where your head was at before we got into this."

"Where are we now that you know that?"

"We're at the favor I'm going to ask you." He leans back in his chair. "You need to tell your girl what's going on, even if it's going to break her heart."

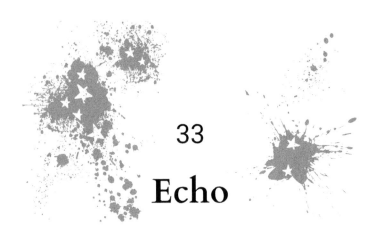

33

Echo

My gum clacks between my teeth. A sound most people find annoying, but it calms me. Chewing. Keeping busy. I'll do anything to resist the need to scratch the flesh from my arms as my anxiety itches to the surface.

When I was younger, I considered less healthy ways of dealing with the nerves constantly skittering around inside me. Watching my mom slowly deteriorate solved that problem because I refused to be weak like her.

I knew I would get out someday, whatever the price. And I would be strong about it.

I'd be free of rat-infested buildings and apartments that reeked of piss and drugs. I'd forget the taunts from the pretty girls at school when I wore dirty clothes and shoes with holes in the bottom. I'd escape.

Not that I wanted Mom to die for that chance. But someday I knew I'd show them I'm capable of something.

And even if now people judge me for different reasons—because my hair doesn't make sense or I'm too inked for a girl—at least I'm myself.

I refuse to be *her*, and I refuse to be them.

That is why, as I sat in Crew's arms this morning, wishing three words would find their way out, I made peace with my decision.

I've been afraid, but no more.

I'm done reducing my happiness for what is safe, just because I've felt pain. Crew doesn't want that for me. *I* don't want that for me.

And my father is going to understand.

"Beautiful service." I smile at Dad as he drops down into the pew beside me.

Just because I'm not religious like he is, doesn't mean I don't enjoy watching him deliver a sermon. There's something about how he fills a room with hope. A belief that things can change and be better.

In front of the masses, my father is a force. People don't gravitate here for God, even if that's who they're searching for. They come here because Dad is a true believer in faith. Good, bad, ugly. He believes in forgiveness and mercy.

"Rhett did a fine job as well, don't you think?" His gaze finds Rhett, who's shaking hands with a group, his usual blinding smile on his face.

"He did fine."

Dad hums, watching Rhett disappear into the crowd before looking at me. "You're not wearing his ring."

I look down to where I'm rubbing my bare finger in my lap. Clenching my hands, I dig my nails into my palms like it will hold me together.

"I can't marry him." A weight lifts with my admission.

"I know."

"What do you mean *you know*?" I turn to face Dad.

"I guess I should say I *assumed*." He offers a gentle smile. "You're in love with his brother, aren't you?"

"Love?" I laugh, clacking my gum between my teeth again. "I mean, I like Crew. But what is love, right?"

"Oh, Echo." Dad shakes his head, reaching out and taking my hand in his. "You're always so logical when it comes to certain things. But love isn't something you can define when it's different for everyone. And the way you love one person doesn't distinguish how you love another. Love is not as clear as you would like it to be."

"That'd be too easy, right?"

Dad shrugs, looking at me with a soft smile. "You wouldn't want it if it was. Always a fighter."

He knows me too well. "Well for the record, I tried to hate him."

"Mm-hmm." Dad squeezes my hand. "Made you fall harder though?"

"I don't even know how—"

I fell in love.

Why can't I say it out loud? Still, when he's not even here?

"What's there to know when it comes to love?" Dad brushes the back of my hand, and I look back up at him. "It's not an emotion defined by rational thinking. It's in your heart—like faith. It's in your soul. You can't *know* love, but that doesn't mean you won't feel it."

"And feelings should be trusted?"

"More than your mind most times."

"Why?" I bite my lip.

"Instinct." Dad pats my hand. "You'll rationalize anything if given the chance, but what really matters can't be explained in simple terms. You knew that walking in here."

I did. When everything rational told me to walk up to Rhett and keep my promise, I waited in the pew to talk to Dad instead. What's safe, what's right—it doesn't matter. Crew is all that does.

"Does he love you?" Dad's expression softens. "Does he make you happy?"

I nod, blinking a tear free from my eye.

"Then there's nothing left to think about, honey." He brushes the tear from my cheek.

"But what about you?"

"What about me?" Dad lets out a light chuckle.

"We made them a promise. Max helped save your life, and I'm just going back on my end of it."

"Echo, one of my greatest regrets was placing that burden on you when you were younger. I was a dying man, scared of the world I'd be leaving you to with your mother also gone. And I let fear drive me to make a bargain I'd take back if I could."

"It got you your heart."

He nods. "It did. But that's beating fine now. I'm fine now."

"You still have expensive lifelong treatments. Max helps with those; he funds the church. He does it because we're going to be family."

"Won't we still?"

I swallow hard, the lump settling in my throat. "I don't know."

Crew and I haven't been clear on what this is. He says he loves me now, but I'm not sure he's any more capable than I am.

"Doesn't matter anyway." Dad shakes his head.

"Why not?"

"Because I could lose it all and it wouldn't matter to me as much as you losing that light I see inside you." He squeezes my hand. "I only went along with it as long as I did because you seemed so happy with Rhett. I honestly believed it until something changed after Christmas."

When I punched Crew for making a comment that forced me to face every buried feeling.

"If you knew, why didn't you say something?" As much as I'd like to believe him, he committed to this deal as much as I did.

"You can lead someone to the path, but you can't force them to take it." Dad pats my hand. "Besides, just because I'm an old man who hasn't dated in years doesn't mean I don't understand it was a delicate situation."

"That's putting it mildly," I mumble.

"You needed to find your way to what you truly wanted. And yes, if you didn't come to me, I would have found the time to ask you if you really loved him. But now..." He smiles.

"What?"

"My daughter of little faith is finally letting her heart guide her."

The brightness in his eyes is nearly heartbreaking. I'm not a believer. But I believe in what I feel for Crew, and Dad must see it.

"Rhett's not going to take it well."

"He doesn't love you." Dad glances at the crowd at the front of the church. "But he cares. And he'll understand. Rhett is a man of faith, and he knows sometimes our paths are guided by other things."

"You really think that?"

Rhett might not want this relationship any more than I do, but we're both benefiting from our situation.

"I do." He pulls back, a smile climbing his cheeks. "And if he doesn't, I'll just have to deal with it. Besides, being a man of God makes me well acquainted with the devil's tricks."

"You're funny now, huh?" I nudge him in the arm, and we both laugh.

Dad shrugs. "Just lightening the mood. It'll be okay, Echo. Talk to Rhett. He understands more than you give him credit for. Besides, he's young like you. He's still finding his own path as well."

A dark current coats my father's expression as he watches Rhett emerge once more.

"He'll make the right choice."

I'm not sure he has much of a choice to make when I'm the one making the decision, but I just nod.

"Tell me more about Crew." Dad diverts his attention back to me. "He's... interesting."

I can't help the laugh that bursts out of me, breaking the tension. "That's one word for him. Crew is Crew. It's like what you said about defining love. You can't define him either. He beats to his own drum."

"Well, he's smart enough to steal my daughter's heart, so he's got that going for him."

"Yeah." I rub the empty spot on my hand once more. "You don't know him well, but he's good to me in his own unique way."

Sometimes unconventional and often messy, but Crew takes care of the needs I didn't know existed.

"He better be; you deserve real love."

"Like you once loved Mom?"

Dad tenses at the question. We don't broach this conversation often. And I haven't brought it up in years.

"Yes, like I once loved her." Dad nods. "I loved who she was before her addiction claimed her. Before I knew she took my daughter away from me."

"I can't imagine the person you met." I shake my head; my memory of my mom is someone he would never have fallen in love with. "I can't picture her as much of anything anymore."

The woman who raised me was hollow—in her eyes, cheeks, heart.

"I wish I'd fought for her." Dad presses his lips together. "Not to save *us* necessarily, but so I would have found out about you sooner. I can't make up for the things I've done wrong, Echo. No matter how long I try to atone for my sins, I'll never make up for your childhood or the burden you took on when you finally met me. I didn't know how to be a father, and because of that, I failed you in every way a man can fail another person."

He closes his eyes and takes in a breath. I should probably resent him, after all, he isn't innocent. But none of us are. Promises, arrangements, bad decisions, they always go one of two ways.

"If it makes you feel better, you're making up for it."

He nods, blinking back at me. "I'll handle Rhett. But you need to do me a favor."

I nod.

"Follow your heart, honey. Don't let the unknown scare you. It's no longer your mother's path or mine. This one is yours. Let it guide you to what is right."

He pats the back of my hand and forces a pained smile.

"And you'll be okay?"

"Always." Dad stands, brushing off his slacks. "Well, I better get up there and handle a few things."

"Dad." I grab his hand. "Thanks."

He plants his other palm over the back of my hand. "Not necessary."

I stand up and smile. "Hey, do you mind if I pop into your office for a minute? I need to print a design out for a tat tomorrow, and the printer at the shop decided to take a shit."

He frowns at my word choice, glancing up at the stained glass Jesus looking down at us.

"Sorry." I grit my teeth.

He shakes his head and chuckles. "Of course you can. I've got a meeting with the contractor after this."

"All right, well I'll just be a few minutes. The girls and I have plans."

Friends, for the first time in my adult life.

"Have fun." He smiles, pulling me in for a hug. "But not too much."

"Never." I grin as he pulls back, and he just shakes his head.

The weight on my chest lifts with each step as he walks away. But I feel another. It was easy to hide behind my commitments. Now there's no hiding. I need to tell Crew how I really feel about him.

I pull out my phone.

Echo: Dinner tonight?

Crew: Only if that's code for me eating you out

Echo: You're perverted

Crew: And you're wet thinking about my tongue in your pussy

Echo: Shut up, I hate you

Crew: Already starting the foreplay, I can get onboard with that. Hate you too, my dirty little slut

I can't help that my thighs clench. The asshole knows what it does to me when he's rude.

Echo: Whatever, seven work for you?

Crew: Yep

Crew: And don't bother wearing panties, I'm just going to rip them off you if you do

Echo: Charming

Crew: You love it

I love you. Not that I'm brave enough yet to type it.

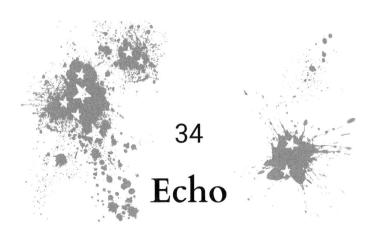

34

Echo

THE DOOR TO DAD'S office opens right as the paper jams in the printer.

"When did you get this thing? It's archaic." I look up, laughing, expecting to see Dad standing in his office doorway.

Instead, cat eyes stare back at me.

A dark, narrow gaze perfectly paired with a disinterested frown. I don't know this girl, but I recognize her from the party last night. She stopped by Rhett and me a few times and tried to pull him aside. But he brushed her off in favor of projecting us as the perfect couple, so she disappeared early in the night.

Her dark hair is pulled up in a neat bun on top of her head, and the blush that coated her cheeks each time she spoke to Rhett has been replaced with a stone-cold expression.

"My Dad's still out there if you're looking for him." I tip my chin to the door.

"I'm not." She crosses her arms over her chest and taps her nails on her forearm. "I'm Angelina."

The darkest smirk ticks up in the corner of her mouth as she steps inside and closes the door behind her. She walks across the room and stops at the desk across from me.

"You know who I am?"

I nod.

"Good. We can skip the general unpleasantries then."

"What are you doing here?" I shuffle the paper until the printer's teeth finally release it.

She plants a hand over the stack and presses it to the desk. "Stopping you from messing everything up."

My gaze moves to hers and it's darker now—focused. Lethal. She's not holding back and that can only mean one thing, she didn't walk in here to make friends.

The hair on the back of my neck stands tall as she pulls her hand back, examining her manicure. Instinct whispers in my ear like I should have seen this coming.

"I overheard your little chat with your father." She flicks her gaze to me again. "Love, happiness, blah, blah, blah. How sweet and supportive of him."

She taps a perfectly manicured nail against her flesh.

"My conversation is none of your business."

"You'd think." She smiles, so dark and empty I'm not sure what Rhett sees in her. "Except, all of this is my business. Rhett is *my man* after all."

"And you can have him." I can't help but chuckle as I start to move around the desk.

If that's what she's worried about, she must have missed the most important points of the conversation.

I'm about to move around her for the door when she grabs onto my arm, stopping me, her nails digging in. But I break free and push her off. If she's after a fight, I'm not the person she should pick one with. I don't come from her world of glass castles, and I have no problem proving it, whether I want what's best for Rhett or not.

"I don't need your permission," she snaps.

"Then what's the issue?" I roll my shoulders back. "Because I don't want him. He's yours. I'm not the enemy here."

"That's where you're wrong." She steps toward me, but I don't back up. I don't bow down, regardless of who this chick thinks she is. "You've always been the enemy. The pawn. The obstacle. But it didn't matter because I was willing to do what he asked, knowing when the time was right, he'd see I was the one he is meant to be with. Except now you think you can walk in and mess it all up just because you're in love? Things aren't ready yet. It's too soon."

I can barely keep up with the word vomit she's spewing at me. "What are you talking about?"

"You're engaged to him, Echo. You're supposed to play house and be happy right now while the church opens and the masses follow. You're the preacher's daughter after all." She rolls her eyes.

"They'll understand."

"They won't." Angelina clenches her jaw. "Not yet. Not until your father steps aside and puts Rhett in his rightful place."

"That's what this is about?"

"Don't get me wrong, Pastor Ryan is a blessing, but Rhett is the only one who can take Eternal Light to the next level. And I'll do whatever it takes to lift him up to where he belongs."

Once more, my spine tingles with her words. "What's that supposed to mean?"

"I've let you have him, Echo. For now, when it matters. Because I understand sacrificing for the ones you love. And you by his side gets him where he needs to be." She narrows her eyes. "But I didn't go through all this just so you can be the one to leave him like you don't even care. You don't leave him. He'll leave *you* once he finally sees what's right in front of him."

"You?"

"Yes me." She's nearly hysterical. Something between a laugh and a cry bursts out as she starts to pace.

"Angelina, if you love him, then tell him." I try to remain calm because if my past has taught me anything, that's the only way to survive unhinged people. "He doesn't care about me like that. This can all be amicable."

She bursts out into a laugh I can't read. It's dark. Her eyes move to the distance. She's drifting away.

"Like you know him."

I'm not sure how to argue with that. I know Rhett as a friend, but clearly she's the one with a deeper connection, even if it is a little terrifying.

"I've played along." Tears brim in her eyes. "I ignored the fact that he was determined to end up with you, no matter how deep our connection is. I waited for him to realize I was the one who would treat him right. I understood God's plan for us. That sometimes you have to be patient to reap the rewards. As long as the two of you appeared happy in public, that's all that mattered. He had his pure, preacher's daughter fiancée, and everyone would love him for it."

I take a cautious step forward, knowing at any moment her calmness could once more slip. "You care about him a lot."

Her fingers clench into fists, and she tips her head back, and a dark smile crosses her lips. "A lot?"

Angelina blinks back at me, and there are tears in her eyes now. A roller coaster playing out with every emotion that rocks through her. And whatever hides on the other side of her statement is darker than the wide pupils staring back at me.

"That's how little you understand love. I *love* him. I'd do anything. It's not like I wanted him to get hurt, but I understood what needed to happen."

"Hurt?" My stomach sinks at her word choice.

Angelina wipes a tear that trickles down her cheek. "Rhett doesn't understand how much I love him. I'm not sure he can. It wasn't easy watching him get shot, but it was for the best. The way they love him more now."

Her face brightens with sick satisfaction.

"I thought that was the protesters." I can't stop shaking my head, barely able to believe it.

She offers a broken smile. "It looked good, didn't it? The threats. The stage. *The show.* Give people easy answers, and they'll always look in the wrong direction. It's actually funny to think about it because my drama teacher said I'd never amount to anything."

She laughs, once more pacing.

"You shot him?"

"Not me." She stops, wide eyes, like my question is the most ridiculous part of this unhinged conversation. "I would *never* hurt him. I love him. I only arranged it, and don't give me that look, it's your fault."

I take a step back. "I'd never hurt Rhett. How is this my fault?"

At least, not like that. I'm not sure how he's going to take the inevitable end of our engagement.

"Because you weren't holding up your end of the bargain." She steps toward me. "You were too busy with his brother, and the protestors were making things difficult for him. He needed more sympathy. He needed their love to lift him higher."

She smiles now, looking up and admiring the memory of her plan. A plan that involved her getting Rhett shot. This isn't love, this is a sick obsession.

The door handle rattles, and my chest floods with relief. I'm not safe in this room with her. And when the door swings open, I've never been so happy to see Rhett's face.

"Rhett." His name spills from me with relief.

His eyebrows pinch as he looks from me to Angelina. "Everything okay in here? Your father's looking for you."

"Rhett." Angelina smiles as she rushes toward him.

"Angie?" But his tone is on edge. Nerves? Something I can't pinpoint as he closes the door behind him.

He closes it.

I'm trapped in here with her, and something about the changing energy in the room has my stomach in my throat.

"I'll go find him." I force a smile, taking a step toward the door.

But Rhett steps to the side and blocks it as Angelina reaches his side.

"What's happening here?" His question is aimed at Angelina.

She clings to his arm, her eyes edging on desperate as she looks up at him. "She's leaving you, that's what. I heard her talking to her father, and he agreed. She's going to ruin everything."

Rhett's gaze flicks to me. A switch of emotion shutting off. Cold, empty orbs that suck me to the center of a drain I didn't see myself spinning around.

"Is that so..." It's less of a question.

A realization?

A threat?

Once more a cool chill runs my spine.

"Yes, I heard them talking. She's trying to betray you." Angelina holds Rhett tighter, but he doesn't move his gaze off mine. "She said she's in love with your brother, that she can't do this anymore. And that Crew is going to have a talk with your father. It's all falling apart. And I told her we didn't do this all for nothing. That she can't back down.

I agreed to let them shoot you for heaven's sake. We had a plan."

Rhett's eyes snap back to her as my stomach sinks.

We had a plan.

Rhett isn't my salvation in this moment. He isn't a savior.

I don't know who he is as all emotion drains from his face and it's replaced with the coldest, emptiest gaze I've ever seen.

While I thought this was Angelina's obsession, I've never been more wrong. Like me, she's a puppet. And Rhett isn't who I thought he was at all.

"What did you say, Angie?" He grabs her arm, tight enough that she flinches.

"I told her the truth." Angelina's eyes beg him for something, but I'm not sure what. "She was going to ruin everything. She needs to understand why we did what we did. Why she can't back out."

"You didn't." It's almost sick amusement.

A cord in his sanity snapping.

A madman he's buried clawing to the surface.

Acceptance.

One moment, his hand is on her arm, and the next, he's grabbing her by the throat and slamming her to the wall.

"Tell me you didn't." He's in her face now, so close his spit lands on her mouth.

Her hands grab his wrist, trying to pull him off her throat. "But I love you."

I think that's what she says. He's crushing her windpipe and words can't make their way out.

Lunging at him, I grab for his arm, but he releases her long enough to backhand me across the cheek. The blow lands so hard I see stars as I fall to the floor.

"I'll deal with you in a minute."

I grab the side of my face, momentarily hearing Angelina sputter something before her breath clogs from his grip once more.

"You never meant anything to me, and you knew that," Rhett says, and I'm stumbling to my feet trying to steady myself, not sure which one of us he's talking to. "You were a means to an end. Just like her. And if you'd all have played your parts, we could have avoided this."

My vision focuses, and Rhett backhands Angelina like he did me, only she doesn't fight it. She stays down. She lets him take her power away as she looks up at him with tears in her eyes.

I rush toward him again. She might not fight, but it doesn't mean I'm going to bow down. I get in one good hit before he catches my wrist and spins me around, slamming me against the wall.

"Don't test me, Echo. Playing rough with my brother isn't the same thing. He's dumb enough to actually care about you—to think he loves you. I don't. You're a tool. And by choosing him, you've just relinquished your importance."

I clutch the wall and turn around, refusing to back down to whoever this man is. The person I thought he was in the hospital, or at the engagement party, has all but faded. The man I've spent years around slips away.

The face in front of me is a mask in an intricate game he's been playing.

Rhett is a psychopath, and I've seen his truth.

"What are you going to do?" I tip my chin up, facing off with him.

He grins, planting a hand on the wall beside my head and gripping my chin. It's not sweet or caring. It's a warning. Evil in his eyes.

"I'm going to get what was promised to me out of this relationship, even if it means I have to take it by force."

I claw at his face, getting one good scratch that draws four lines of blood down his cheek before something connects with the side of my temple, and everything goes dark.

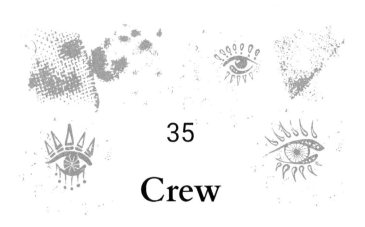

35

Crew

WALKING INTO THE CHURCH, the flames of Hell feel just past the horizon. My blood boils and my fingers clench. There's nothing but rage as I hit Echo's number again and it goes straight to voicemail.

She always answers her phone. Even if she's mad at me, she'll pick up simply to say something snide to piss me off. And when she can't, she'll text back with whatever her feisty little mind is running away with at any given moment.

All things I didn't appreciate enough until I couldn't get her to manifest on the other end of the line.

The church is still half full from Sunday service. People are mulling around and talking, but I make a beeline straight to Echo's father.

"Crew." He nods when I stop in front of him.

I can't help but laugh. "I'm going to fucking ruin you for what you're doing to her. She trusted you."

His smile falls and his face pinches. "What are you talking about?"

"The money." I dip my hands in my pockets. "You're messing with Kingsleys and you really think you can hide it?"

He sets down the Bible he's holding and steps to the side, shuffling us to a quiet corner. "You're going to have to elaborate. What money?"

"Lying in the house of God is a sin, right?" I chuckle. "Although I suppose funneling money from a church is as well."

His face pales, and I'm not sure what to think of his expression.

He's either a great actor or genuinely shocked.

"I don't handle Eternal Light's finances." His jaw clench-es.

"Then who does?"

Ryan's eyes dart around the room. Panic, frustration. A carousel of emotion. "Your brother."

His stare lands back on mine and truth cements between us. My stomach turns and my fingers clench.

"Rhett?"

He nods. "So you're saying he's stealing from the church?"

"Fuck." I nod, raking my fingers through my hair.

How have I been so blind? Rhett's always been the golden child. The good boy. The holy son. He's the one people rely on and look to for guidance. And all that has given him the greatest power of all.

Belief.

It's stronger than money. Stronger than influence.

"Where is Echo?" The realization that she's not an-swering her phone spins a web of tension inside me.

"In my office, why?" But then his eyes widen, and I feel him having the same thought I am. "She was going to end it with him."

I nod, brushing past him, even if I feel him following.

I thought I knew my brother. And even if we didn't get along, I still thought he was the safer option. But pieces are clicking into place from as far back as I can remember. Echo ending things with him might be the final thing to set him off. Everything is going to come to a head once she tells him she's leaving him, and I have to find her before that happens.

Storming down the hallway that leads to Ryan's office, the walls are tunneling in on themselves. The ceiling shrinks downward, and the sides of this box are caving around me. The tightening in my chest only worsens when I finally reach the door to Ryan's office and it is cracked.

Gasped crying comes from the other side as I push it open.

"Echo?"

But it's not her. It's the dark-haired girl who talked to me at Rhett and Echo's engagement party. She's curled in a ball with her knees pulled to her chest. Dark bruising is forming on her neck and makeup smears like bleeding paint down her cheeks.

Her eyes freeze me in place. Emptiness. Not sad even if she's crying. They're a void and she's lost. She's a pawn like everyone is, in a game we didn't know we were playing into.

Rhett's been hiding behind a cross, using it to shield the truth.

"Are you okay?" Ryan's expression pinches. "Crew, call—"

"Where is she?" I ask, cutting him off.

His eyes snap to me, then widen, as he realizes the state Angelina is in, and that Echo isn't here.

Both of us look back at Angelina, who's staring at me with pity. She let Rhett use her—break her. And she's paying the price.

"Is she with him?"

Please say no.

Please say no.

"I—" She reaches up, rubbing her neck. "He said he loved me."

She's avoiding the question, and I have to dig my fingernails into my palm to ground me. To remind me she has answers, and if I push too hard, she'll retreat like my brother likely trained her to.

"He doesn't love you, Angelina." I try to keep my tone steady, even if the truth will likely hurt.

She's in shock, and she needs to come back to reality before something terrible happens to Echo.

I squat down in front of her, and sadness coats her eyes. It leaks down her face. She's pretty, naïve. Rhett's type.

"Tell me what happened."

Ryan stands, threading his hands through his hair and pacing the room. He's in shock, and repeating Echo's name through his mumbles. He's falling apart like I want to—like the pieces shifting around inside.

I can't.

For her, I need to do what I do best when faced with a worthy opponent—maintain my focus and don't take my eyes off the enemy.

"She was going to end it with him *for you.*" The way the last part spits out makes it clear she's still a little disillusioned over her relationship with my brother. "That's not how it was supposed to happen."

"How was it supposed to happen?" My blood boils at the question. At the thought of them using Echo as some kind of pawn in whatever sick game they've been playing.

Angelina isn't upset that Rhett was with Echo. She's mad that Echo was going to end it. And everything about that fact is concerning.

"Once he got what he wanted, he'd finally be happy, and he'd realize he was meant to be mine." It's nearly a whisper, the faintest smile ghosting her lips. "I did everything he asked of me. I pretended we meant nothing to each other. I let him try to convince himself he still wanted to marry her. I even hurt him when he asked me to. He knew I didn't want to, but he needed it, and I love him."

"You hurt him?" I grit my teeth and try to pretend to give a shit because at least she's talking. I need to keep her talking to figure out why Echo is gone, and Angelina looks like she's been hung up by her neck.

"I told him there had to be another way."

"But he wouldn't listen?"

Angelina shakes her head. "Echo was too busy with you to care. And people were starting to notice she didn't spend any time with him. At least the shooting diverted their attention."

"You two planned that?"

"I didn't want to." She sounds disgusted at the accusation. "I *had to*. He was only with her to get what he needed."

"Which is what?"

She shrugs. "He didn't tell me everything."

Of course he didn't. He's an evil asshole, but he's not stupid.

Angelina's eyes darken the longer she watches me. Some kind of wickedness slipping out with her gaze. And even if my brother used her, she's not innocent. Whatever twisted things play in her mind have her pupils blown wide, edging on excitement.

"Does Rhett have her?" My gaze once more falls to the darkening bruises on her neck.

Angelina pulls her lower lip into her mouth and nods.

He has her, and if she's not answering her phone, it's not good. While I thought he was the one brother who escaped the poison laced in Kingsley DNA, he's no better than me or Adam. He's worse even. A psychopath who's been hiding in plain sight.

A monster who has Echo.

"Where would he take her?"

Angelina shrugs. "Don't know and it doesn't matter. He'll realize his mistake. He'll find me once he's done."

It's something she shouldn't wish for, but she repeats it because she can't help letting the delusion settle in. It's more comforting than the reality of the bruising around her neck. More peaceful than accepting Rhett no longer has any real use for her.

"He'll find me." Angelina closes her eyes and tips her head back against the wall. "He'll love me."

Blind faith when all the proof says otherwise. Doesn't matter. She can drown in her delusions. All I care about is Echo.

"Fuck."

I walk up to Ryan, who's staring at a cross on the wall, while he grips the one around his neck.

He's probably in shock from the overload of information. Ryan trusted Rhett. He was willing to hand his church over to him. He sees people for the best and can look past any darkness. Something that betrayed him in this situation.

"Ryan." His name comes out sharp, but I need him to snap out of it so we can focus on the situation at hand. "I need you to focus so I can find her."

"What's happening?" His voice shakes.

Fear.

The most dangerous of all emotions. All consuming. And I recognize it in myself as I hear it in his tone. The fear that this situation is spiraling, and she might not be okay. But I bury it down before he finds a mirror because we can't both fall apart right now.

"Rhett has Echo." There's so much more to it than that, but anything else might officially tip him over the edge. "I need you to stay here and take care of Angelina. I'll keep you updated."

I brush past, but Ryan grabs my arm, stopping me. His grip is tight, the most broken edge to his eyes when I look back at him.

"Crew."

One word housing all the questions I can't answer for him right now. Asking me for more than I might be able to give him.

"I'll find her." I grind my teeth. "Nothing is going to happen. I promise."

A promise I can't break because I won't survive it. I held her in my arms this morning. Shards of glass that cut me straight through. I had her in my heart and promised I'd be there for her. And then I let her go.

Ryan tightens his grip, mulling me over, before releasing me.

"I'm trusting you." Each word might as well be its own sentence. Hitting like a hammer inside me.

I swallow hard, not sure how to feel about the only other man in Echo's life handing me something so important.

"I know."

Ryan nods, turning back to Angelina.

I pull my phone out and head back down the hall. There's only one call to make, no matter how much it sickens me to do it. Only one person who's going to know where my brother might have taken her. One person who hides every dirty family secret.

The line only rings twice before his voice comes through.

"Crew." Dad sounds almost amused, if not a little surprised. I barely text him—never call him. It takes me swallowing every ounce of my pride to not hang up the second I hear his voice.

I skip the hellos. There's only one reason I'd make this call.

"Dad." I tighten my fist at my sides and pause. "Where would Rhett go if he needed to hide something?"

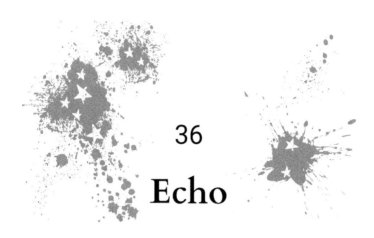

36

Echo

POUNDING THUNDERS BETWEEN MY temples. Heavy knocks clatter at the inside of my skull as I curl my fingers and my nails drag against an unforgiving surface.

It's cold in this room, and I try to blink the darkness into focus as spots dot my vision. Attempting to pull myself up, I fail, and my knees scrape against a hard floor.

Darkness cloaks the details, but there's a single light overhead that casts a cool glow at the cement under me. Shifting again, something clatters, and that's when the weight around my ankle becomes clear.

I blink my vision into focus and look down to see a shackle around one of my ankles. The rusted chain tied to a metal loop bolted to the floor. It only has a couple of feet of slack, so there's nowhere to go.

Tugging at the lock, it doesn't budge. The metal digs into my skin and leaves a rusted coppery tinge.

"There's no use trying." Rhett's voice comes from across the room as he slowly makes his way into the light.

His face is placid. Serene even. The opposite of what I saw before something hit me over the side of the head. And the calmness might be more terrifying as the memories flood back.

The church.

Angelina.

Violence.

And Rhett stands here looking at me with the same expression he did when he was in the hospital. Soft, unaffected. Like someone I should be able to trust.

"Why are you doing this?" I scoot back as he gets closer, but the chain only allows me to go so far, and my back strikes a wall.

Rhett crouches down in front of me, skimming my bare legs, before looking back up at me. "You're a little troublemaker, you know that?"

He tilts his head to the side, narrowing his gaze, but I don't dare to respond. Because if I had to guess from the scene in my dad's office, one wrong thing could set him off.

"You seemed so sweet back then. Innocent. You could have been the perfect little prize if you'd just stayed that way."

Reaching up, he tries to graze my cheek with his thumb, but I pull away. A swift movement that draws an amused smirk across his lips.

"Your father should have kept a tighter leash on you."

"I'm not an animal." I can't help but spit it out as my anger boils to the surface.

"Unfortunately." Rhett stands back up, pacing to the other side of the room. "Animals are much easier to tame. And your father let you run wild far too long. Do you know what happens to a dog without the proper training? A dog who refuses to behave."

I'm not sure what's more concerning, that he's scanning something on the table in front of him, or that he's comparing me to a dog like this is casual conversation.

"Do you?" he asks again, firmer this time.

I shake my head. "No."

I shouldn't answer, but I'm out of options if I'm chained up, and he's unhinged.

"I'll tell you." Rhett spins around, and there's something in his hand, but I can't make it out from this far across the dark room. "They get put down."

My back stiffens, and I swallow hard. The fact that he doesn't seem to be drawing a line between me and an animal isn't a good sign, especially considering where this is going.

"Why are you doing this, Rhett?"

I hate the tear that rolls down my cheek. I hate my blurred vision making it hard to see what's right in front of me. I hate that I never told Crew I love him when I'll never get the chance.

"Because when my mother died, I saw my destiny." Rhett lets out a long breath. "A calling. I'd spent years burying what I felt just beneath the surface. Denying what I deserved. My father and brothers like to think they're so important when really they're pointless. They don't understand true influence. Adam chases money. Crew chases whatever he's interested in at any given moment. But I'm the smart one. Nothing is more powerful than faith."

"And that's why your father helped mine. So you could play God?"

"I don't *play* anything. I *am* their God."

He's so lost in his own fantasy, I see the situation clearly. He truly believes every word, which makes him the most dangerous monster there is. A devil who thinks he's a god. And I'm chained up like a sacrifice for his egotistical cause.

My only hope for survival is to try and lean into it. Pray for mercy, even if I doubt he'll show any.

"They already love you." Tears brim in my eyes, but I try to fight them back. "Nothing will change that."

It's a lie. If they knew the truth, he'd lose everything. Which is why I'm in this situation.

"You can be with Angelina. I'll say that publicly. You can blame me. Make me the bad guy."

"You had your chance to play your part, and like the selfish bitch you are, you refused."

I can't help but flinch at his words—the delivery. How he's nothing like the man I sat with at the hospital.

"I don't trust you anymore, Echo. You broke your promise."

I almost laugh at the irony of his comment, but I manage to hold it back.

"You told me you understood what had to be done. I even let you play out your little forbidden desires with my brother. I gave you everything you could ask for. And you betrayed me by deciding to not follow through with your commitments. You're worse than a fucking dog because at least they're loyal."

My heart is racing. We're back to the dog references, and I can't help the nerves that prickle with whatever that might mean to him.

"You remind me of her." His teeth grit.

"Who?"

"My mother," he spits the words out. "I thought my brother was stronger than that. But he's just like my father. Letting a worthless woman ruin him. I should have seen through it."

"Please let's just talk about this. I care about you, Rhett. Even if we aren't together, I can still help."

Rhett lets out a terrible laugh. Walking the line between untethered and wicked. It rises like bile from his stomach and spills out into this dark room.

I'm in a basement maybe?

It's cold, and I don't see any windows.

"You still don't get it." Rhett shakes his head, walking closer to me. "You *will* help me, regardless. That's why you're here. You'll be the catalyst of it all."

"All what?"

Rhett once more crouches down in front of me. "Power. Control. Devotion. Them bowing down."

"That's not faith." Even if mine falters, I know a false prophet doesn't make a God, and that's what he wants to be.

"I've spent the past eight years studying faith. And do you want to know what I learned?"

I don't move or answer, knowing he'll tell me anyway.

Rhett leans in close. "Desperate people will believe in anything."

"You're sick."

Of all the times I've called Crew the same thing, this is the first time I've actually meant it. There is something wrong with Rhett. Something I don't think can be fixed as he smirks in response to my comment. A darkness that isn't playful.

"If you've already brought me here and made up your mind, what are you going to do?"

Growing up the way I did, I've seen bad situations. But this one is inescapable. I'm stuck. Caged. At the mercy of a madman.

"At least now you're asking the more important questions." Rhett scans me over, reaching for my ankle.

When I try to kick him, he grabs my foot and holds it down, striking me across the face with the back of his other hand.

So hard my head spins, and for a second, I'm her. I'm my mother, as I watched her dealer beat her for not having the money to pay him for the drugs she'd already used. For a moment I'm my past, and there's never really any escaping that.

"Don't fight me when I know you can be so compliant." Rhett pulls my ankle, and I'm having a hard time seeing straight as he grabs me between the legs. "What's wrong, Echo? You can be my brother's toy, but I'm not allowed to touch my fiancée?"

I try to kick at him again, but he pulls back laughing.

"I'm not your fiancée."

Rhett stands up, still laughing as he makes his way back over to the table. Even if I shouldn't, I relax my head against the wall and close my eyes, trying to catch my breath. One touch and I feel dirty. Invaded. I'd rather he just kill me.

"You are my fiancée, and there's no backing out of that."

"Watch me." I face him again.

There's no use playing nice at this point. Rhett's shown me his true colors. He's not letting me get out of this. At least if I piss him off enough to kill me, I don't have to fear the worse things he could do.

"Your fight used to be one of your more interesting qualities." He hums. "Now I'm bored. And while this worked out at first, you've become more trouble than your worth. Just like all women."

"What's that supposed to mean?" I'm not sure what ignites my hate for him more, the nerve or his comment.

"Women are a distraction—at least for those too weak to use them for only what you need."

"You're disgusting."

"Hate me all you want. Doesn't really matter now, does it?" Rhett reaches for something on the table, before turning to face me once more.

This time, my vision is clearer as he holds it up and the light glistens off the needle in his hand.

"What's that?" Doesn't matter how many tattoos I've given or received, syringes make my skin itch.

Watching too many go into my mom's bruised, frail arms makes it impossible to see anything else.

"I think you know what it is, Echo. After all, your druggie, whore mother had you around them all the time, didn't she?"

"Don't say that."

He's trying to kick me where it hurts. Remind me of the parts of my past that erase some of my worth. Digging into wounds when he knows nothing about them. Like I'm insignificant and a piece of trash.

I've been looked at that way too many times in my life. And while Crew has never judged me, his brother is like the rest of them.

"It's the truth." Rhett starts walking over to me, and I try to back up. But there's no going anywhere. "You can't run, baby. There's nowhere to go. This is where we end."

"What are you going to do?"

"What your mother did." He squats down in front of me with the needle sitting like a threat between us. "I should be thanking you for giving me such an easy out. I'll be sure to mention my appreciation at your memorial."

My fingernails dig into the concrete as he smirks darkly at me.

"You're going to kill me?"

"Of course not. But I can't help it if my fiancée is a drugged-up piece of trash like her mother. That she couldn't handle the pressure, so she turned to something to make her feel better. That she got in so deep her dealer came after her and shot me for her mistakes. I can't help that her addiction is going to take her from me." He laughs. "No, I won't *kill* you. I'll set up a foundation for you. Mourn you. Make you an example of what happens when you lose your way. And they'll love me for it."

"You can't."

Sure, I smoke pot and drink. I enjoy a good time. But I've never touched anything harder. I wouldn't dare after seeing what it did to my mother. I've avoided what Rhett holds up between us my entire life, and my skin itches at the sight of it.

"I can, baby. And I will." His eyes pinch with forced sympathy, and I'm not sure how I'm only now realizing he's a psychopath. "Nothing draws devotion like a dead fiancée. With you out of the way, I can ascend with a woman who understands what it means to be my wife. Someone who isn't distracted with her own dreams and isn't interested in opening her legs for my siblings."

"But Angelina—"

"Will say what I ask of her." Rhett cuts me off. "Or I'll find a way to get rid of her too."

He grins, and I nearly vomit.

I've only seen pure evil a few times in my life and now is one of them. I can't help but wonder if Crew knows this about his brother.

Crew.

I'm going to die without ever telling him how I feel. With him thinking I gave up. With my father believing I turned into *her*.

"Please don't do this," I whisper.

Rhett can slit my throat or put a bullet in my head. Anything is better than turning me into my mom.

Tears run in rivers down my cheeks.

"So good at pretending to be sweet." He lifts his hand to my cheek, roughly smearing his wet fingers across it. "Don't worry, you'll go feeling real good."

A sob rips from my throat, and I hate that he's making me cry. That I'm letting him see me like this. That I can't fight back because there's nowhere to go, and with these chains, I have limited movement.

His hand moves from my cheek, down my neck, between my breasts, and I think I might really throw up. My insides shut down even without the drugs.

He's going to empty me. Take me. And then, he'll end me.

"Rhett." My vision snaps into focus at the voice. I don't ever pray, except right now I can't help it. Because I hear Crew, and I don't want to be imagining him.

And when my gaze lifts, he's there—in the doorway—rage in its purest form, looking directly at the back of Rhett's head.

"Get your fucking hands off my girlfriend."

37

Crew

IF IT WEREN'T FOR the needle in my brother's hand, too close to Echo's perfect flesh, I'd hurl myself at him and beat him until he no longer had a face—or a skull, for that matter.

He put his hands on her, and all I see is red burning so hot it's nearly white.

"Wondered if you'd find us, brother." Rhett doesn't look at me, but from the fear painting Echo's eyes, I can imagine his expression. "Let me guess—dear old Dad decided to be helpful for once."

I don't bother responding as he just laughs. Rhett's always had this ridiculous idea in his head that I'm the favorite. That role is reserved for him.

Finally, Rhett stands up, but when he does, he pulls Echo up with him. She's weak as she climbs to her feet, and he wraps his arm around her throat, pinning her to his chest to use her like a shield between us.

It's pathetic. Can't even fight his own fights.

Worse, he's using her.

The needle in his hand is still firm in his grasp, close to her arm, but she's pulling away as best as she can. Her eyes, terrified at the sight of it.

"What are you doing, Rhett?" Something about the scene isn't right. If he wanted to just kill her, he could have.

It took me too long to get here. Something I'll hold against myself once this is done. For right now, I need to focus.

"Giving her a little present." Rhett smiles at me.

"Please don't." A tear rolls down her cheek with her words.

It cracks something inside me. Breaks me open as I take a step forward.

"Now, now, brother." He draws the needle closer to her arm, and she flinches away. That little flinch she's always had around him, like her body sensed his true nature before her mind woke up to it.

I wanted to believe Rhett really was the good brother. That while our mother's death and our dad's arrogance ruined me and Adam, Rhett survived whole. I wanted to believe he cared enough about Echo to take care of her if she refused to be with me.

I was mistaken to think he'd keep her safe.

His lips curl in a smile I haven't seen in years, and memories flood me. The same look he had the split second before he saw me walk into the room where he was standing over our mother's body.

I was five, and I thought I imagined it because it didn't make sense he'd be happy to see her dead. Only someone truly sick and broken would.

That moment didn't break him as it did me and Adam, it revealed something he was trying to hide.

"Just set the needle down, and we can talk."

Rhett laughs. "You're a shit liar. I know you too well for you to try and use your head games on me, Crew."

He's right, I am lying, but I'll say and do anything to get him away from Echo right now.

"Where is this going to get you? Adam told Dad about what happened with Angelina. Ryan knows about the money. You can't walk away and pretend nothing happened."

"Then fuck them." The unhinged crack in his tone makes Echo jump. "They still need to learn a lesson."

I take a single step, but it causes him to flinch, so I'm forced to stop. At least I'm getting closer. Just not close enough.

This basement is too large. Too dark.

The family hasn't used this property in years, and the house is falling apart on top of us. I should have guessed this is where he'd bring her since Adam uses it on occasion for some of his not-so-legal business. But when Dad confirmed my gut feeling, my stomach was in knots.

You don't bring people to this house for them to walk away. And when I walked in and saw her chained up like an animal, my patience nearly snapped.

The last thing you do to a girl like Echo is chain her down. She's wild. She burns so hot, she's the sun in my universe. You don't bury her; you orbit to her gravity and pray she draws you in so you can dissipate into her oblivion.

She's everything, and I'm not prepared to lose her for my brother's sick revenge.

"What lesson do they need to learn, Rhett?" I keep him talking, like I did with Angelina, hoping it's enough to distract him until I figure out what to do to get Echo out of this.

"That women are a worthless distraction. No one learned after what happened with Mom, but maybe this will do the trick."

"Mom?"

"Do you know she was leaving him?" Rhett's fingers tighten their grip. "I heard them fighting. She said she was taking us away. That and half his fortune, and we both know which of those things is more important."

"He would have made more."

"That's not the point. She tried to make him look like a fool after all he'd done for her. As evidenced by his pointless little rampage of revenge he dragged us on after she died. Women always get in the way. I tried to show you all back then, but you didn't see it."

My eyebrows pinch as his grip on the needle tightens so hard his knuckles are white.

"You tried to show who?" I'm not sure I like where this is going.

Or the sick smile, distilled by the darkness in the room, even if his evil still finds a way to shine through.

"Why do you think Dad never found who killed our mother?"

Echo's eyes widen, and it's like her realization is what offers me my own. My stomach turns, and I try to remember what I saw all those years ago. A foggy vision through five-year-old eyes. A scream that cut through the night.

Footsteps ran away, but then I heard something else. They ran back.

Whoever did it was in the room with her not once, but twice. Rhett killed her and then ran to stash the weapon before returning to the scene of his crime. He stood there basking in what he'd done like it was art. Our mother's body, bleeding out in the living room.

"You killed her?" It's nearly a growl that rips from my throat as I take two steps forward, momentarily forgetting the needle in his hand.

"Don't." He draws it to Echo's throat, the needle barely poking her flesh, and she freezes.

"Crew, it's okay," Echo's voice cuts through my darkened vision.

Her eyes are liquid gold they're so dark. Melting me from the inside. Burning hot and saying all the things I don't want them to right now. Because it's not okay, none of this is. And she can't give up on me like this.

I shake my head.

"I promise it's okay," she says, another tear streaming down her cheek.

The most beautiful path I'd like to kiss better until there are no more tears trying to wash her away.

"I'm yours." She chokes on those words. "No matter what happens."

Rhett laughs behind her, but she doesn't break her stare on me. She holds me with her gaze like it's her arms gripping me tight. She hands me her soul so no matter what he does in this moment, he doesn't get it. Echo gives herself to me because she trusts me, and I refuse to fail her.

"It's going to be okay, Goldie." I steady my words, trying really hard to believe them so she will.

"Don't make promises you can't keep, brother."

"I'm not." My gaze once more finds Rhett. "No matter what happens here, you're done. The truth is out there. It's only a matter of time before Adam recovers the money you've been funneling. And Ryan already has the cops talking to Angelina."

"And you don't think I have a backup plan?" Rhett grits his teeth. "The moment this little toy of yours started fucking you, I knew it could be a matter of time before she got attached. What you've found is only a fraction of what's out there. I'll survive. I'll reinvent myself. I always get what I want. You can't touch me."

Except I will. The moment I get my chance, I'll beat the holy light out of him.

"You think you're the only one who can be free, Crew?" Rhett is shaking with his rage. "That you're the only one who can do as they please? I'll be free too."

"I'm not free, Rhett." None of us are.

We're all chained to something. Obligations, histories, women with dual-toned hair and beautiful tattoos.

A door opens upstairs. Dad and Adam were a few minutes behind me.

"Let her go, Rhett." It falls to the empty silence between us.

We both know he won't. He'll fight this until the end, and I'll help him reach it.

A door slams and he jumps as it catches his attention. Just long enough that he looks away and I make a move for him.

One of his hands wraps into Echo's hair as he stops her from trying to get away. She's held by that and the chain, but my focus is on the needle and keeping it away from her.

I manage to grab his arm and steady him, but he's still got too good a hold. She must sense my thoughts as our eyes connect, but her gold eyes shimmer, and she does the exact opposite of what I want her to do.

Echo reaches for Rhett's arm and wraps both her hands around his wrist, pulling it in as she ducks down. And in that moment, I use my body's full force to shove Rhett's arm forward, the needle stabbing into my brother's neck.

I push his hand, releasing the drugs into his system as he chokes on blood.

He releases Echo with his surprise, and she crumples to the floor. But I don't loosen my hold on Rhett, shoving him to the wall so he doesn't fall on top of her. My hands hold his arm, pinning his body to the wall, while the needle sticks from his throat, and his eyes start to get hazy.

I'm not sure what drugs he used, but they hit him hard and fast as his blood spills out of his neck. And in his dark haze, his eyes focus on mine. He grins and blood pools between his teeth.

Sick satisfaction like he got what he wanted all along.

His eyes roll back and the grin falls. His cheeks pale, and all expression fades. His body goes limp, and I shove him in the opposite direction from Echo.

"Crew." She's looking up at me with tears in her eyes, and I drop down to her.

I wrap my arms around her and pull her into my lap as best I can with her still chained to the floor.

"You're okay." I hold her tighter, her body shaking in my grasp. "I've got you. You're going to be okay."

I'm choking on the words as they fight their way out. I hold her shivering body in my arms and try to keep her together. I bind us as one and hope it's enough.

"It's going to be okay," I whisper again.

"What happened?" Dad walks in, Adam right behind him.

They both look from Echo and me to Rhett's body.

"Find the keys to this thing." I tug the chain.

Adam nods and starts looking around, but for the first time in my life, my father is frozen. Speechless. In shock.

Echo shivers, and I pull her into my grip tighter.

"Thank you for getting to me." She starts to cry, sobs out big tears as she buries her face against my chest. "He was going to—"

She can't finish her sentence, and I hold her through it.

"I'll always get to you. I'll always protect you. I promise. I'll keep you safe."

She looks up at me, blinking with tears streaming down her face, and she reaches up to cup my jaw in her hands.

"I was scared I'd die before I could say it," she whispers, pulling me close through her cries. "I love you, Crew. I love you. And I need you."

"I know." I kiss her lips, her nose, her cheek, her jaw. "I love you too."

She buries herself in my arms, and I rock her as she repeats it over and over. As Adam releases her ankle. As I carry her from the basement.

"I love you too, Echo. I'll never let you go."

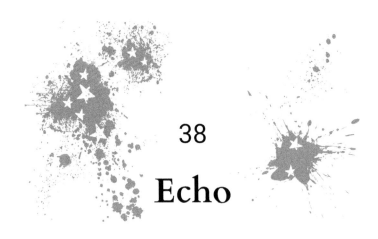

38

Echo

"Welcome back!" Fel and Maren jump up from behind the counter, even though Jude and Sage are both standing against the wall shaking their heads at them.

"You guys were supposed to hide." Fel walks over and pushes Jude's shoulder.

He grabs her wrist and tugs her to him. "Not going to happen, Red."

I can't help but smile at the familiarity of being back at the shop, the one place that feels like home after everything that happened with Rhett.

It took a week before I could even get out of bed, and another couple before I felt strong enough to face anyone. Crew took care of me and brought me anything I needed, refusing to come to work the first week himself while we both processed everything that happened. He finally returned a couple of weeks ago, under the condition I'd still be there when he got home each day.

There's nowhere I would rather be.

"I'm not back *back* yet. But I'm working on it."

Jude tips his chin up. "Take all the time you need. We've got this."

Crew wraps his arms around me and pulls me close to his side, before planting a kiss on the top of my head. "Don't worry, princess. Fel is keeping us all in check while you're out."

"Someone has to." She rolls her eyes, but Jude pulls her in and whispers something in her ear that's distracting.

"Well, it's good to be back, even if it's just to say hello. So thanks for the banner."

A bright yellow sign hangs over one of the doorways, reading: *Echo's return to Hell.*

I can't help but grin at the reminder of the club Crew and I went to when we were in Oakland.

As if he senses my thoughts, he steps behind me and wraps me in his arms again. My safe place. And I sink my head back against his shoulder, holding onto that feeling.

After what happened, years of fears and traumas brewed to the surface. My unresolved issues with my mom and my past couldn't be avoided any longer. For the first time, I've had to accept if I don't face this, it will forever live inside me. And even if I'll always be broken, it doesn't mean I can't soften the sharp edges.

Just because I've been hurt doesn't mean I can't heal.

With Dad's encouragement, I started seeing a therapist. And even if I've only been twice, I'm on a path. One I hope leads me in a better direction.

I'm lucky to have a father like mine. He's strong for me even when these past few weeks haven't been any easier on him.

After what happened with Rhett, Eternal Light is still reeling, and he's been busy rebuilding what Rhett was slowly taking apart behind everyone's back. He's still trying to track all the money Rhett hid, while regaining the trust of the congregation in the process.

The fallout has taken its toll on everyone, but at least I have Dad.

And Crew.

He's supported me through all of it. He and Adam organized to have my apartment emptied, and all my things brought to Crew's place. I didn't even fight him on it.

So many years I had spent pretending to be happy with the choices I was making, but it was all fake. And now that I have someone who loves me, accepts me, protects me. I'm not letting him go.

The fact that Crew had never invited a woman to his apartment before we met, and now he refuses to let me leave, feels like breaching a first with him. In our own ways, we hand each other pieces of ourselves we haven't trusted with anyone.

"No clients today?" I ask, looking around. It's past eleven and usually, at least a couple of us are already locked in our rooms.

"Not until later. We wanted to catch up first," Jude says.

Fel nuzzles against him. "Look at you, being all sweet."

"I'm not sweet." He narrows his eyes. "It's a fact. It's busier when she's not here."

I roll my eyes, knowing he's lying to himself. The guys love to act tough, but they've both been texting me as often as Fel and Maren.

"And the fights have been too easy without you around, man. When are you coming back?"

"Soon," Crew says. "We'll see."

"A hundred hearts broke the moment the ring girls learned Crew Kingsley was off the market." Maren laughs.

"Good." I wiggle and Crew grabs me tighter. "He's mine."

Crew dips his mouth to my ear. "You know it, Goldie."

"All right. Enough of the small talk, who wants a drink?" Maren pulls out a bottle of champagne and walks around the counter, handing it to Jude.

He pulls his knife out of his back pocket and flips it open, taking it to the bottle and popping it open in one swift motion. A move Fel seems to appreciate as she pulls his mouth to hers the second he hands the bottle back to Maren.

"Gross." Maren frowns at them. "Get a fucking room."

"Okay." Jude tries to tug Fel down the hall, but she plants herself in place.

"Later." She grins, rubbing his arm.

Sage looks as disgusted as Maren, turning his back on the happy couple.

I can't help but wonder if that's what Crew and I look like to them. Not that I care.

Maren pours glasses of champagne, and everyone takes one for the cheers. But when they turn away, I hand it to Crew, not taking a sip. Instead, he walks it back over to the counter and Jude drags him into an argument he's having with Maren about if Fel should be allowed to walk the ring at another one of his fights.

"Saw that." Sage knocks my shoulder, stopping beside me. "Please tell me he didn't knock you up already."

"He didn't knock me up."

"Good." Sage smiles with relief, and I'm not sure he'll ever be one to settle down or think about a family. "Then what's the deal?"

"I don't know." I rub my arms. "It's not like I'm done drinking. It just doesn't feel right at the moment. I'd rather stay in my head."

The threats of Rhett taking away my power still lingers with me. Him saying he could so easily turn me into my mother. And even if logically I know I'm not her, it's been easier to have clear thoughts as I process everything that happened.

Sage pulls out his phone, frowning at whatever's on the screen.

"What's wrong?"

"Nothing." He pockets it, crossing his arms over his chest.

"Sure." I poke his arm. "I'm not believing that for a second."

"It's really nothing." His eyes dart to the shop window. "Kane just asked me to stay late tonight so we can catch up about something."

"Something?"

Sage shrugs. "He just wants to talk."

"About what?"

"Nothing important." Sage wraps an arm over my shoulders and shakes me. "Stop worrying about me. I'm a grown ass man."

"Debatable." I elbow him in the side. "You know I don't like you spending too much time with the Twisted Kings. Don't let Kane drag you back into his shit."

"I won't."

"Promise?"

"Promise."

But as he says it, I feel the truth in his gaze. Even if he pretends ties are cut, everyone in this room is aware there are still strings. Sage's past is where he hides all his secrets, and I can't help but wonder which ones are waiting to come full circle.

"Where's the new front desk chick?" I change the subject. "I thought she started a couple of weeks ago."

"She did." Sage grins.

"Oh my, God. You're disgusting." I shove him off me.

"Hey, she knew what I was offering." Sage shrugs, walking off as Crew circles back around and wraps me in his arms.

"Did he actually fuck another employee into quitting? He has a problem."

"Lots of them," Crew agrees. "How does it feel being out of the house? We can leave if you're not ready."

"I'm good," I assure him. "I can't hide forever."

"You can if you want to. I won't judge." He kisses the side of my neck.

"You just want to keep me all to yourself."

"Damn right, I do."

He kisses a path up to my lips and claims them, before pulling back to look at me. Those steel-gray eyes, so cool they take my breath away.

"Have you talked to your father?" I ask.

"Way to kill the mood." Crew frowns, caught off guard by my sudden change in subject. "Let me guess, Adam asked you to check in on me?"

"Technically, Lakeyn."

"Not sure how I feel about the two of you being so buddy-buddy all of a sudden."

I just shrug. As close as I am with Fel and Maren, Lakeyn is the only person who really understands what's going on right now. Beyond my personal trauma, the Kingsley family has been rocked to the foundation with the loss of Rhett, and the revelation of all his secrets.

Crew, Adam, and their father are still trying to process all the awful things he did. For years they all believed an outside enemy killed their mother, but it was her own eight-year-old son.

Nothing erases that kind of pain, and nothing logical explains it. He was sick, and he did things beyond comprehension.

Lakeyn has been there for me like the sister I never had, and we've grown close because of it. She's been helping Adam through the same things I'm dealing with when it comes to Crew.

Kingsley men aren't great with their emotions.

And their father isn't dealing with anything. He holed away after that night and still hasn't left the house. If it weren't for Adam still running the family business,

I'm pretty sure his entire empire would have started to crumble.

"You should call him." I wrap my arms up around Crew's neck. "I know you guys haven't been close, but there's no one who understands what he's going through except for you and Adam."

"Then let Adam do it."

"He is." Lakeyn said he had been there earlier this week. "But he might need both his sons right now, Crew."

"He's not innocent."

"I understand." I'm still unsure how I feel about him myself given the eight-year arrangement our fathers had regarding mine and Rhett's relationship. "But I don't want you living with any more regrets. So just consider it for me, okay?"

Crew tips his head back and lets out a groan. And when he lowers his face back to me, he rests his forehead on mine. "Fine."

"Thank you." I kiss his lips. Once. Twice.

"You're still too sweet for me, you know that?" He kisses me back, this one deeper. His fingers dig into my lower back, and he pulls my body flush with his.

When he breaks it, I can't help that I'm catching my breath, and my mind is spinning.

"I'm aware." I brush my nose back and forth, grazing his. "Guess you're going to have to dirty me up then."

"Fuck, that's it." He releases me and grabs my hand, tugging me to the door.

"Hey," Maren yells behind us. "Where are you two going?"

"Home." Crew doesn't even look back as he pulls me from the shop.

"Sorry." I wave at her and Fel, but I can't stop laughing. "We'll catch up later."

Right now, I'm going home with my boyfriend. And there's no place I'd rather be.

Epilogue

Crew

"WHERE ARE WE GOING?" Echo's devious little smile is so gentle and cute. She tries to use it to balance her wicked edge, but I know the real her. She's secretly hoping I'm taking her somewhere to slam her against a brick wall and fuck her.

Not tonight. As much as she enjoys it when I bend her over where anyone can catch us, we have somewhere to be.

"I need to ask you something." I tug her hand, pulling her around the corner, surprised she hasn't figured out where we're headed.

It's probably more that she doesn't expect it.

She pops her gum, looking a little nervous at my answer—quiet as she lets me lead her to the shop—only pausing once we're standing directly in front of the blinking *Closed* sign for Twisted Roses.

"Work?" She frowns.

I nod, unlocking the door and opening it for her. It's dark this late at night, but when I flick the light switch and the room illuminates, so do her eyes.

Glancing around, I've never been so thankful for Echo's friends, because Fel and Maren did exactly what I asked them to. Toffee rose petals cover the floor and paint the shop with a golden hue. A few are in vases on the counter. They're everywhere. Yellow on the edge of gold, as close as roses can be to the color of Echo's unmatchable eyes.

"Crew, what is this?" Tears are already pooling in her lashes as she looks back at me, while I drop to a knee and take her hand.

She presses her lips together and a sheen coats her eyes. For a girl who never used to cry, she's opened up so much since starting therapy. She's no longer afraid to let me see her wear her emotions—each one more beautiful than the last.

"Do you know why I started the wall of eyes, Echo?"

She shakes her head, glancing behind me at the wall in the shop I've spent years adding to. I'm sure she's expecting me to ask her something else, but she needs to understand this first.

"No."

"Look in the center."

She squints but doesn't seem to see it because there's no hint of recognition as her eyes pinch.

"In the middle of it all is a picture of you, of your eyes. The most beautiful ones I've ever seen."

Her gaze darts around, before she finally lands on what I suspect are the right ones.

"It's from that first barbeque we had when Blaze brought you on at the shop. Some chick was running around snapping pictures, and she took one of you."

"I remember her. She wanted you to fuck her."

The little hint of jealousy is so cute I'm tempted to lay her out and remind her why no girl matters to me but her.

"All I saw was you that day." I squeeze her hand. "And you're the only girl who's ever been worth fucking."

"I know, I'm not jealous." She lies to herself, and it's adorable how she bites her lip when she does it.

"Well, that's good because I am." I kiss the back of her hand. "And if another man touches you, I might be tempted to do things I promised not to do again."

Her cheeks heat at my comment.

"My point is, your eyes are unmatched, Echo. They're the center of everything."

"I don't understand... when did you add them?" Her nose scrunches as she looks down at me kneeling in front of her. "And why are you down there?"

"You already know the answer to one of those questions, Goldie." I can't help but smile at the blush that warms her cheeks. "But as for the first one. They've always been there; you just didn't notice them until today."

Her eyebrows pinch in confusion as she looks back up at the wall again.

Her golden eyes were the first ones I put on that wall. And even if I added to it every day for years, none drew my attention away from that pair.

"Echo, you've been the center of all I see from the moment I met you. And even if it took me too damn long to understand why, it was always you. Deep down, I knew. Your eyes are the sun, and I can't escape them. I tried to look in every other pair, put them all on that wall behind me, and none of them saw me like yours. None of them drew me in like yours. None of them are yours."

I squeeze her hand, brushing where her purity ring used to live, while gripping where it still hangs from my neck. She used to ask for it back, but now she's accepted it's mine. Just like she is.

"You gave me a ring before I got the chance to give you one, and I need to correct that mistake."

Releasing her purity ring, I take both her hands in mine. "Echo Gwendolyn Slater, will you marry me?"

She gasps at the question. And I love that she's still surprised even if she sees it coming. It's the innocence she still holds deep inside, no matter what kind of darkness she's been through.

Her fingers tremble as she brings one hand to her mouth and nods her head.

"Yes?"

She jumps up and down, and into my arms, almost knocking me over as she sits on my knee and wraps her arms around my neck.

"Yes, of course." She giggles.

I wrap my hand in the back of her hair and pull her mouth to mine. I could live in this feeling—her breathing me to life with her kiss. My tongue finds hers, and she tastes like bubble gum, so I steal it straight from her mouth.

"Hey." She pulls back, swatting at me. "You stole my gum again."

"What's yours is mine, Goldie."

She frowns, but it's forced, and she doesn't look the least bit annoyed. "Fine, and where's this ring you mentioned?"

I run my thumb over the back of her finger. "Already told you, when I put a ring on your finger it would be permanent. Hence our location."

She smiles, her eyes darting around. "You mean...?"

"Yep." I nod. "You said yes so there's no backing out."

Echo leans in and brushes her lips against mine. "And what about you?"

"What about me?" I grin. "I'll go first if you'd like."

The way her eyes light up is enough to make me consider tossing her to the floor and fucking her in the golden rose petals.

"You're going to let me tattoo you?" she says, pulling back.

"Goldie." I pick her up to standing, wrapping my arms under her thighs so I can lift her up all the way. She wraps her legs around my hips, and I start to carry her into the back. "You can tattoo your name over my entire body if you want to."

"Ooh, don't tempt me, Crew Kingsley." She licks my ear, sending a shiver down my spine. "I might be tempted to take you up on that."

"Whatever you desire, princess." I drop her into the tattoo chair and kick the door shut. "But first. I'm going to give you something better than a ring."

"Oh yeah?" She grins. "What's that?"

"My cum." I reach for the button on her jeans and strip them off her. "Let's get to marking what's mine."

She giggles as I flip her around, and I'm not sure what I enjoy more—her moans as I fuck her through two orgasms, or the ones she makes while I ink her finger with the ring that's never going to leave it.

Echo

Crew's eyes darken the moment I step out of the bathroom. His gaze traveling the full length of my body, before flicking back to my face again. One look from him, and this ridiculously tiny piece of white lingerie is worth every penny.

The lace dress is see-through, hitting just below my ass cheeks, and I'm not wearing anything beneath it. My bare skin is on display, apart from my thigh-high leather boots. The ones Crew can't get enough of, even if it pisses him off every time I wear them in public and some guy looks in my direction.

I can't help that I enjoy watching him break someone's face when he's feeling territorial.

"You're a fucking wet dream, princess." He leans back, planting his hands behind him on the bed and perusing me once more.

"You're one to talk."

He's in nothing but his underwear, and his rock-hard dick isn't hiding beneath the tight fabric. His tattooed chest flexes as he shifts forward. It's not fair for a man to look like that.

"Come here." He skims me again. "Let me get a closer look at my present."

"You think this is your present?" I brush my hand down the center of the chest, where it dips to my belly button, keeping my other one behind my back. "I got you something much better."

He smirks, his smile darkening. "Better than my dirty wife in a slutty little outfit desperate for me to fill her up with my cum. Not sure that's possible."

I finally bring forward the tiny bottle I've been hiding behind my back. "You tell me."

He lifts it from my palm, reading the label before tipping his head back in a giant laugh.

"Did you actually get me lube as a wedding gift?"

I bite my lip and nod.

Crew leans forward, snaking his hand around my waist and pulling me to him. "Best wife on the fucking planet. Is this for what I think it is?"

I climb onto his lap, wrapping my arms around his neck and tipping my mouth to his ear. "I want you to take my virginity one more time, Crew."

"Fuck." He shivers at my words, his grip on me tightening. "Are you sure?"

Crew can be downright crude with me. Degradation is one of his favorite games we play in bed. But when we're broaching certain things, his caring, loving side comes out. Like right now.

"I'm sure." I kiss his jaw—peppering more along the scruff there. Making a path to his mouth and then sinking my lips to his.

I wrap my hand around the chain around his neck and pull him closer. I love that he still wears my purity ring. He holds it like it's a gift. He keeps it safe, like he does me every day.

"I need this." I kiss his lower lip, murmuring against it. "I want to give myself to you any way I can."

"Goldie." He wraps his hands up in my hair. "You give me the best gift every day—you."

It's almost sweet until he tangles his fingers in my hair and grips tightly, pulling me until his mouth is by my ear.

"But you better believe I'm going to claim every fucking inch of this beautiful body if you offer it to me."

A shiver runs my spine, and I can't help the rush that floods my veins as he slips a hand up the backside of my lingerie and grabs my ass.

We've been experimenting with toys, and I'm still nervous as he pulls me closer.

But I want this. I need to be Crew's in every way. Since the moment at his fight when I made the decision I wanted to hand this man my virginity, he's the only one I've wanted to give every first to.

Raking my nails over Crew's shoulders, I trace the pattern of the demons that reside there. Angry faces that match the darkness in my husband's soul. I love the broken sides of him because his cracks are where I fit, and it's how I'm whole.

Crew stands up with me in his arms, and I can't help but giggle as he spins us around and pins my body to the bed. My legs stay wrapped around him as he grinds his steel length against me.

"Crew," I moan.

"Yes, Goldie?" He kisses my lips, down my neck, biting me at the base of my throat.

"I need you."

He lifts up, grabbing one of my legs and using it to spin me around until I'm on my stomach, before tugging my ass in the air.

"Don't worry. I'm going to give you all of me."

His fingers drag under my lingerie, peeling it up over my ass, before he drags his hands back down and teases the line my leather boots hit me at mid-thigh.

"My little whore..." He runs his palms back up again, over my ass and up my back, before grabbing the hair at the back of my head, pulling me up to kneeling so he can whisper in my ear. "You want me to fuck your ass like the slut you are for me, don't you?"

I nod as his hand trails down my stomach, running a circle on my clit before he shoves two fingers inside me.

"Your greedy pussy is crying just thinking about how I'm going to fill you up." He shoves in another finger, and it stretches me until I gasp. "I barely need the lube."

He pulls his fingers out and shoves my chest down to the mattress, pressing his wet fingers against my tight hole and toying with it.

Behind me, I hear a pop, then something warm and slippery drips over my ass. Crew tosses the lube to the side and rubs it over me.

He pushes a finger in. "Fuck, Echo."

The vibration of his tone relaxes my nerves. His free hand grips my ass and something about how I have this power over him makes my head spin. He wants me—only me—in every way possible. A man who could have chosen anyone to be his wife. And I want to hand him every experience of mine in return.

He pushes his finger in deeper, warming me up, and my core starts to churn with the pressure. My skin prickles, and I can't help but rock my hips back as he presses forward.

"Naughty girl." He toys with me some more, and my body slowly starts to relax for him. "But you're going to take a lot more than this today."

He adds another finger, and I lose my breath.

"That's it." He's playing with me, slowly working me until I start to relax. "Your body knows who it belongs to."

He palms my ass with his free hand, calming circles as he fingers my tight hole and prepares me.

Reaching down, he grabs the lube once more, drizzling more over me. I can't help but moan as he slides his fingers in and out of my ass with slippery ease.

Crew tosses the bottle to the side once more and withdraws his hand before a greater pressure is against me. The head of his cock pushes as he rocks his hips forward, and my body reacts by moving toward him.

He hums. "That's it, you want this cock in your ass?"

"Yes." I grip the sheets.

Crew presses forward, gripping my ass cheeks as he moves through the resistance, and I lose my breath. My eyes tear, and for a moment it burns as he presses deeper. He starts with just the head, before pushing in again, and again, slowly forcing his length in until I'm so full I'm on the verge of blacking out from the pressure.

When his hips hit mine, he squeezes both ass cheeks, and spreads them wide for him.

"This might be the most beautiful sight on the planet." He rocks back, before driving forward again. "Your ass taking my cock. So tight and desperate for my cum."

He pushes in, and I bury my face in the blanket, holding it tight. The pain starts to fade as his slow pace quickens and the pressure starts to detonate something else deep in my core.

"Crew." His name is a plea, and I need him to keep going.

He folds forward and grabs one of my wrists, pulling my hand under me. "Finger your pussy while I fuck your ass, Echo. Let me feel your fingers inside you."

I groan because he has a way with words that feels so dirty that I want to listen to him talk like this all day. I want him to degrade me. Defile me. Make me absolutely filthy.

When he releases my wrist, I reach under myself. My pussy's wet from lube and my excitement. Dripping onto the bed as he fucks me slow and steady. And even as I climb, I need to get there faster. My body clenching with desperation.

I push my fingers in my pussy, and it's tight with his dick fucking me from the other side. He must feel it too because he groans, pulling out and then shoving himself back in.

His dick rubs against my walls with every thrust.

"Deeper," he commands.

I shove my fingers in further, and he lets out a low growl. His cock pumps inside me, and I'm soaking my fingers at the sensation of it. My legs are shaking so hard I feel like I'm going to collapse, but he holds my hips so my ass stays in the air for him.

"Finger yourself, let me feel it."

I pick up my pace at the same time he does, and being fucked both ways has my vision spotting. I bury my face in the mattress and my body relaxes as much as it's tightening. A release I can't help that I'm chasing, and if I don't get there, I'm not sure how I'm going to stand it.

Crew shoves in deep, and it presses my fingers against a spot that sparks a bonfire. It rips a scream through my lungs as he hits it relentlessly.

My body shakes as my climax rocks through me, and he fucks me through it. He picks up pace, and I can no longer think as I'm bursting from every pore.

"Fuck you're tight." He grips my ass harder and grunts as he hits me deep and hard, and his body shakes.

We're waves in the ocean, crashing. He releases himself into me, and I've never felt so dirty or alive. A balance only Crew can offer.

When he relaxes and my climax fades, he slowly pulls out. But he stays kneeling a moment with my ass cheeks spread.

"Beautiful." He holds me like that as he rubs the back of my thighs. My ass and pussy a dripping mess for him.

After a moment, he rubs me once more and peels my lingerie back down, before sitting on the bed and pulling me into his lap.

I'm still shaking from my release. A high that has me crashing. But he wraps his arms around me and holds me through it. Burying my face in his chest, inhaling his cedar scent, I'm home.

"You okay?"

His entire demeanor shifts as I come down from the high. He might fuck me rough, but afterward, he knows how to be gentle. A caring side only I get to see.

"Yes. That was..."

I'm not sure how to finish that sentence. It was more than I expected.

Lifting my head, I look him in the eyes and can't help the smile that fills my face at the sight of him this relaxed and happy.

"It was perfect." I decide.

Crew hugs me tighter, planting a quick kiss on my forehead. "I'm all your firsts, Echo. And I'm going to be all your lasts. 'Till death."

"I love you."

"Love you too, princess." He brushes his lips over mine and pulses his hips between my legs. "Now let's wash off because I'm going to make my wife come on my cock the rest of the night."

I expect nothing less.

Choose Wisely

XOXO

Acknowledgements

Crew and Echo will always hold a special place in my heart. Everything about these two is chaotic, complex, and messy. They break each other, heal each other, and become each other's safe space. And ultimately, they show that love is accepting a person for who they are.

I want to start with a special thank you to my readers. Crew and Echo's story was one of the most difficult ones I've written. They have such strong personalities and deep flaws; I was worried I wouldn't do them justice. But hearing how much you already loved them and were excited for their story, helped me push through. Thank you for continuing to read and support. It means more than I can put into words.

Chris, thank you for talking through this ending a million times and never getting tired of it. You are my biggest supporter, and you always push me to do my best. I'm thankful to have you by my side in love and life.

My boys, even if I secretly hope you never read my books, I will always thank you and say how much I love you at the end. You are my heart walking around outside of me. I love you both more than anything.

Mikki, every time I start a new book, I think about that blank page I sent you. That moment where there's nothing but an idea and I feel like I'll never be able to write it. You reminded me that day what I'm capable of and continue to do so. As far as sister's go, I have the absolute best. I couldn't do this without you.

Mom, you've survived another chaotic anti-hero, another round of texts of shirtless cover models, and another cheers when I reached *yet another* "The End". It's all those little things that mean so much to me. It doesn't matter how small the win; you want to be a part of it. I love you.

Alba, thank you for the kind of friendship that makes us family. We've shared over a decade of laughs, tears, family, and life. I'm thankful for every minute.

Autumn, the way you care about these stories and work to bring the vision to life is so appreciated. I am endlessly thankful for your guidance and support. To you and the entire Wordsmith team, I'm beyond grateful.

Kat, I'm so lucky to call you an editor and a friend. I love the messages you send while you're working through my stories, and how your excitement at the end of each one motivates me to write the next. Thank you for all you do to make this possible.

Vanessa, I know you said you were worried your heart wouldn't survive Crew, but here we are. It did. And your love for him makes me so happy! Thank you for polishing my stories and catching those tiny details I've missed. It's all those little things that add up to something big in the end.

Sam, I survived! When I got your initial notes, I wasn't sure it was possible... Talk about a rough first draft! Thank you for never taking it easy on me. Your honesty pushes me to do better and dig deeper each and every time.

To my ARC team, I'm so lucky for all of you. Handing over my stories when all is said and done is one of the scariest moments. Your genuine love for my characters keeps me motivated. Thank you for spreading the word about my books and helping me send them out into the world.

Books By Eva Simmons

Heart Break Her

(*Celebrity Crush*)

Forever and Ever

(*Opposites Attract*)

Heart of a Rebel

(*Second Chance*)

Worth the Trouble

(*Forbidden Love*)

<u>Twisted Roses (Dark, Taboo Romance)</u>

Lies Like Love

(*Stepsiblings*)

Heart Sick Hate

(*Boyfriend's Brother*)

Cold Hard Truth

(*Her captor*)

<u>Reckless (Kinky, Dark, Billionaire Romance)</u>

Reckless Games
(Hot, Holiday with a Billionaire)

Reckless Promises
(Mafia heir, forced marriage)

Find a complete book list at www.evasimmons.com

a amazon.com/Eva-Simmons/e/B07MMX2MLB?ref_=dbs_p_ebk _r00_abau_000000

f facebook.com/AuthorEvaSimmons/

g goodreads.com/author/show/16225312.Eva_Simmons

BB bookbub.com/profile/eva-simmons

(O) instagram.com/evasimmonsbooks/

♪ tiktok.com/@evasimmonsbooks

About the Author

Eva Simmons writes hot, heartbreaking romance with complex heroines, and broken, dirty-talking bad boys who fall hard for them.

When Eva isn't dreaming up new worlds or devouring every book she can get her hands on, she can be found spending time with her family, painting a fresh canvas, or playing an elf in World of Warcraft.

Eva is currently living out her own happily ever after in Nevada with her family.

Printed in Great Britain
by Amazon